HUNT DOWN HARRY TRACY

A Western Story

W. R. GARWOOD

Five Star • Waterville, Maine

WES
Garwood

First Edition
First Printing: May 2006

Published in 2006 in conjunction with
Golden West Literary Agency.

Set in 11 pt. Plantin by Christina S. Huff.

Printed in the United States on permanent paper.

Library of Congress Cataloging-in-Publication Data

Garwood, W. R. (William R.)
  Hunt down Harry Tracy : a western story / by W.R. Garwood.
  —1st ed.
      p. cm.
    ISBN 1-59414-335-8 (hc : alk. paper)
    I. Title.
  PS3557.A843H86 2006
  813´.54—dc22   2005036153

HUNT DOWN
HARRY TRACY

Chapter One

Harry got down from his grandpa's buggy on that warm, still, August night of 1889, and watched the Silver Star rig wheel around in the wide road opposite his home, then set off back down the pike as the judge, with a flick of his limber crop, touched up his high-stepping bay mare, Diamond. "Tell your pa I said you're to keep that little Sure Shot!" the old man called back. "You're big enough for something beside a dinky air gun. You're going on fourteen now!"

Harry waved at the dwindling black smudge of the buggy and proudly hefted his prized gift—the little single-shot .22 rifle. Grandpa was right. When he'd celebrated his thirteenth birthday the day before at his grandparents' Pittsville home, he'd stepped out of the little kid class. In some 300 odd days or so, he'd really be fourteen.

The moon, just rising, balanced itself, for a moment, spang on top of his house, a glowing bull's-eye. Before it could mount higher he whipped up the barrel of his .22 and plugged it dead center three times. Of course he didn't have any cartridges yet, but he knew he could talk Pa into a box of them.

Pa was real good that way. If it hadn't been for him, he'd never even have got that air gun, because Ma was dead set against guns and hunting and all that. She even raised a fuss when Harry had owned up to building that little cabin out in the woods. Not that it was much—just a log lean-to. But it was his, and a good place to hide out when Ma went on the warpath. It was also a great spot to read his dime novels, never allowed in the house, and to play the harmonica his pa had given him. His half-brother Ervie, a year younger than Harry, had followed him all of the past summer, trying to discover what was going on out in those woods, so as he could peach to Ma. But Ervie was just a plain town kid, and couldn't track for sour apples. No gumption, that's what Mike Tracy usually said. Mike, their neighbor who batched in a small box of a house a quarter mile up the road, was a fine hunter and woodsman when he wasn't off logging. Mike Tracy just couldn't stand the sight of Ervie—said he'd never make a border scout in 100 years. Mike did say, though, that he, Harry Severns, had the makings of a real pathfinder, and showed him ways to track game and how to survive in the really big timber. Mike even took him squirrel hunting a couple of times, Harry lugging along his pa's old top-lever breechloader when Ma had gone off to a Pittsville Temperance meeting.

"Harry!" It was his brother breaking in on his daydreams out in the middle of the moon-washed roadway. "How long you been back from Grandpa's? Ma's just fit to be tied. Your pa stoled a heap of money and the sheriff's been here twicet already!"

Harry followed Ervie through the side door of the narrow clapboard house to where his mother sat in the dim light of the dining room, rocking back and forth in her spool rocker.

"You heard?" Her voice, normally subdued and resigned for such a big woman, was harsh and raspingly shrill. Gone was her usual martyr-like air, and she seemed like a possessed person—at least the way possessed folks were said to take on in the Bible. "You heard?"

"Yes, Ma." Harry's throat was so dry he had trouble opening his mouth. "It's a lie, ain't it, Ma?" He waited, but she only rocked back and forth, her own lips compressed into a thin line as she stared from him to Ervie. Ervie, who'd been standing beside Harry, moved away as he sidled over behind his mother's rocker.

"Bad blood always tells!" she rasped so suddenly that Harry, in his growing anxiety, dropped the little rifle.

"Look, Ma!" Ervie pointed at the Sure Shot where it lay gleaming in the lamplight. "Harry's got that gun! He says old Grandpa Severns give it to him for his birthday. You always tol' us we boys couldn't have real guns, and Harry's defying you, like you always say. And now his Pa's run off like a thief. That's bad blood for sure, ain't it, Ma?"

"Bad blood," Mrs. Severns repeated in that strange, harsh voice. "The good Lord help us, for sorrow's come to us through bad blood." She threw her checkered apron over her head and momentarily subsided rocking away and moaning to herself.

"But what's happened to Pa?" Harry asked his half-brother, clasping his hands together, tears filling his eyes.

Ervie momentarily wavered through the filmy-blur of amber lamplight, pudgy face all askew, as he patted his mother's shoulder and scowled at Harry.

"Your Pa took all the money they'd saved up to build our new school and left home. Ma said he never come home last night."

"He wouldn't do that. Pa wouldn't!" Harry stood with clenched fists, looking from his mother to Ervie. "You're a suck-egg liar and I'll thrash you plenty!"

He made a start for his half-brother, but his mother suddenly threw off the apron from her face and stood up. A large, stoutly-made woman, she towered over her son. "Harry, if you touch Ervie, I'll do some thrashing. Now march upstairs to bed!"

He turned without a word, picked up the Sure Shot, as his trembling legs took him to the upstairs doorway and up the creaking, uncarpeted steps to his small bedroom. His mother had made no attempt to seize the little gun, despite Ervie's accusing finger. He'd have whacked that tubby sneak a good one if Ervie'd opened his mouth one more time.

Although he'd had no supper, Harry didn't care. He didn't think he'd ever be able to eat again. He unlaced his shoes, and got out of his shirt waist and knickers, then sat on the edge of his bed in the attic bedroom, staring out the south window at nothing.

Orlando Severns, his father, had been head bookkeeper at the North Star Logging Company ten miles north of town. A well-educated man, who could play the mandolin, harmonica, and zither, he was always so neat and successful-looking that folks in the growing village of Chittamo voted him to be school treasurer. And now, he'd gone off with the money raised for the new schoolhouse—if Ma and Ervie were telling the truth. That was one thing about Ma though, for all her Bible talk, she did tell the truth.

Harry thought it was funny about that "bad blood". Although Grandpa and Grandma Severns weren't much on prayer meetings and hymn sings, Grandpa was a judge and they always went to church. But Ma had her own ways, and it seemed she'd just never got over her first husband, Ervie's own pa, though he wasn't nothing but a fat farmer who drank too much. He'd gone and fell out of a haymow one 4th of July and broke his fool neck. And even if Ma had gone and married pa about a year later, she was always twisting any talk around to some mention of that God-fearing man, her first husband. Now Pa, for all his church-going, was somewhat of a freethinker, and thought Colonel Bob Ingersol was a blue-ribbon winner—and that didn't set well with Ma, who feared so-called atheists like rattlesnakes. But Harry just wouldn't believe that Pa, or even Grandpa, had anything like bad blood. There had to be a good reason for Pa's sudden departure. Come to think of it, maybe Ma was somewhat at the bottom of it, with her "Old Rugged Crosses", and "Beautiful Isles of Somewhere", and her continual harping on the goodness of Jeremiah Baggot, that drunken farmer, Ervie's old man.

Harry gave it up, and watched the sheet lightning flickering away in the south. A wind, blowing up out of nowhere, flared the trees around the house, while the moon, big and full, when he'd come home, seemed battered and hunted as it raced in and out of the growing packs of wolfish-looking clouds that rolled ominously across the sky.

He tried a tune on his harmonica but just didn't have the heart and put it away. A muffled growl of thunder came drumming down from the northwest, where the great primeval forests stretched away toward Minnesota. To the sleepy boy it sounded like the pounding of giant horses loping through the windy night, following that fleeing moon. And his pa was out there somewhere in that wild darkness. Harry dug fists at his eyes once or twice, then drifted off to sleep as the rain began to lash its whips across the wooden roof shingles.

For the next year Harry studied his *McGuffey's* at the log schoolhouse out on the Minong Road, and had more than one scrap with some of the larger boys when they insisted upon teasing him over his father's departure with the school money. But the majority of the pupils didn't hold that affair against him. His mother, after that one outburst on the night of Orlando's flight, had subsided back into her usual martyr-like existence, keeping house and attending Temperance meetings. However, she insisted that he and Ervie attend church each Sunday, with several prayer meetings thrown in for good measure during the month. On the other hand, Ervie never let Harry forget it was his father who'd darkened the family name, although he stayed well out of Harry's reach and never walked the two miles to school with him.

There was nothing more said about Harry's single-shot rifle. The judge, who handled his daughter-in-law's affairs after the decamping of his son, made it clear his grandson was capable of handling a hunting weapon. The old man even saw to it that Harry had a few cartridges from time to time. As a Civil War veteran, the judge believed that guns were a natural part of everyday Wisconsin life.

When Harry couldn't get over to his grandparents, he took to spending more time out in the woods after school. He also ranged the local timber with Mike Tracy on those summer week-ends when that young bachelor returned from the logging camps around Prairie Lake.

"How old are ya now, kid?" Mike asked one lazy August afternoon as they sat upon a couple of stumps at the edge of Silver Lake, fishing lines dangling like spider's gossamer into the shining water. Off to their left a flock of blue-winged warblers in a nearby stand of aspen were showering each other with a torrent of bubbling song.

Harry turned from trying to capture the bird music on his harmonica, and eyed the speaker. Mike Tracy, sub-foreman at the Ryan and Duff lumber outfit, was a small, red-headed man, not more than five feet two, weighing in at around 130 pounds. But he was tough and quick in all his actions—a real holy terror in a fight—and a man Harry was proud to tag after.

Harry mentally counted the weeks, then straightened up on the stump and squared his shoulders. "Going on fifteen."

"Got yourself a birthday comin' pretty soon, ain't you?" Mike squinted at a flight of black duck as the birds whirled up from the far shore in an explosion of fast-beating wings and rapidly lofted toward them. Lifting his fishing rod, he aimed it at the oncoming flight. *Whang-kabang!* He grinned at Harry. "If this here cane pole had been a shotgun . . . then good bye mister duck. And that's my birthday present in advance. Always be ready for what jumps out at you." He flicked his hook and line back into the rippling water and took a long puff on his cob pipe. " 'Course we didn't fetch along our weapons today, 'twouldn't have made much sense to carry shotguns on a fishin' trip. But y'gotta remember that life's chock-full of surprises, y'never know what's comin' next." He paused and took another drag on the cob, then rapped the dottle from it on the side of his stump. "Just like last year when your pa lit a shuck outta town. Knocked the wind outta your sails somewhat, I know. But ya got sand, Harry, and that's why I take to you. You don't let things get ya down."

"Grandpa said soldiers never know what's happening one day to the next. They just weather the storms and keep marching." Harry suddenly had a picture of Pa hiking down a long road leading nowhere, his good clothes all dusty and torn, and he furtively rubbed his eyes—then gritted his teeth. Where was Pa, and why hadn't he ever dropped them a letter?

"Pull 'er! Pull 'er!" Mike was yelling.

Startled, Harry tugged and hauled back on his bending, whipping pole—and a great whopper of a muskellunge landed on the bank, thrashing madly over the grass in a rainbow spray till Mike knocked the glittering fish on the head with a rock.

While the muskie lay stretched out, goggle-eyed and jaw agape upon a bed of moss, a scarlet bead of its blood sparkling jewel-like on a lady slipper's yellow leaf, Mike relighted his pipe. "Y'darn nigh lost that one, kid. That's just what I always say, be ready for the unexpected."

Harry nodded silently, then, seeing Mike's bobber doing a jig, pointed at the twitching cork, while the logger dropped his pipe and tussled with his line to land a runty brown trout fingerling.

Unhooking the little fish, Mike heaved it far out into the lake and grunted: "Like I said, be ready for the unexpected." He picked up his cob, reloaded, and got it lit again. "Goin' on fifteen, eh? Well, I'm movin' over to a new company, so how'd you like to come up there until school starts? Then you could work at the camp week-ends, too. Think your ma would go along with that?"

In the late fall of 1890, Harry went to work at the Wright and Ketchum Company logging camp as cook's helper, staying out at the site, thirty miles north of Chittamo, the month around. His mother had made little objection to his leaving school in the sixth grade now that he was actually going on fifteen. She only insisted he take his Bible along and read a verse each day, and attend services whenever a sky pilot, or itinerant preacher might strike camp.

At odd times during the summer of 1891 he still ranged the woods with his friend Mike, now a "bull of the woods" with a nearby lumber company. Mike's elevation to the rank of foreman had done little to stop his famed Saturday night fisticuffs. Still quick as a cat, he took on any work stiff that came along looking for trouble—defeating one and all. He'd

passed along many of his tricks to Harry over the past years—
"Get in that first punch!" To Harry and the rest of the Shanty
Boys, Mike Tracy was the "damned state's best man."

By 1892, when Harry was nearly sixteen, he'd taken to
traveling to the Dakotas with some of the teamsters
working with the threshing crews after the lumber camps
were shut down for the summer. It was a change from the
cool, deep green world of the forests to the wide, dusty
prairies with the mile upon mile of tawny-yellow grain, all
sun-browned by the blazing sun. But it seemed that everything was changing.

Word had come that a man answering to the description
of Orlando Severns, working on the Kansas railroads as a
section foreman, had been killed in an accident. Old Judge
Severns didn't think it was his fugitive son, and neither did
Harry. But it was good enough for Harry's ma, who
promptly married a fellow church-goer by the name of Ed
Goodwin. Goodwin, a part-time surveyor and logger, immediately moved into the Severns' homestead. Although Harry
never came back to the place, save for brief visits, he could
never hold any strong feelings against Goodwin, for he sym-
pathized with anyone trying to live with Ervin Baggot
Severns.

It was while he was laboring under the fiery Dakota sun as
a driver and stacker that Mike Tracy met his match.

Fat Sol, the old cook, told Harry about it when he returned to camp in the fall. "Mike was one of the best in the
whole dumned woods, like you know. He was off work for the
month, so Old Man T. E. Dorr hired him on as a looker to
check out that range of timber forty miles west of here. Mike
took his compass, his pack, maps, and a bottle of tangleleg
and rode over there. They think he took himself a little drink
in a stand of old pine. Then . . . while he was dozing it off . . . a

15

big windstorm toppled a devil of a whopper tree, and that was the end of Mike Tracy."

So that was the way the world went—for Mike hadn't been ready for the unexpected, after all.

Chapter Two

Harry came to work on the railroad by way of a fluke. That summer of 1893 he'd been driving a wheat wagon for the threshing gangs in South Dakota when his half-brother Ervin Baggot Severns had got himself properly threshed by a Chinese track worker at Devil's Lake, North Dakota.

The chain of events leading Harry northward to the aid of his bothersome kin began with Judge Severns's attempt to run down the rumored demise of one Orlando Severns, thought to be a railroad employee in the Dakotas.

Grandpa Severns had written to a Union Pacific superintendent but was unsuccessful in learning anything, although this official turned out to be a G.A.R. veteran and properly sympathetic. In fact, he offered work to any of the judge's relations—something the old man passed along to Ervie, being aware of Ed Goodwin's determination to rid himself of this unwanted stepson.

Ervie, who'd been loafing around, doing odd jobs in town and keeping clear of farm work, snapped at the offer like a frog grabbing flies. He'd packed and caught the train for the North Dakota construction site as soon as the judge had wired his veteran friend and received a work offer for his shirt-tail relative.

Ervie arrived at Devil's Lake and, being a big, beefy fellow, was put to work moving supplies from the camp out to the section gangs. As some of the crews were Orientals, he found himself hauling huge bales of rice from the warehouse over to the track's end.

A great reader of William Randolph Hearst's brand of yellow journalism, together with the *Police Gazette*, Ervie was familiar with the alleged "Yellow Peril". Getting half tanked one night at a local saloon, he began cursing the hordes of "half-starved chinks" who were invading the U.S., and eating their fool heads off, while pipe-dreaming during the day at the end of some pick or shovel.

Unfortunately for Ervie, one of the Chinese interpreters and labor bosses, quietly drinking at a corner of the bar, heard the drunken diatribe and heaved Ervie over his head as easily as one would toss a twenty-pound rice bag!

Laid up with a broken leg in the local hospital and bereft of wages, Ervie sent a sorrowful letter to his mother, asking for enough money to buy a railroad ticket home. As he'd already boozed and gambled away his previous month's pay, he inferred that some slippery John Chinaman had lifted his poke.

But the new stepfather balked at sending money and suggested that Harry should go up to Devil's Lake and look after his half-brother.

When his mother's wire reached him, Harry turned in his time and caught a short line northward. He wasn't particularly enthused about coming to Ervie's aid, but he'd been getting itchy feet over the past few months and was fed up with both the blazing prairie sun and the monotonous work. He felt himself looking forward to a change, even if it meant being in the company of the lumpish Ervin Baggot Severns for a time.

At the end of the 500-mile trip he detrained at a small wooden station, in the midst of a real North Dakota duck drowner, and was soaked to the skin before he could hire a hack to take him out to the ramshackle house doing duty as a hospital.

Making himself known to the gaunt, warty-chinned dragon of a nurse, he was shown into the charity ward, a cramped room with four cots, and found his half-brother, leg in cast, reclining on the middle bunk with a pair of badly-bruised vagrants lying on cots on either side. The end bunk was empty.

The startled Ervie tossed down the tattered dime novel he was in the process of devouring and raised himself up stiffly, while the two bums squinted through tremendous shiners.

"Gawd, Harry, if you ain't a sight for sore eyes! How'd you find me?"

Harry briefly told him of the letter, the trip, and inquired into the facts of Ervie's accident.

"Here's a hell of a tough place, Harry. All three of us been jumped when we wasn't lookin'. It's them damned chinks from the gradin' teams. They're pure pizen. Turn your backs on 'em and good night, Miriah!" He reached down to finger his cast with a pained expression, while the two bearded derelicts waggled battered heads.

"Sure it wasn't your big mouth?"

"Hell, no. Been mindin' my Ps and Qs ever since I come here."

"How long will you be laid up?"

"Doctor says three weeks. But, Harry, you git me outta here!" The broad, doughy face puffed with anguish. "Y'gotta git me a room somewheres." He lowered his voice. "Woke up last night and found one of 'em there goin' through my duffel bag. They even rolled their pal in that empty bunk before he croaked."

"Who's pulling your shift with the supply wagons?"

"Dunno. Don't give a damn. Just want to git outta here."

★ ★ ★ ★ ★

Harry got the straight of Ervie's downfall from his ex-foreman, but moved him out of the hospital and into an inexpensive hotel room uptown. In the meantime, one of the vagrants had died of the d.t.'s while the other decamped with Ervie's best boots just before he was moved.

There was no trouble filling in for Ervie's job as the foreman. A big, lanky Irishman welcomed an experienced teamster, and during the next month, with only half a day off on Saturdays, Harry hauled supplies from base camp out to track's end.

He'd carried his shotgun out to the Dakota wheat fields from the lumber camps, and, when he came up to the railroad, he'd fetched it along with his duffel. Often, as he freighted the big wagons across the rolling plains to the current terminus of the lengthening steel ribbons, he'd pull up his team at the edge of a marshy hollow to take a sudden snap shot at some sitting flock of waterfowl.

Whenever Harry arrived at the railhead, he was welcomed as much for the braces of birds along with some goodly bags of rabbit, as he was for the expected sacks of beans and rice and boxes of tinned goods.

By making friends with the company cook, he was always invited into the mess tent for some extra grub, plus a snort or so of good rye whiskey.

"That your brother the Chinee road boss whupped?" the drooping-mustached cook wanted to know one night as the two sat in the tent making short work of a roast Canadian goose.

"Relative . . . of sorts," Harry answered, digging away at his plate.

"A real flannel-mouth, that one," grunted the cook. "And if you hang around him you're damn' well bound to git into trouble y'self. Have another drumstick."

The cook soon proved to be a good prophet, for, as the days went by, Ervie was up and around on a crutch, while living off Harry. Spending most of his time in the local saloons, he'd resisted Harry's advice that he take a train home. "I'll be back on my pins in another week or so, then I'll take over the hauling again," Ervie informed him.

"I don't think they'd want you to come back to work," Harry answered. "At least not on the wagons. If you ever fell off, you might break that leg again, and they'd be responsible . . . this time."

"To hell with that," Ervie mumbled as he craw-fished away on his crutch, heading for the nearest saloon.

That Saturday night, when Harry got back to town after an extra haul, he went looking for his brother. He'd made up his mind to ship Ervie out, even if it meant hog-tying him.

There'd been a string of complaints from saloon owners, and even from the small hotel where Ervin Baggot Severns was registered. It seemed he was forever getting into rows at the saloons, and then coming back to his room so loud and disorderly he usually disturbed the other guests. Harry, who'd been bunking down at the livery stable to save money, figured that was just about enough.

Searching for Ervie, he found him at the Free Silver Saloon embroiled in a heated argument with a knot of railroad men. Harry felt the tension as he came through the batwings. Several patrons had already risen from nearby tables to seek a safer clime along the bar, while the remaining card players were having heavy going to hear each other's antes.

"Damn fools!" Ervie was weaving around on his crutch like a kite tethered to a pole. "Always said railroaders got nothin' between their ears but a head of steam. Everyone from that slippery weasel of a Jay Gould to old Jim Hill's nothin' but a bunch of high-rollin' bandits . . . grabbin' off rights of way from patch-tailed farmers for just pennies and. . . ."

Whatever point Ervie was about to make was rebutted by a hefty uppercut, delivered with great emphasis by one of the grading crew. Ervie went down with a clatter, bouncing off the bar rail—to lie stiff as a pole-axed beef.

Just as one of the others hauled off to plant his number ten in Ervie's ribs, Harry sprang forward and landed a tremendous clout alongside the fellow's head.

The man jackknifed headfirst into the mahogany with a resounding *thump* and lay side-by-side with Ervie. But there was a major difference, instantly apparent—Ervie was stirring slightly, but the railroader lay motionless—not breathing.

For a long moment clammy silence filled the room as water fills a sponge, then the muttering crowd moved purposefully toward Harry and the recumbent Ervie.

After a glance at the dead man on the floor, Harry recovered Ervie's crutch and got his brother onto his feet.

"Hold on," Harry addressed the nearest patrons with such flat command they suddenly stood motionlessly while the ones coming on from behind bunched up against them. "This was a fair fight. That one there got just what he was trying to hand out to my brother . . . no more or less. Only thing, he wasn't lucky."

"Luck be blowed," one of the graders gritted, reaching into his back pocket to yank out a big jackknife, flipping it open with practiced ease. "Luck be blowed," he repeated, starting for Harry.

"Come on if you want a dose of the same!" Harry shoved the wobbling Ervie aside and, grabbing a whiskey bottle from the bar, smashed it, leaving the neck with its deadly, jagged shards menacing the crowd.

Seeing the men hesitate, Harry yanked Ervie's arm and backed him out of the barroom. "Some of you know me. I haul freight to the railhead, and bunk at the livery, so you know where to find me when you roust out the law. I'll not turn myself in to anyone else . . . and you can believe that."

"Marshal's out of town. Won't be back afore tomorrow," the barkeep spoke up. "I'll put in a telyfun call to him over to the county seat tonight."

"All right, I'll be waiting. The rest of you keep your noses out of this until then." Leaving the dead man in the sawdust, Harry hurled away the broken bottle and piloted Ervie down the steps and along the street, looking back over his shoulder, but no one seemed overly interested in following.

Once at the hotel, he got his brother's imitation-alligator gladstone bag packed and the both of them over to the railway depot. An eastbound passenger train was due at eight o'clock, and it was now just a quarter to that hour.

"Gawd, Harry, I don't wanna go off this way 'n' leave you facin' them damned fools." Ervie, still groggy, pawed at Harry's arm as they sat on the station baggage cart, awaiting the oncoming train—now visible as a wavering plume of steamy black, drifting toward them through the moonlight.

The thin wail of the engine's whistle grew deeper and throatier as it rounded a last curve, its blazing headlight throwing into high relief the little station, the nearby livery barn—and the silvered shape of a knot of men, moving toward the tracks from uptown.

"That's the bunch from the saloon," Ervie groaned, rubbing his head. "They're gonna make trouble you can bet."

"Come on." Harry hustled him across the rails in front of the oncoming express as it came, glaring and pounding, toward the depot. Then it was coasting to a panting halt,

spewing steam and chuffing hoarsely to itself, momentarily
blocking the view.

"Here." Harry boosted Ervie up the steps of the first passenger coach, handing him his crutch and traveling bag.
"You've got more than enough traveling money and a ticket.
That will tide you over until you can get a job." Waving a
hand at the staring, moon-child face of his half-brother, he
crunched along the cinders to the end of the train.

When the express had bellowed out a series of shuddering
whistle blasts, and began to jerk and bang itself into motion,
Harry was already in the shadows of the baggage shed,
watching the train's green and red running lights dwindling
eastward.

In the ensuing stillness, shouts and curses rang out into
the night. "Where's that damned murderin' rascal?" There
came more yells and curses. Then someone fired off a pistol,
its cracking explosion reverberating among the sheds.

Still Harry waited. All of a sudden he saw vague moonlit
silhouettes drifting down the tracks. For another moment
they didn't spot him, then they did and hooted to the others.

It was high time to get out. Ervie was gone, thank the
Lord, and now he meant to light a shuck as well. As the clamoring crowd fanned out toward the baggage shed, he ran
across the road to the livery. Old Man Paxmore, the owner,
had sauntered out of his small cubbyhole office, and was
leaning against the doorjamb, holding a lighted kerosene
lamp, peering out into the darkness.

"What in tunket's goin' on?" he called as Harry ran up.

"Just drunks." Harry brushed past and on into the empty
stall where his cot and possessions were placed. The first
thing he did was to haul out his Forehand & Wadsworth
shotgun from under a stack of blankets, check its two loads,
and flip off the safety.

"Mister Paxmore, get in here."

"Said what'n the world's goin' on?" The old man bow-legged into the barn, still holding his lamp. "Hey, what's that weapon fer?"

"Paxmore, just button your lip and hustle yourself." Harry barred the stable doors and thrust a roll of bills into the other's hand. "Saddle that bay mare and don't ask questions. I'm leaving before there's more trouble."

The fat proprietor looked from the money to the leveled shotgun and promptly busied himself. Long before the first of the mob had begun to hammer upon the locked door, Harry was mounted and ready.

"Open up," he ordered, yanking his hat down and buttoning his coat against the night coolness. With shotgun butt resting easily on his thigh, he spurred the bay straight at the knot of men who hesitated, squinting into the barn.

"Clear out, boys, he's got a shotgun!" In the ensuing scramble to get clear of the oncoming rider, the clustering mob parted like the Red Sea to give Harry clear passage. As he thundered out into the night, another pistol cracked, followed by shouts and curses, but he ignored the commotion and spurred his mount into a gallop, heading out of Devil's Lake as fast as the bay could take him.

All that had happened about eight o'clock the past night, and by the time the first red streaks of dawning were burning across the night-darkened horizon he was a good forty miles westward. He'd not thought which direction to take when he'd first galloped out of town but instinctively headed for the railhead camp where he rousted out the cook.

"Tol' you that so-called relation of your'n was plain bad medicine, didn't I?" The cook tugged at his grizzled mustache, then patted the nose of Harry's bay. "You're plumb

lucky to git away from there without gittin' your neck
stretched by them bustards."

"You don't have to tell me that."

"Well, then I'll tell you somethin' else. Iffen the wind's a-
blowin' back that way, you best not linger. That bunch'll yelp
that you was the one at fault, and the law'll come lookin' for
you hot and plenty heavy."

Shaking the cook's hand, Harry strapped the supplies he'd
given him behind his saddle, swung aboard the bay, and rode
on west while the rising sun warmed his back.

He spent the second day traveling across rolling, broken
prairie, sheltering that night in a shallow coulée. It wasn't too
unpleasant as he'd knocked off a brace of prairie chickens,
and was near enough to a branch of the Souris for coffee
water.

Next morning he rode into the village of Surrey, where it
nestled in a bend of the Souris River, northeast of the rising
folds of the Missouri Plateau. There he discovered something
that effectively halted his westward trek. Eating breakfast in
one of the town's two restaurants, he happened to pick up a
day old copy of the *Minot Optic Reporter* and was idly scanning
through it when he came across an item on an inside page:

Hunt For Killer of Jacobs

Search continues for the slayer of Henry R. Jacobs,
an employee of the Union Pacific Railway, killed in the
Free Silver Saloon at Devil's Lake two days ago.

According to witnesses, the assailant, Harry
Severns, a teamster employed by the railway, attacked
Jacobs without warning in a barroom altercation, using
a club, which fractured the victim's cranium.

Funeral arrangements were in progress for Jacobs at

press time. It is thought that Severns's early arrest will be accomplished as law officials of all towns within several hundred miles have been furnished with detailed descriptions of both Severns and the stolen bay horse he used to accomplish his escape on Saturday night.

Harry paid his bill, and, untying the bay from the hitching rail, rode out of town without picking up any supplies. Heading the six miles over to Minot, he arrived an hour before train time.

Wary of attempting to dispose of the horse, he left the bay tied to a picket fence near the railroad bridge and walked five blocks up to the Great Northern depot at the end of Central Street.

Retaining only his gripsack and shotgun, which he'd wrapped securely in a blanket, he boarded the eastbound Flyer along with a scattering of drummers and some ranchers. No one on board seemed to have the look of a lawman, but Harry was watchful, for the bay mare was sure to be found and common sense told him that someone might prove shrewd enough to wire down the line to be on the lookout for the rider.

Sometime in the night he dozed off in the smoker and awoke with a crick in the neck, staring at the flickering, crisscrossing shadows of the railroad bridge as the Flyer chuffed across the wide, chocolate-tinged expanse of the Mississippi between Minneapolis and St. Paul.

There being an hour layover at St. Paul, Harry stepped down onto the cold stone platform, gawking at the big buildings and the droves of people, then walked over to the nearby Harvey House for breakfast. Carrying along his grip and the blanket-wrapped shotgun, he deposited them beside his stool in the steamy, noise-filled hall, and worked his way through a plate of ham and eggs, washing it all down with the world-renowned Harvey House coffee.

Replete at last and feeling somewhat at ease for the first time since leaving North Dakota, he reached down to take up his luggage and grasped empty space. Startled, he stared around, but everyone seemed intent upon their own business. A big, beefy patrolman, standing by one of the doorways, picking at his teeth and joshing some of the cashiers, was looking over the breakfasting throng incuriously. He merely glanced at Harry when he went up to the cash register and settled his bill as rapidly as he could without causing any attention.

Once outside, Harry stood flat-footed, peering about, but there was no one in sight with his particular bag or weapon. Baggage men were rushing past, trundling carts loaded with grips and suitcases, while train men and passengers walked this way and that. But there was no sight of his vanished property.

There were several letters in the gripsack, together with various items capable of alerting the authorities to the fact that a fugitive killer was hundreds of miles east of the Dakotas—and then there was the vanished shotgun. He cursed that unknown thief as he got back on board the Flyer.

As the broad fields and timber stands of Illinois spun away past the southbound train, Harry felt a growing sense of tenseness sweeping through him. He was on the way to a real honest-to-john big city. St. Paul had been downright overpowering with its crowds and bustling street traffic—just about the largest place he'd ever struck, but the drummers had bragged-up Chicago as ten times as big. It was hard to feature such a place.

Golden gleaming house windows and silent blue flares of small town stations were now blending into a rushing constellation of lights as the train dashed along, moaning through the suburbs of a giant city. Staring through the rattling plate-glass window at his wavering reflection, Harry saw the chains of yellow squares and oblongs sweep upward toward the actual stars, then the fast-blooming lights were blacked out when the Limited began easing into a clattering, long-protesting halt as it puffed steaming and clanking into the echoing depths of the great, barn-like Chicago and North-western Union Station.

Emerging with the other passengers into the chilly, Lake Michigan night, Harry stood on the corner of Madison and Canal, staring up along the stone streets at the light-flecked, mountainous buildings, and feeling, despite the elbowing crowd, more alone than if he were deep in the great, shaggy forests of home or far out upon the vast expanse of the loneliest of prairies.

Chapter Three

Harry had been in Chicago six days before meeting the one person who made him happy he'd decided to dare this huge, sprawling city—the girl, Janet Warrington.

With less than $20 left in his pocket, he'd economized by staying at a run-down rooming house on South Halsted, near the stockyards. Eating Spartan meals in small, neighborhood restaurants, he spent the days seeking work with little luck. His first break came when he got into a game of cards with some hangers-on at a saloon near his rooming house. Using skills honed to near perfection in bouts with the Wisconsin lumberjacks, he managed to part his fellow players from nearly $120.

But his most immediate good fortune arrived with a sightseeing trip he'd taken downtown on the electric cars. Wandering into the lobby of a very elegant hotel, The Congress, on South Michigan and blandly ignoring the inquiring stares of the desk clerk and lounging guests, Harry stopped at the cigar stand and purchased a pair of Havana Nuggets and came nigh forgetting his change, when he looked into the blue eyes of the lovely, young attendant.

Lingering, he tried out some small talk, but the blonde girl, with a quick glance over at the sleek-haired desk clerk, turned away with a quiet smile. Yet that was enough for Harry!

She was everything he'd dreamed about women and carried secretly in his head since a tad. In fact, the more he thought of it, the more he was certain she looked exactly like the golden-haired angel on the front of his mother's *William Vaughan Moody's Collection of Inspirational Messages*.

Now he felt he might have something really to live for at last, and he could forget the rough life he'd had on the prairies and such bad times as those up at Devil's Lake. Somehow, some way, he'd meet this young lady, get himself a decent job, and all the rest would follow in the best Horatio Alger or E. P. Roe tradition.

Immediately upon leaving the hotel lobby, Harry had lingered on the sidewalk, looking back through the huge plate-glass windows without appearing to do so. He was apparently interested in the constantly passing drays, hacks, and wagons all rolling past, the clatter of their hundreds of wheels competing with the staccato whirring of the South Michigan electric cars. It was mighty overpowering, this big city life—but he could make his way in Chicago, he was positive.

The first move in his campaign was simple; he merely walked around the corner to LaSalle and into a clothing store. When he emerged, he was togged out in a brown, small-check, single-breasted sack suit in the latest square-cut style, topped off with a white shirt, turkey red necktie, blucher gaiters, and a stylish blue-black fedora. Harry was willing to bet that no hunky from the railroad or lumber camps would recognize him, even if they met him face to face. It was $16.25 well spent.

Carrying his old clothes and underwear in a paper bundle, he made a few saloons in the neighborhood, eating the free lunches and fortifying himself.

When the clock across the street on the front of a jewelry store stood at five, the young blonde girl came out of the hotel. Moving through the swarms of people along the street, she caught an electric car marked LAKE SHORE DRIVE.

Harry hurried down to the next corner and got aboard the same vehicle, standing near its front and looking everywhere but toward the girl. For the next half hour, throngs of passengers got on and off as the trolley crackled and swayed its way through increasingly affluent neighborhoods.

Viewed through the rows of trees, the huge Victorian mansions, drifting backwards, seemed to bask in the golden afternoon light like benevolent stone dragons.

Despite his new clothes, Harry began to grow uneasy. This girl lived in one high-toned neighborhood. He thought she must work at that hotel for some sort of lark. She could be one of those "liberated" women he'd read about in the papers. But far more disturbing, she might be some sort of an heiress.

The sun was now low, a flattened red ball, constantly rolling in and out of the passing elms to their left, while a vast, watery prairie that was actually Lake Michigan, stretched sparkling on forever to the right.

The blonde girl still hadn't noticed Harry, being involved in an on-going conversation with a young man in a gray, three-button cutaway and pearl gray derby. Suddenly she stood up in the aisle of the swaying car and started for the door. Just as she reached Harry's seat, the car clattered around a steep turn and the girl fell into Harry's lap with a gasp.

"Oh!" Her face flushed as she attempted to arise, while Harry, arms about her curvesome waist, set her back on her feet.

The car ground to a halt and, with a swift backward glance at Harry, the girl descended to the ground, the skirt of her navy blue Newport Suit lifted high enough to give the briefest glimpse of a pair of trim ankles, encased in dainty, high-button boots.

Before Harry could decide to follow, the young man at the back of the coach shouldered up the car and was on out the door.

The car had again started upon its whirring way, when Harry yanked the bell pull and leaped off after the pair, now half a block behind him.

He was standing near the massive iron gate of an enormous stone building, more like a medieval castle than a house, when the couple neared him, still carrying on their hushed, intent talk. For an instant they didn't see him, then the young man stopped short, while the girl brushed past, head down.

"Here now, what's this?" The man, who appeared to be half sheets to the wind, stood legs apart, rattan cane in a gloved hand. "Y'don't belong out here, eh?" He looked over his shoulder at the rapidly retreating girl, almost at the front gate of a huge red and yellow brick house beyond the castle.

The fellow took a step toward Harry, cane raised as if about to thrash a dog. "So, what'd you want, Charlie Cheese? Make a noise like a hoop and roll off!" And with that he lashed out the cane, the whistling blow missing Harry's face by scant inches.

In that instant Harry saw the girl start back toward them, then the sport made another cut with the stick. This time Harry was ready, ducking under the rattan's brittle slash to plant a solid right onto his assailant's jutting chin.

The man went down with a grunt, landing on his rear end, cane clattering one way and the pearl gray topper rolling the other.

"Oh! Ogden are you hurt?" The girl's voice was concerned

but the smile, hidden behind her gloved hand, was less sympathetic.

Harry stood motionless, hands raised to let the fellow have another one in case he pulled a weapon—but the man only staggered up, rubbing his jaw and muttering. Retrieving his hat and cane, and with a milk-curdling look at Harry, he turned and stalked off through the massive, wrought iron gate.

"Sorry for the trouble." Harry raised his hat while trying to smile, and finding it hard going—being so near this lovely girl.

"Oh, it wasn't any trouble . . . in fact, the trouble's all with Mister Ogden Palmer. Like his family, he thinks he can have about anything he wants, or what his money can buy." Her blue eyes flashed. "But he'll never buy me, and I've told him so."

"Then he was"—Harry tried to think of the phrase he'd read in one of his dime novels—"he was forcing his attentions on you?"

The girl laughed aloud, eyes crinkling at the edges with sudden merriment. "Well, that's one way of putting it." As she spoke, her smooth forehead creased slightly with recognition. "You're the young man who bought those cigars this afternoon. But you look, somehow, different." And she stood, hands on curvesome hips, smiling at him with a questioning look in her brilliant eyes.

Admitting he'd followed her from work, Harry grinned, hoping he'd not made a complete fool of himself.

For a long moment the two stood silently as the great houses about them silently stretched their shadows across the wide lawns, leaving the cast-iron deer and intricately trimmed shrubbery awash in welling pools of dusk.

"I must go in." The girl indicated an adjoining, yellow and

red mansion. "Mother's expecting me. And you'd better catch the next car back. Ogden's mean enough to call one of his friends on the police force. He's even had a detective named Dan Doherty follow me he's so jealous."

"When could I . . . ?"

"Tomorrow's Saturday. I only work half a day, and I'm off at noon. If you'd like to meet me outside the hotel, we could go down to the Exposition Grounds. Ogden wanted to take me there, but I really don't care." She turned and was gone up the street and through the mansion's gate before he could nod his head.

Harry, waiting outside the Congress just before the noon hour, was sure he'd seen Ogden Palmer strut into the lobby with a rumpled-looking tough who had to be the gumshoe, Doherty. He eased along to the next building where he studied a log jam of bonnets cluttering the show window in a kaleidoscope of shapes and colors.

In less than a minute he felt a light touch on his arm, and quickly turned to find the blonde girl at his side, dressed in a white summer frock and holding a little blue parasol. "Well! Did you think Ogden was after his revenge for that trouncing last night?"

"Could have been a pickpocket. These big towns aren't my cup of tea." He grinned sheepishly, looking over her shoulder toward the hotel entrance.

"No need to rubber that way. Mister Palmer and his plug-ugly friend have gone." She snapped her fingers. "I told him I'd other plans. And here's our car right now." Taking Harry's hand, she ran with him through the crowds to board an electric coach, marked TO THE EXPOSITION GROUNDS.

It was the start of one of the most delightful days of Harry's life.

★ ★ ★ ★ ★

On the long swaying, jangling ride southward to 57th Street and the lake, Harry and the girl were elbowed this way and that by the press of holiday makers, all equipped with wicker baskets, straw hats, sofa pillows, and blankets. Notwithstanding the late season, the crowds were out in force as an autumn sun, large and golden as a glowing pumpkin, burnished the afternoon with mellow warmth while the benevolent sky over the vast, gilded lake surface was one huge dome of melting blue.

By the time they'd descended from the Exposition trolley at the grounds, Harry had told the girl he was Harry Tracy. In turn he'd found she was a Miss Janet Warrington, and far from being some pampered blue blood was merely the daughter of the Rockefeller-McCormick's housekeeper.

"So that's why this Palmer's always on your trail?"

"That's right. Just up to his usual tricks of chasing the housemaids." With that, Janet flipped open her small parasol and led the way from the car stop into the Exposition Grounds.

Harry tried to imagine the Exposition when in full bloom with all its domes and halls crammed with examples of art and industry from across the globe. Janet, who lived within thirty blocks of the grounds, recounted some of the vanished wonders, including Hagenback's trained lions, the glamorous Streets of Cairo, and all the rest. The original giant wheel of a Mr. Ferris still lofted up over 250 feet into the sky from its base among the groves of trees.

Together they strolled along the red brick footpaths winding through the mazes of green shrubbery, and lingered to buy hokey-pokey ice cream under the feathery willows that surrounded the trio of grotesquely picturesque Japanese pavilions.

36

Later in the afternoon, after they'd threaded their way around innumerable picnicking families who bedecked the grounds with blankets, tablecloths, and running, shrieking droves of children, Janet paused in the seclusion of a tawny gingerbread and rococo wooden building. This, she said, represented the Convent of La Rabida in Spain, where Christopher Columbus had found shelter.

For a time she was silent, but he knew what she had in mind as if she'd spoken. This girl was as direct and straightforward as the prairie wind. She was, he thought, the kind who knew exactly what she wanted and took it with pleasure once she'd made up her mind.

Sitting upon a convenient bench in the shadow of nearby shrubbery, Harry clasped her in his arms and was delighted with the girl's response. Kissing her again and thrilling at the wonder of it, he looked out across the glittering lake to see three white gulls curving over the water's golden surface, rather like faraway angels on the edge of some distant paradise. And then his own immediate heaven was enfolded in Janet's arms.

For the next week and a half, Harry and Janet planned to meet as often as they could, which was nearly every night. Together they dined out at some of the better restaurants, such as Thompson's on Madison, and Brevoort's along the street, as well as attending several plays at the downtown theaters, including *Leave It to Jane* and *Good Gracious Annabelle*.

And at each outing, they grew to know more about the other, as they exchanged confidences and life stories. Janet had come from a well-to-do family out state, but her father, John Warrington, a Chicago stockbroker, had gone broke in one of the recent depressions. Her mother, an early debutante, and a friend of such Chicago society belles as the Connelleys, Gillettes, and Fieldses, and herself a cousin to the Gillettes, was taken on as a housekeeper-companion to Mrs. Edith Rockefeller-McCormick.

Janet had studied at several exclusive girls' schools and, upon graduation and the death of her father, had coaxed her mother into letting her work downtown, first as a secretary, and then as a manager of the tobacco counter at the famed Congress Hotel.

Lacking such experience, Harry had woven himself a background out of whole cloth. He was in town, he told Janet, to look over the cattle situation, the reason for his out-of-the-way lodgings near the stockyards. He was also investigating the possibilities of taking a partner to expand his ranch holdings in North Dakota.

This much they'd told each other, and then returned to concentrating upon the immediate present which, to Harry at least, was certainly more satisfying.

Deprived of such a companion in his prior years, Harry reveled in knowing and possessing this wonderful girl. But this dream world relationship came to a sudden conclusion with their visit to Chicago's rather notorious Peacock Alley theater.

On Thursday night, less than two weeks after Harry had walked into the Congress lobby to purchase a cigar, he stood outside the hotel, waiting for Janet. Forever fascinated with the never-ending flow of the crowds streaming up and down Michigan, together with the *clang* of the electric cars and rattle of drays and hacks criss-crossing every which way, he was always ready to bet that all would, shortly, come together in one almighty smash-up.

Nothing unusual had happened by the time Janet emerged at five o'clock—except she seemed somewhat on edge and not quite herself.

"Where'll we go tonight?" Harry asked, hoping she might suggest some inexpensive eatery, for his ready cash was about depleted. There was barely enough left to cover his room rent for the coming week. And, in addition, his gambling efforts at the neighborhood saloon had met with one steady run of bad luck. One of the regulars, a huge hog butcher from the stockyards, even had the gall to suggest that Harry must have lost his marked deck of cards.

"Tonight?" Janet repeated his question, eyes downcast, then she stiffened with a short laugh. "If that Ogden Palmer could have his way . . . there wouldn't be any tonight." She turned to Harry, sapphire blue eyes blazing. "He had the nerve to tell mother's employer, Missus Rockefeller-McCormick, that I'd been seen with undesirables and needed taking in hand. The old lady's a dear, but a perfect stick-in-the-mud, and she's insisting mother keep me home till I find some responsible Christian employment. In other words, out of the cigar stand and away from all the sports and mashers."

"If I could get my hands on that chump!" Harry doubled his fists.

"But that's not all," she continued. "Ogden's already got the day manager's promise to replace me as soon as he can." She took Harry's arm, regardless of the passing crowds, and pulled him into a shop entrance. "Harry, why don't we get married and you could take me back West with you?"

"I don't know."

"You don't know?" She dropped his hand and stared, then smiled. "You're joshing, aren't you? Anyone with a ranch and cattle needs a wife to help about the place."

"I guess you're right." Harry took her in his arms and, without a thought of the jostling throngs on the sidewalk, kissed her. "Where'd you like to celebrate our . . . engagement?"

She paused, smiling up at him, considering. "We've never been to that new dinner theater, Peacock Alley, on Fourth near Dearborn. They say it's very beautiful and there's private wine rooms."

Harry had heard gamesters around the Halsted Saloon call the place the devil's delight and stopped in his tracks. "Fellows tell me it's a pretty fancy layout."

"No, you goose, just lively. Sylvia Starr just opened there in her American Venus Review with a chorus of two dozen dancers. But I hope you won't have eyes for them alone." Her own blue eyes were glowing.

It had been over a week since that day at the Exposition Grounds and now Harry burned to repeat the lovely experience. In fact both were so intent on getting away from the world again they failed to notice a familiar face during their five block walk to the imposing new three-storied theater building.

From the minute Harry and Janet had left the vicinity of the Congress Hotel, they'd been trailed through the shoulder-to-shoulder crush of evening crowds by the ill-matched duo of Ogden Palmer and the detective. Doherty wore a seedy brown suit while Palmer was stylish in a black worsted outfit, with a hard-crowned fedora, and toting his perpetual rattan cane. This pair silently entered with the late comers to Peacock Alley and seated themselves in a corner of the rapidly filling theater, keeping an eye on their quarry far down the aisle.

With a roll of drums and blare of brass the great red curtain parted and Miss Sylvia Starr pounced out with all the animality of some jungle cat. From that moment the stage was alive with the ebullient rowdiness of some three-ring tent show. The red-tressed Miss Starr sang one cleverly off-color song after another, postured and danced superbly at the head of a small squad of flashing-eyed, high-kicking young women in the scantiest of costumes while the audience noisily applauded its approval.

When the hour and a half of unending musical mayhem reached its finale, Sylvia Starr, strangely motionless at last, was to be seen posing center stage as noted sculptor Lindstrom's famous statue of "Light".

Palmer's pale, hatchet-face creased in an ugly smirk as the curtain closed on that vaguely risqué scene. "Now where's our pigeons off to?" he asked as Harry and Janet headed toward a nearby door.

"Probably dining in one of the upstairs wine rooms."

"Good. We wait for a while and then. . . ."

"We bust in and haul out your filly while I knock the daylights out of young Lochinvar. That'll bring her to heel."

Seated in the small upstairs wine room with its rose-shaded lamp, Harry and Janet tackled their order of lobster Newberg and smiled at each other while a sleek waiter poured their champagne.

For a time both applied themselves to the meal, then Harry cocked his head at the muffled racket coming from the next room.

"I think our neighbors are raising too much Cain. That's not the style for folks like us."

Janet took another sip of her champagne and giggled. "I'm afraid I've lured you to a low-class grog shop, after all."

Although enjoying the show and the first-rate meal, Harry had decided Peacock Alley's other main attraction was its secluded wine rooms as places of assignation, but he shrugged it off although the night had put a great dent in his dwindling bank roll.

Before he could do more than reach across the table for her hand, the locked door crashed open.

"Here you are, you conniving strumpet!" And Ogden Palmer lunged in followed by Dan Doherty waving his Smith & Wesson.

Teeth bared, Palmer yanked at Janet, scattering plates and glasses while Doherty swung the weapon to buffalo Harry.

The battle joined, Janet furiously scratched Palmer's face as Tracy evaded the clubbed pistol and hurled the detective to the floor where he lay stunned. Then he went for Palmer.

"C'mere you chalky-faced bastard and take your medicine." With the detective's Smith & Wesson in hand, Harry poked the big pistol straight at Palmer's shrinking belly.

"Now let's talk this . . . ," Palmer began, hands stuck out stiffly, but that was all before the long-barrel landed on his head with the sound of a thunked melon.

"Pardon us!" Tracy slammed the door on the collective faces peering in from the hallway, locking it with the dead bolt. "We'll be out in a minute!" he called through the heavy oak paneling.

"You were wonderful, dear." Janet's voice was trembling with mixed excitement and laughter. "What are we going to do now?"

"This." And Harry tugged the belts and galluses from the downed duo and, rolling them over, lashed them together, back-to-back, like a pair of unpleasant Siamese twins. "And this." He yanked off their cravats and, stuffing their handkerchiefs into their respective mouths, gagged them tightly just as the detective was groaning back to life.

Doherty's eyes, bulging like a tromped on frog's, flickered from the girl to Tracy and back, leaving little doubt but that he was indelibly engraving Harry's face and description upon his policeman's memory.

Ogden Palmer, made of less sterner stuff, still slumbered noisily at the officer's back.

"That rascal there's got my number." Harry took Janet in his arms and kissed her. "Chicago's going to be too hot for me, darling. So, I guess it's going to be twenty-three skidoo for now." He went over to the room's one window and, heaving it up, was relieved to find it opened onto a fire escape. Following a resounding kick to the groaning Palmer's ribs, he led Janet through the window and down the rickety iron ladder into a dark alley, just as the room's door commenced to resound to a volley of blows delivered from the other side.

Two hours later, Harry was occupying a scuffed, yellow plush seat on a westbound passenger train. After leaving Peacock Alley, he'd taken Janet over to Michigan to catch a late night streetcar, spending their fifteen minute wait in a doorway, locked in a tight embrace as they swore eternal devotion.

"Don't worry about Ogden Palmer," she'd told him. "I can lie as well as he can." She'd smiled slightly as she'd reached up on her tiptoes to kiss him. "And a darned sight better."

Remembering her warm lips, Harry shifted the detective's gun in his waistband, and silently renewed his vow—to send for her as soon as he could get up some money. When they parted, she still believed him to be a successful rancher, and now, somehow, he had to make that yarn come true.

But, staring at the train's rattling glass window, he saw the other Harry Tracy reflected in the black, rushing night—shaking his head.

Chapter Four

Two days after parting from Janet Warrington, Harry was forced to stop off at Little Rock, Arkansas. He'd intended traveling as far as Dallas, Texas to look for work on one of the outlying ranches. But his plans were altered when he lost nearly every cent to a pair of cardsharpers who got on at St. Louis.

With nothing left but a six-shooter and a $20 bill, hidden in his shoe, he swung down onto the Little Rock platform at noon the first day of September, 1894. He walked the sunny streets, looking over the big hotels, the bathhouses, and strolling crowds, killing time until nightfall.

Still believing in his luck, despite the trimming he'd taken on the train, he managed to get into a game of five-card stud in the back room of one of the smaller saloons on Arkansas Street. From seven o'clock onward he watched his pile grow as he outplayed a trio, including a hotel operator, an off-duty policeman, and a cotton broker.

By nine o'clock he was $400 to the good, but, with the advent of a local Little Rock jeweler into the game, his luck began to fade. By eleven he was flat broke, and, although he knew it wasn't smart to kick up a row with a policeman in the game, he was positive the jeweler had been cheating.

Folding, he went up to the bar to think about things. There was just $5 left, enough for three drinks—and he had them. It was a fool thing to do, but he was half tipsy from a combination of whiskey and lack of food, and sullenly determined to get even with that slick-fingered trinket merchant.

Following his bout at the bar, Harry walked across to the next block on South Street and looked over Erastus Keeny's Jewelry Emporium. The place stood in deep shadow, with the nearest street light eight buildings off. Thus it took less than a few seconds to knock out the door glass with his Colt barrel, reach inside, throw the dead bolt, and walk in. Lighting a series of matches, he'd barely begun to look over the assorted geegaws when the policeman from the game, accompanied by another officer, gum-shoed through the door and covered him with their service revolvers. And by twelve o'clock that night he was locked up tight in the Little Rock jail.

From the time he'd left Chicago everything had seemed jinxed. For simple breaking and entering, a first offense, Tracy drew a one year stretch in the state pen at Little Rock. It wouldn't have gone quite so hard if they hadn't found that six-shooter under his coat. But he was still thankful they'd accepted his story of being an out of work cowpoke from Montana named Harry Bass. He'd picked that moniker out of thin air, probably from some dime novel he'd read about that old time Texas bandit, Sam Bass.

Assigned to the prison jute mill, he kept out of trouble and watched his step. But he was bound to run into some hardcases during those long months, and his jinx held, for when he was released on good behavior May 15, 1896, two of his fellow cons walked out through the big iron gates at the same time.

Lanky Jack Bennett and pudgy Bill Pigeon had knocked around the frontier for years, doing as little work as they could do to get by, and most of that outside the law. They had a good dodge, they'd told him, bootlegging whiskey to the Indians, and they meant to head back to Idaho and go into business again.

Taking the Pacific Northwest Flyer, the three landed at American Falls at the end of May, and for the first time in over a year Harry sent a letter to Janet Warrington. He wrote her that he'd been as far south as Mexico, looking for a good strain of beef cattle, and hoped she'd received the letters he'd mailed from around the country. But whether she believed him, or whether she didn't, Janet never replied. It was as if they'd never met—and never loved.

Shrugging it off as ancient history, Tracy applied himself to the fine art of bootlegging and for several months all went along swimmingly. The trio, having taken over an abandoned cabin in a hidden hollow just off the main road to Fort Hall, began to ply their trade with the motley settlement of Indians camping near the fort. Mostly Paiutes and Shoshones, with a few Nez Percés, they hunted sporadically, but in the main lay around their teepees waiting for beef issue day.

As junior member of the firm, Harry was deputized to drive their recently purchased buckboard twenty miles over to American Falls and purchase their stock of tanglefoot from certain saloonkeepers. Aware of where the liquor went, the barkeeps asked for and got the high dollar. But that was all right, for the triumvirate charged their customers enough to ensure a hefty profit. When one of the natives was unable to come up with the ready cash, either Bennett or Pigeon were generally amenable to working out some swap for the night—usually one of the prettiest squaws. Bennett soon became so taken with the daughter of the old Shoshone Chief, Wild Goose Jake, that he built another lean-to onto the cabin and moved in his copper-colored mistress. Naturally her concerned parent visited the establishment on a regular basis—to get his weekly whiskey rations.

Things had been going so briskly that Bill Pigeon, the business head of the company, began to talk one morning of establishing a regular hog ranch and importing several more young squaws, along with a couple of white saloon girls from town.

"We give the soldier boys their choice." Pigeon cocked a boot up on the dinner table and chewed at his cigar. "Then we git it both ways. We peddle our goods to the Injuns and the troopers git their fun here . . . so they'll look the other way when the redskins kick over the traces and go on a high lonesome."

"Yeah, but Spotted Fawn says their new commandant at the fort is a hellbender." Jack Bennett nodded at his squaw, where she sat on a stool, plucking the feathers from a pair of sage hens Harry had dropped with a shotgun before breakfast.

"Oh, he'll look the other way, too, like the last one, providin' he gits his bottles of Old Crow oncet in a while." Pigeon lifted his other boot up and rubbed his fat legs reflectively. "Let me worry about business . . . and you can break in the chippies, you 'n' Harry."

Harry, who already had his eye on one of the American Falls saloon girls, grinned. "Fine by me, if we can get that red-headed Pearly Mae out here . . . the one at the Bird Cage."

That was the last meeting of the firm of Pigeon, Bennett, and Tracy. Around dusk, on his return from hauling over another load of wet goods, Harry was nearing the stand of aspens enclosing the cabin when he saw a wavering pillar of black smoke bending eastward over the quivering grove. He reined in the buckboard and looked around. A horse whinnied somewhere nearby and voices called to each other. His first thought was there'd been a raid by reservation bucks, then a noise in the underbrush brought his six-gun out of its holster.

"Hold on! It's me!" Jack's voice sounded from the dense shrubbery, then with a rustle, Bennett's long neck poked out of a creambush thicket, with the dark face and glittering eyes of Spotted Fawn behind him. "We been waitin' for you to get back from town. Git rid of that wagon and ride outta here! They gobbled that damn' fool Pigeon when he went to the fort to make peace talk with the new brass. Then that big muckety-muck of a major came back here with a passel of troopers and set fire to the whole shebang."

"Where'll I go? Where'll you go?"

"Anywhere but here. You stick around and git caught by them bluebellies . . . it's back to the old stone hotel. And this time you'll do more than nine months."

While Bennett was talking, Harry had been unhitching the horse, throwing a blanket over its back, and making a bridle from a piece of rope taken from the canvas covering the whiskey load.

There came a series of shots and more hoots from over the hill where the cabin and lean-tos were now roaring with flame. "That damned major must 'a' gone back and his troopers hev got into the red-eye," Bennett growled, emerging from the brush leading a horse with Spotted Fawn astride the animal. "Well, good bye, old sport, we're headin' down inter Utah. Got me shirt-tail relation at Brigham City."

Harry shook hands with the lanky bootlegger and swung up onto the mare and rode away, leaving the abandoned buckboard. There was a sheep ranch ten miles east where he could get a meal, put up for the night, swap the wagon mare for a riding horse, and buy himself a saddle and bridle.

Hunt Down Harry Tracy

After that? He didn't know, but he'd head on into Wyoming, and try for a job on some ranch—somewhere where they didn't know Harry Tracy, or Harry Bass. Maybe this time that jinx would be left behind in the ashes of the cabin.

Three weeks after crossing the Wyoming line, Harry arrived at Casper, Wyoming on July 3rd and put up at the town's single hotel. With less than $50 in his pocket, he kept firmly out of the poker games, while letting his mount rest up at the local livery.

While lounging in the Wolcott House bar on the afternoon of July 4th, he struck up a conversation with a young fellow in shabby range clothes who was teetering on a three-legged chair, intently watching a poker game in the room's corner.

"Bottom's fallen out of the ranch game, stranger, due to this golblamed depression and that's why I can't introduce myself into that there game," the swarthy-faced young cowpuncher said in answer to Harry's question. "Nope, ain't one ranch between Lander and Lusk doin' more than keepin' its nose above water."

Harry bought a round and discovered the cowboy, who called himself Kid, was on his way to northern Wyoming. The fellow seemed more than willing to discuss just about everything, from the merits of the White River saddle as opposed to the Wyoming model and the advantages of Ralston breakfast food over plain flapjacks.

"Do me any good to stretch out that way?" Harry bought another round, feeling this drawling expert on just about everything might be worth riding with.

"Y'can far as I care," the Kid replied, staring longingly at the busy card game, then hitching at his belt as he teetered back on the chair to face Harry. His dark restless eyes swept over Tracy and lingered where Harry's six-shooter bulged under his vest. "Y'ain't supposed to carry arms into a town, but I guess you know that?"

"I was just about to remind you of the same thing." Harry grinned, staring at a corresponding bulge under the Kid's own vest.

The Kid looked thoughtfully at Harry. "You asked if it would be worthwhile to ride up Powder River way . . . and the answer is . . . maybe, that is if you ain't afraid to use that hardware . . . if you have to."

"My own answer is . . . maybe, if the money's right." Disgusted with his failure to find work, Harry had also been thinking of his luck. Again maybe, just maybe, if he could make a raise with this high line rider he might come up with a stake, then return to Janet—and remind her of their promises. No doubt this Kid was some sort of owlhoot, but he wouldn't have to ride with him long—just long enough.

"I can see you're chewing that over pretty good," the Kid muttered, staring at the noisy card game. "Where's your horse?" the young cowpuncher suddenly asked.

"Why down at the livery," Harry replied.

"Mine's out front . . . the bay with front stocking feet. Go get yours and tie it beside mine. Got any baggage?"

"Just what's on my back."

"Then we'll travel fast. Now move, *pronto!*"

As Harry was going through the door, the Kid called after him. "Ain't this the Fourth of July?" At Harry's nod, he waved him on out and let his chair *thud* to the floor—eyes glued on the poker game.

When Harry had paid the livery man and brought his horse up to the hitching rail beside the Kid's black, he heard the *crack-slam* of gunfire and met the Kid running, head down with a sombrero clutched to his breast, six-shooter smoking.

Tugging the reins loose, Harry vaulted into the saddle and

followed the Kid's mount up the street in a head down gallop as the barkeep's double-barrel blasted another charge of buckshot. With blue whistlers screaming past his ears, Harry glanced over at the Kid, shouting: "What the hell are we doing?"

"Leaving a dead burg with something more than we got here with!" The Kid's swarthy face split in a white-toothed smile as he spurred on his mount, long dark hair streaming, banner-like, behind him.

Easing up at Caspar's shabby outskirts just past the slaughterhouse, the Kid reined in long enough to dismount hurriedly and stuff the contents of the Stetson into his saddlebags.

"You stood up the poker game?" Tracy looked over his shoulder at the distant Wolcott House where the bartender was still out in the middle of the dusty street waving his fist and empty shotgun.

"Thought we'd kill two birds with one stone . . . put some pep into Casper's Fourth of July and take along some traveling money."

Tracy stared at the Kid. "Well, then, we'd better get traveling."

The Kid looked toward town, clapped the empty Stetson back on his head, swung into the saddle, and spurred up his horse, with Tracy following suit. Far behind came a series of shots.

That night, as they sat at a small campfire in a coulée finishing the last of Harry's coffee and beans, the Kid leaned back against a boulder and rubbed his belly with contentment. "Ah, the end of a perfect day."

Tracy rolled a cigarette, lit it with a twig from the fire, then nodded. "All your days like this one?"

"Some." The Kid grinned, teeth flashing in the firelight.

"Guess you're wonderin' what's next . . . after we hit Hole-in-the-Wall?"

"Hole-in-the-Wall? That's Powder River Country?"

"Keep forgettin' you ain't from around these parts . . . y'ain't, are you?"

"Think I said I came over from west of here."

"Yeah, and with a six-shooter tucked away for an ace in the hole?"

Tracy merely grunted and puffed away on his makings.

"Well, Hole-in-the-Wall, spang out in Powder River territory, is a hang-out for some folks like me . . . and maybe you. Only one way into the place, and that's guarded by jaspers who don't care much for tin stars. A real peaceful place to winter mavericked stock and cipher out some raise or other. They say all sorts of longriders, from the James boys on down, have used the place in the past."

"When do we get there?"

"If we start out early in the morning, we should make 'er in two days easy-like."

Tracy lay long in his blanket staring at the contracting red fire circle before he drifted off. If this Kid had some raise in mind, and it went right, there just might be a chance to get enough money to buy up some small ranch—that ranch he'd fibbed to Janet about. It wouldn't be easy, he knew that from the way this wild Kid seemed to go off on the half cock, but the fellow certainly had sand, and there had to be someone in his gang to keep a short rein on such a young rooster.

They rode side-by-side, hour after hour, across the lonely high plains, with the Big Horn range lofting along the horizon like a chain of blue-tinged clouds. And as they rode, the Kid, monopolizing the talk as usual, proposed and disposed of a wide variety of subjects including: William Jennings Bryan—

"Confounded puppet of the Silver Trust!" Buffalo Bill—"Big four-flusher got his name firin' point-blank at the woolies that was so thick even he couldn't miss!" Tammany Hall—"Greatest gang of highwaymen in the country . . . includin' the Hole-in-the-Wall bunch." President Grover Cleveland—"Never make a longrider . . . just think of some poor cayuse totin' that heavy weight . . . any posse'd grab him off in the first mile." And so on—*ad infinitum.*

For all of his talkative ways, the Kid never had much to say about himself, and Harry didn't pry for he had no desire to re-hash his own faults and failings. But the Kid did reveal something of his beginnings on the outlaw trail when they stopped about sundown near a small ranch close to a fork of the Powder.

As this was the first habitation they'd come upon in the all day ride, the Kid remarked they might as well stop for the night. "But not too blamed close," he told Harry as they reined in 100 yards from the bunkhouse and corrals.

The Kid dismounted in the scarlet light and opened the swing gate, closing it behind after they'd passed through. Slipping toward the buildings, he lingered near the corrals and gave a series of short whistles.

Tracy saw a vague figure drift forward and stop at the corral. He caught the subdued mutter of their voices, then both came toward him.

"Here's Elzy Lay," the Kid told Harry, who reached down and shook hands with the man. "Elzy's a retired streetcar magnate." The Kid chuckled, dodging a slap from the shadowy cowhand.

"And this maverick's always jealous of folks that rise higher than some light-fingered wide looper," returned the other. "Ain't you, Mister Sundance?"

"Can the chatter and fetch some grub," the Kid grunted,

ignoring Lay's sarcasm. "We're bedding down over in the north pasture."

Lay turned away with a quiet laugh. As he neared the bunkhouse, a hulking wide-shouldered figure silhouetted itself in the orange oblong of the lighted doorway.

"Damn! That's the foreman, old Bob Divine himself," the Kid muttered. "Let's get ourself out of sight."

As they walked their mounts across the pasture toward a shadowy grove of trees, the Kid filled Harry in on Lay, Divine, and the CY Ranch. "Elzy's a right good fellow, but laying low, same as me. He signed on with that hard-nosed Divine, when I rode down southwards."

At Harry's unspoken query, the Kid continued while both stripped the horses of saddles and extra gear. "Elzy and me ran off a string of quarter horses from some ranches in the Big Horn Basin, hopin' it would be blamed on the Jack Bliss gang. Bad part of the deal was another pal of ours, named Cassidy, got nabbed for the job. Butch, that's his name, drew two years in the state pen. He ain't out yet, but you bet he'll have something to say when he gets back to the Hole."

"Get rid of the horses?"

"Yeah, we peddled 'em off around Miles City, except for a few Elzy fetched back to the CY Ranch."

"This foreman, Divine, on the take?"

"Not generally. Just when he can get by . . . and he knew Cassidy was takin' the jolt, so he welcomed Elzy and the extra horseflesh more or less with open arms. Even though the ranch was in slow times, Elzy's a top hand with horses."

By the time they had a small fire going, Lay was back with a couple of plates of fried potatoes, beef steaks, and coffee. "Old Bob's leery of you roosting out here. He's got a good idea who you are, Sundance, and, knowing your itchy trigger finger, don't want to get in Dutch for letting you camp on the ranch."

"Well, darn his picture anyway," the Kid glowered. "He makes me sound like some wild Indian." Then shrugging, he turned his attention to the meal. " 'Sall right, we'll be long gone by morning. Want to hit the Hole by dinner time." Between mouthfuls, he exchanged gossip with Lay, while Tracy, eating in silence, kept his ears open.

Names such as Flat Nose George Currie, Matt Warner, Tom McCarty, Bill Madden, and Bub Meeks arose to the surface of the quiet conversation, usually marked by chuckles or low whistles, while others, including some deputy named Calverly and a feisty little stock detective called LeFors, drew muffled curses and sounds of mutual disgust.

Finally Lay arose from the campfire, took the empty utensils, and, bidding them good night, walked back to the bunkhouse.

Rolling up in his blanket, feet to the fire, Tracy inquired about the peculiar nickname Lay had used.

"Sundance?" The Kid cursed morosely and spat at the sinking red eye of the fire. "That's the fool handle he and Cassidy wished onto me after they found out I'd done time in the pokey at Sundance, Wyoming on a drummed-up horse theft charge a couple years back. It's a name I sure wish everybody'd forget, let me tell you." He rolled over in his blanket, burying his head in its folds. "Now let's get us some shut-eye. We gotta get some ridin' done come daylight."

Chapter Five

Next morning they were saddled and out of the CY pasture before the tardy sun had begun to lance its golden beams across the rolling, night-wrapped horizon.

Riding steadily toward the Big Horns where they loomed up at the feathery cloud masses in the north, Harry and the Kid arrived about noon at a deepening gorge in the steeply rising hills. Here the middle fork of the Powder River carved a deep path into the hidden valley of Hole-in-the-Wall. Entering a towering cañon, so narrow their stirrup leather brushed both sides of the sheer, red granite cliffs, they rode down a gorge to the west, coming at last where the rocky trail cut abruptly back toward the east, ending at a huge notch in the vermilion walls.

"Here she is at last," the Sundance Kid, who'd been unusually silent, suddenly sang out. And in another moment, with his guide ahead, Harry rode around a great upthrust boulder and was descending a good trail into the lovely valley.

Shifting cloud shadows slowly drifted over the enormous green vista, now dappling a few weather-beaten cabins in the near foreground, then sweeping its violet-tinged patterns onward over the scattered group of brown flecks in the verdant distance that were stock at browse.

"Pretty, heh?" The Kid jerked a thumb back over his

shoulder at the massive stone opening behind them. "And mighty well forted up, too."

Harry, looking back toward the enormous Red Wall, caught the glitter of nooning sun on rifle barrels, and dropped his hand upon the butt of his Colt.

"Don't get edgy," Sundance snickered, and waved his sombrero in the direction of the riflemen.

In a moment, two men came from around a pile of boulders and ambled toward them. The taller of the riflemen was turned out in good store clothes with a white shirt, string tie, vest, and dark broadcloth pants tucked into red, tooled leather boots. He wore a pearl gray sombrero and packed two nickel-plated six-shooters. Tracy decided that he wasn't a bad-looking sort save for a mighty flat nose and a pair of the most piercing black eyes he'd ever seen. He was introduced as George Currie. The other, a big open-faced tow-headed fellow in rough range clothes, was hailed as Walt Punteney.

"Welcome to Hole-in-the-Wall Ranch" Currie laughed shortly, indicating the shabby layout. "Used to look better in the days when old Nate Champion's Red Sash Gang was here."

"But we do our best to please," Sundance quipped as they dismounted in front of the largest of the three buildings. "Say, where's the rest of the boys?"

"Nobody here just now except for George 'n' me and Tom O'Day," Punteney answered. "He's pullin' his turn up on Eagle Peak. He's the one signaled down here it was you-all."

"Figured you knew it was me," the Kid replied, lounging down on one of the wooden benches in front of the cabin. "Where you off to?" he addressed Currie who'd gone into the building to reëmerge with a coat, slicker, and bedroll and strap the outfit behind his saddle.

"Business at Buffalo." Currie swung up onto his claybank

mare, shoving the saddle gun down into its boot. "Got to find a buyer for those cattle down there." He turned to Tracy. "Can't trust these itchy-footed saddle tramps here. They might be here a week, and then gone tomorrow. I was wonderin' if you'd help out with the herd just in case I have to run it here for a spell longer?"

Tracy replied he was agreeable. "Haven't got any long-range plans that I know about."

"Right. Then you'll get your cut when we move them out." Currie kicked his horse into motion, then pulled up short. "Contrariwise to what you might think, that's a legitimate herd down there. They came from my place over at Crazy Woman Creek." He spurred his horse on up toward the Hole.

"Flat Nose's right," Sundance offered as they watched the rider dwindle in the shining afternoon light, bending and distorting in the brilliant glare finally to vanish into the gray maze of distant boulders.

"Yeah," Punteney agreed, "George sure got the dirty end of the stick from them Buffalo bankers. He was nearly wiped out in the big snow of 'Eighty-Seven, then this panic didn't help. He tried to hold on but the blamed banks foreclosed on his notes last fall, and impounded the ranch and herd."

"But old Flat Nose's a fighter," Sundance picked up the tale, "and he up and run off the stock one night last spring. Walt, Elzy. and me helped him. We was all workin' for him at the time and that's the way we lit in the Hole."

"Some boys on the dodge was already in here layin' low from rustlin' charges, and they welcomed us with open arms," Punteney put in. "Fellas like Tom O'Day, Bill Madden, Matt Warner, and Tom McCarty."

"But they're the kind that just won't stay put for long, like Currie says." Sundance grinned, getting up from the bench and leading the mounts to a rough pole corral around behind the cabin.

"And you can add your name to that roll," Punteney called after him, "you and that Elzy Lay, or McGinnis, or whichever he's callin' himself." Punteney also arose and motioned to Tracy. "Come on, seein' you're here for a spell, I'll take you over to the bunkhouse. Me and O'Day stay here in George's cabin, but there's plenty of room down there." He paused and squinted at Tracy. "Just one thing, George and Tom's been gettin' mighty tired of my meals. Y'ain't any sort of a cook be you?"

For the next two months, until Elzy Lay rode back into the Hole, having got the itchy foot and quit both the CY and Bob Calverly, Harry served as camp cook to the fledgling Wild Bunch. Having been cook's helper to old Sol Simpson back home in the north woods, he'd picked up a few tricks to transform such plain fare as biscuits, beef, spuds, and coffee into something extra special. And every so often he'd take time to turn out dried fruit pies that tasted just right from the judicious dollops of bourbon cooked up in the filling. After watching George Currie roll his glittering dark eyes up to the bunkhouse's cobwebbed ceiling as he cursed feelingly with pleasure over roast quail and rice, and Elzy Lay compare the canned peach and cracker pie to any of the finest desserts taken onboard when a streetcar driver in Denver, Harry felt he was earning his particular share of Flat Nose's cattle, fair and square, without ever riding herd.

Another talent making him popular with the fugitives and outlaws passing through the Hole was music. Retaining his old harmonica over the years, Harry would often sit down after supper and cut loose with such tunes as "Shanty Boys", "Golden Slippers", or "Dan McGinty" and soon everyone's toes were tapping. One of the jingles picked up at the bootleg-gers' camp became a great favorite with Sundance and the others:

> Oh, the chickens they grow tall in Cheyenne,
>   in Cheyenne,
> And they eat them claws and all in Cheyenne,
>   in Cheyenne.
> Oh, the women wear the britches in Cheyenne.
> Yes, the women wear the britches in Cheyenne.
> Oh, the men are sons-of-bitches in Cheyenne,
>   in Cheyenne,
> Yes, they're dirty sons-of-bitches in Cheyenne.

Although the meter limped a bit, Harry sometimes varied the lyric's locale to Buffalo to get a laugh out of George who'd been chased headlong from that town by a sheriff's posse on a warrant filed by the Buffalo County bankers.

Flat Nose still had the herd boxed up in the Hole with no money to show for his efforts. And that eventually led to the first train robbery by the longriders from Hole-in-the-Wall.

Elzy Lay and the others, with the exception of Sundance, who always had his own version of how food should be cooked, often lauded Tracy for his efforts with the pots and pans. In spite of such approval, Harry became bored with the long weeks as camp cook, and promptly resigned when George Currie announced his plan to take the herd south to Medicine Bow on the Union Pacific.

All the riders in camp, except Sundance, expressed their willingness to go on the drive to the railroad construction camp. "A mite too close to Casper," the Kid told Currie. "I don't think they forgot our little Fourth of July powwow."

He turned to Harry, where Tracy was putting a batch of

sourdough in the fireplace's Dutch oven. "I shouldn't think you'd want to show up in them parts, either. Somebody's bound to spot you, too."

"I'll take my chances," Harry answered, winking at Elzy Lay. "And Kid, seeing you want to sit home, I guess you're cook. Now you can try out some of those great recipes you've been bragging on."

The herd, when gathered, was worked slowly down the valley in the direction of the great V-notch that was the Hole's main entrance. Another entrance lay at the northern end of the valley where Beaver Creek snaked out of the Red Wall, but that passage was far too narrow for such an out-pouring of this bawling, jostling river of beef on the hoof.

With the exception of a few yearlings, which Currie left behind, on Monday, September 8th, the entire herd of 200-odd cattle was trailed out of the Hole and on down the winding passage to the outside plains. Currie rode at the point with Walt Punteney, while the swing riders consisted of Tom O'Day and Matt Warner, a sardonic sort of fellow on the dodge from a successful shoot-out back in Utah. Harry and Elzy brought up the rear, riding drag and eating their peck of dust.

Sundance and Bill Madden, a drifter on the scout from Colorado for horse theft, remained at Hole-in-the-Wall Ranch, holding down the fort. As Harry and Elzy rode past the bunkhouse at the end of the bellowing cattle parade, Sundance, lounging on the cabin bench with Madden, waved an ironic farewell. "Say hello to our old friend Honest Bob Divine on the way."

Once past the Hole and stretching out into a day-long drive, Tracy exchanged reminiscences with Lay, learning some of his background. Hailing from back East as did most of the range riders, Lay first landed in Denver in 1889, taking on the job of driving a horse-drawn streetcar. This didn't last long as he'd lit into a masher who was making life miserable for a woman passenger. "Guess my dander got the best of me." Lay chuckled. "I pitched that sport, headfirst, from the car and damned nigh killed him. Then I parked the contraption and headed out of town as fast as I could hike. Got a horse on the sly from a neighboring farm and drifted over in Utah, eventually going to work on some of the ranches thereabouts."

Using the alias of McGinnis, he'd worked with a young fellow called Cassidy on several ranches in Brown's Park and took to him. "Butch, same as a lot of fellows, got the dirty end of the stick though. Sundance and I lifted some dandy saddle stock, and it just worked out that Butch got the blame. But we'll try to make it up to him when he gets out."

Tracy, taking to the quiet cowboy, particularly for his whipping of the masher, related some of his own adventures in the lumber camps and with the bootleggers, throwing in something of his escapades in Chicago but barely mentioning the one person who remained constantly in his thoughts.

Lay, aware that Harry seemed to be skirting around his Chicago days, grinned to himself as he spurred up his black mare to haze a two-year-old steer back into the moving herd. "Know what you're saying . . . or not saying. There's only two things that spook me, too . . . a woman, good or bad, and being afoot."

For the rest of that long, dusty day, Harry and the others were busy until they reached a small branch of the Salt River called the Black Snake. There they went into camp, watered the stock, and bedded them down on the north side of the shallow stream by dusk.

The country had such a familiar look to Harry that he mentioned it to the leonine Matt Warner, who sat drinking a cup of Arbuckle's at the fire. Warner stretched out his bowlegs and shrugged. "Ought to, hadn't it? This is the way you and the Kid came to the Hole. And you stopped by the CY over that ridge there and got yourself a hand-out from old Bob Divine, didn't you?"

Harry nodded and glanced across at Elzy Lay, who was squatting on the far side of the fire, cradling a Winchester. Suddenly Lay stood up, and Tracy saw the rest of the crew following suit—weapons in hand. Then he caught the thudding of an approaching horse, and in another instant both rider and mount were silhouetted against the orange bars of the sunset.

"Aha! Divine himself, and about as welcome as a polecat at a picnic." Warner stood beside Tracy, hand on the butt of his six-shooter. "Keep your eyes on Flat Nose."

Currie lofted a hand in greeting, waving the rider on in.

The burly CY foreman swung down from his mustang and spoke in a low tone to George Currie, then the pair walked off a distance to stand in animated conversation. At last Flat Nose barked an order to Punteney and O'Day, and, as Harry watched, the pair, along with Divine, mounted up and rode over to the far side of the herd. There the trio cut out a dozen steers and headed them up a rise toward the CY Ranch. When they were out of sight in the enveloping twilight, Currie, who'd stood hands on hips, staring after his vanishing cattle, turned back to the remaining crew. "Well, if that ain't like some goldamned Injun taking a cut for crossing his bailiwick. Gone. Over four hundred dollars' worth of stock." He cursed feelingly and fingered his pistol as Harry and the others waited.

"Say the word, George, and we'll ride over and take that beef back," Warner gritted, while Elzy and Harry nodded.

"Like to boys, like to," Flat Nose growled. He kicked a

brand out of the fire, the sparks whirling upward to mingle with the evening stars. "But, no, we'll camp here and leave at crack of dawn . . . then we'll get our innings."

Good as his word, George Currie was up and had roused out all his riders a good hour before the eastern stars began to fade. The drive was well under way by the time they reached the south limits of the CY range. Here Currie halted long enough to send Elzy, Harry, and O'Day off toward the rolling foothills of a spur of the Big Horns.

"There they be!" O'Day called, pointing toward a dark mass of animals vaguely outlined beyond a shadowy drift fence. As he spoke, the first gleams of sunlight poured over the farthest hogback and the black silhouettes of the cattle were suddenly rimmed with gold.

"Let's get that wire cut there!" Lay barked. He and Harry spurred forward to the barbed barrier, where O'Day had already dismounted to work with a pair of wire cutters on the triple wire strands.

"Guess that'll do," O'Day snorted, remounting his paint pony. "Now we can get to work and even up the score for Flat Nose."

They rode on through the downed fencing and began to drive out the unbranded yearlings. Within less than an hour they'd culled out a bawling herd of two dozen unbranded yearlings and were soon chousing them down the trail to the south, following Currie's herd.

O'Day lingered just long enough to rewire the severed strands, and then loped on to rejoin Elzy and Harry. "Feel like some Texan barb-buster!" he called. "But she's back together, ship-shape, for ain't no use lettin' the rest of that CY stuff loose on the open range."

Elzy slapped his lariat at the bobbing rump of a diverging

beef, driving it back toward the compact little herd. "Yeah, let's hope old Bob Divine don't tumble to us swappin' a dozen scrubs for two dozen of his prime stock . . . leastwise until someone rides along that drift fence."

By the time the sun was noon-high they'd reached the main herd. Flat Nose had been pushing his cattle along at a steady, mile-eating pace that fetched them up at a small water hole, twenty miles northwest of Casper.

Once Harry and the others had reached the main herd with the stolen stock, Currie put Matt Warner, the group's artist, to work with his running iron. While Elzy and Punteney acted as roper and bulldogger, respectively, with O'Day helping Walt as a flanker, Warner traced Currie's brand—the C-Bar, looking like a sideways turkey track, on each of the bellowing, struggling beeves. Flat Nose tended the branding fire as Harry, the greenest of the trail drivers, circled outside the herd to keep them gentled, while he also kept watch on the rolling plains to the north.

Branding done to both Currie's and Warner's satisfaction, the new stock was wedged into the midst of the original herd, and members of the drive sat down for a cup of Arbuckle's brewed on the branding fire by Punteney, and whatever food was left in their chuck bags.

But Currie didn't waste time allowing the crew's meal to settle. As soon as they'd finished, he was mounted and, with an eye cocked back toward the CY range, had the augmented herd strung out again toward the railroad camp at Medicine Bow.

They reached the north bank of the Platte between the towns of Goose Egg and Mills an hour before sunset. The muddy, yellow river was down from lack of recent rainfall but still stretched out an ominous distance to the south bank.

Currie, who'd seemed to grow increasingly more on edge

as the afternoon wore on, rode his brown mare down into the water, then turned in the saddle. "All right, we're gonna push on over. Git them point steers down here and let's move 'em out."

As the cattle had been dry and thirsty, it wasn't long before they all were in the river. Being a small herd it didn't take a lot of hooting and shouting to guide the animals across, and Harry and the other riders gained the other bank without swallowing much water.

Once across, Currie ordered the herd moved along as far as possible before nightfall. When that came, they bedded down the cattle just beyond Jackson Cañon. After the crew had wolfed down the last bits of food from their respective war bags, filling out the scanty meal on hot coffee, Currie rode off to the nearby town of Mills for supplies and information.

While the others settled down at the fireside, yarning and playing cards, Harry, who'd won the cut, guided his black gelding, Midnight, around the resting herd.

Listening to the idle talk and laughter of the Currie bunch while watching the moon ease up its big, silver-dollar face westward over the dark, jagged waves of the Wind River range, Harry thought of Janet back in that place he was beginning to picture as a dream city—Chicago. Recalling his last night with her, he wryly considered that rough-and-tumble finish to the entire Chicago episode. And as to Janet herself, did she ever dream of him?—he surely wondered. One thing was certain, he'd given that high-and-mighty sport, Ogden Palmer, and his plug-ugly Mick flatfoot something to dream about themselves.

Gazing upward where the shoals of glittering stars blazed out in all their diamond-like brilliance despite the moon's growing fierceness, Harry took out his harmonica and played a mournful little tune Pigeon and Bennett often sang after they'd sampled their own bottled wares too often:

> Last night, as I lay on the prairie
> And looked at the stars in the sky,
> Got me wondering if ever a cowboy
> Might drift to the sweet by and by.

He'd been at his reedy serenade to the bedded down stock less than an hour when Currie came loping up out of the star sheen. "Any trouble?"

"All's quiet, except for me," Harry told him.

"Well, it won't be long if we don't light a shuck," Currie growled, wheeling his mount and riding toward camp through the suddenly milling cattle. "That damned Joe LeFors is over to town askin' too blamed many questions."

Within five minutes the entire camp was up, saddled, and heading the lumbering, bawling herd on southward through the chilly moonlight.

Chapter Six

The remainder of the drive took another day and a half, but at last Currie'd let up his hard pushing and the Hole-in-the-Wall cowhands had time to talk over things as they rode along at a more leisurely pace.

"Flat Nose gets into a real sweat whenever he crosses trails with Joe LeFors," Elzy Lay offered. "But now he seems to think he's lost Joe back in the dust."

"Who in tunket's this LeFors?" Harry wanted to know.

"Oh, just another cow waddy that ain't got enough gumption to run a spread of his own, so he hangs around the big cattlemen, snitching for them or doing their dirty work . . . like dry-gulching some poor devil who tries a little mavericking on the side."

"Sounds like a busy little bastard."

Tracy and the rest of Currie's cowpokes soon learned how busy Joe LeFors could be, when they drove the herd into the sprawling cattle pens beside the U.P. tracks at Medicine Bow that blistering hot afternoon of September 12th.

While Currie, backed by Walt Punteney, got down to business with a portly, walrus-mustached fellow in a hard hat, named Jenson, who repped for the firm of McCreary & Carey of the Union Stockyards of Omaha, Harry and the others stabled their horses at Tisdale's Livery on Reno Street and walked up to the town's small business section.

Hunt Down Harry Tracy

Strolling into the shady depths of the Monte Carlo Saloon, they elbowed themselves a space at the busy bar, ordered up a round, and fell to debating the forthcoming profits from the herd's sale.

Harry abstained from the discussion, not wanting to display his inexperience in cow country finances, and listened as he drank.

According to Elzy Lay, due to the current depressed market, Currie would be lucky to get more than $30 to $35 per average beef on the hoof. "Which'll make a tidy seven thousand dollars . . . if Lady Luck smiles," he concluded, staring through the gleaming amber of his whiskey glass at the fading sunlight coming through the batwings, for the day was clouding over.

"Now that'll make about three thousand dollars fer George as owner, and he can ransom his Cee-Bar spread away from them weasel-faced bankers with such an amount," Warner observed, also squinting through the golden depths of his diminishing rye.

"And leavin' the rest of that money . . . ah, let's see. . . ." O'Day peered into his own nearly empty glass, futilely seeking the correct amount.

"Forty five hundred," Tracy broke in, not hesitating to display his schooling.

"Correct you are," Lay answered. "And with a five-way split, we could each take away about eight hundred dollars . . . a damned fine round figure!"

Grinning at each other, the Hole-in-the-Wall Cattlemen's Association turned, as a body, and voted themselves another round. But before they could apply themselves to their drinks, Walt Punteney slipped in through the batwings, along with a swirl of windy dust.

"Phew, looks like a storm coming"—Walt held up a finger for the barkeep—"and not just one kinda storm at that."

"Don't tell me," drawled Matt Warner, "Flat Nose's got you gawkin' over your shoulder at shadows."

"Call it shadders if you want," Punteney muttered, "but I call it that four-eyed sidewinder Joe LeFors."

"LeFors' here?" Elzy and the others scowled at this bearer of unwelcome news.

"Yeah, and right now he's queerin' George's deal. Jest rode up to the pens flashin' some kinda warrant."

"Fer who?" Warner eased his six-shooter out of its scuffed holster, thoughtfully spun the cylinder, then shoved it back.

"Don't know for sure, 'cause I got me outta there on the double. Didn't hear much, but I caught George's name, and Elzy's. That warrant was swore out by Bob Divine of the blamed CY."

"Damned sore old loser," O'Day grumbled, ordering another shot of rye.

"Well, you can stay here and drown your sorrows iffen you want, but I vote we either git down there to help Flat Nose or ride," Warner gritted.

"My vote's for the cattle pens." Elzy smiled.

"Say, no use lookin' fer trouble," O'Day countered, hastily downing his drink and waving for a refill. "Maybe George can talk his way out of this and we'll still git our cut."

"I still say those Buffalo bankers are after George's herd." Lay's even voice took on a hard tone. "And it looks like they're going to get it at last."

"Yeah, waited fer him to come outta the Hole like a batch of tomcats, then let LeFors do the pouncin'." Warner pushed up the brim of his sombrero and stared at Elzy. "Still vote fer the pens?"

"Seeing my name's on the warrant, I've either got to get my hands on it . . . or. . . ."

"Or ride?"

"Maybe I'm not named on that ticket," Harry spoke up. "Think I'll go and see what I can do."

"I'm coming." Elzy Lay tossed down the remainder of his drink and grabbed O'Day by the arm. "And you've had enough. Get to the livery and fetch our horses over to the tracks."

"I'll give him a hand," Punteney said, shoving the lagging O'Day out through the Monte Carlo's batwings.

"Let's hustle before George's dander gits the best of him and he starts actin' wild-like," Warner put in, heading for the door.

"I know LeFors pretty well," said Elzy as they hurried toward the cattle pens, the buildings' false fronts throwing dim slabs of shadow across the sandy street, for the cloud packs were now scudding bleakly overhead. "He can be foxy when he's got the upper hand. But I've never heard him mixed up in any gun play . . . unless he's got the firepower on his side."

"That's the smart way to play it," Warner grunted, easing his Colt in its scabbard again.

Rounding a street corner, with the wind kicking up dust devils about their boots, they approached the tracks and the cattle pens. Looking for Flat Nose, they saw him standing with a foot cocked-up on the bottom rail of the cattle-jammed corral, having words with a pair Tracy took to be the stock detective and the cattle buyer.

"Hello, George, looking for us?" Elzy asked, clapping Flat Nose on the shoulder and nodding to a short, broad-shouldered man dressed in a store suit, enveloped in an oversize linen duster. The fellow had just removed a black, square-crowned hat to fan his round flushed face. At Elzy's voice he turned like a startled owl to stare at the newcomers, thick glasses flashing.

"Elsworth Lay?" Joe LeFors clapped back his headpiece and reached carefully into his coat pocket.

"That's the name, LeFors. And I sure hope you're reaching for a warrant and nothing else."

The stubby stock detective nodded as he slowly eased out a paper and unfolded it. "This is a warrant for your apprehension, and detention, along with George Currie and others involved in stealing stock from the CY Ranch . . . as well as that herd in the pens, driven off illegally from the C-Bar, despite the fact that said ranch and all livestock thereon had become the sole property of the Mountain National Bank of Buffalo, Wyoming."

"Damn. You sure make great speeches, pardner." Matt Warner wagged his head with apparent admiration. "And please tell just how you ever figgered out who stole them CY cows?"

"Warner, isn't it? Matt Warner?" LeFors glanced down the dusty street that led west out of town as if seeking something. "I've seen your name on more than a few dodgers together with the McCarty brothers. I've already informed George Currie, here, that I've been investigating cattle losses throughout central Wyoming for the past year."

"And?" Both Elzy and Matt stepped over to flank the glowering but silent George Currie, while the cattle buyer, Jensen, tugging at his red mustache, backed away toward his office beyond the pen's double gates.

Despite the rain-threatening storm clouds now close-herding overhead and the rising wind gusts, Joe LeFors was sweating. Fanning himself with the official-looking document, he glanced again at the west. "Well, Warner, I've been trailing you and Currie's bunch ever since you-all left the Hole. I was within rifle shot when Elsworth Lay, Tom O'Day, and this other fellow, here, cut the CY fence to run off the stock."

"Say, you really are a busy bastard." Harry folded his arms and stared at LeFors. He was burning inside. If this puffed-up little gumshoe on horseback had his way, not only would George Currie lose the entire herd, but he'd be doing time as well.

"You're who?" LeFors ruffled up at Tracy like a wind-blown owl. "What's your name cowboy?"

"Harry . . . Bass."

"Well, Harry Bass, I'll enforce the warrant by saying every man jack of you-all's under arrest right damned now!" And like some sleight-of-hand artist, a self-cocking Colt appeared in LeFors's fist—appearing with snake-like suddenness from a shoulder holster, under the voluminous duster.

Things happened in a hurry. As the wind blew the paper into the corral and LeFors's eyes swerved toward his vanishing warrant, Harry lunged for the gun hand.

While they rolled in the dust, a pair of horsemen appeared out of the dust storm to the west—with drawn pistols. The reinforcements LeFors had been awaiting. "Hold on there!" one shouted. "Git up and reach!" The older of the riders, a grizzle bearded oldster in faded range clothes and a straw skimmer, shrilled out: "Hold on! This here's Sheriff Jeff Carr and deputy!"

"You hold on there, too . . . Jefferson Davis Carr!" Walt Punteney and Tom O'Day rode up, extra saddle horses in tow, and with Winchesters leveled on the surprised lawmen.

Tracy arose, self-cocker in hand, and pointed it at the turkey-necked oldster and his deputy.

For a long moment there was only the noise of the rising wind, gritty swirling of flying dust, the jingle and stamp of horses, and the lowing herd in the cattle pens. Then came the mournful coyote howl of an approaching train from the west.

"Git down from those plugs, Carr, you and your hop toad

deputy . . . right now!" Warner emphasized his order with a shot in the air.

The two lawmen dismounted without a word. While Warner lashed both to the corral rail with a stake rope, Elzy shoved LeFors beside them. Fishing around in the officer's pockets, he produced a pair of steel cuffs, and, locking him securely to the railing, he stood off and admired his work. "There, that should hold you till we make our departure . . . wouldn't you say?"

"And now I've got me some hurry up business with friend Jensen." George Currie was off on the run toward the buyer's shack, both cocked six-shooters in his fists.

Punteney and O'Day, having dismounted, had tied the horses to the railings, and were keeping an eye on both depot and warehouse, where several loafers and hangers-on were now gaping at the activities along the cattle pens. In the distance the inbound train whistled again.

"Gonna be hell to pay when that train gets here and they see what's going on!" Warner shouted, ducking under the corral railing, and then coming back out with the trampled, muddy warrant. "Guess this is what you're looking for!"

Lay took the crumpled ball of paper, glanced at it, then stuffed it back into the pocket of LeFors's duster. "Keep this for a souvenir. And next time don't try pulling a gun on that gent there." He grinned at Harry.

The Union Pacific Flyer was now pounding in upon them, shooting out jagged spears of steam and chuffing up a towering black smoke pillar, which broke apart and flattened in the rising winds. By the time the engine had pulled its line of yellow coaches to a shuddering, creaking halt down the line at the depot, Currie was back.

"Damned Swede didn't mean to give me a red cent!" Flat Nose's black eyes glittered with rage.

"But you got the money, George? You got it all right?" Tom O'Day's voice was husky with more than wind-blown dust. "We'll get our split, hey, George?"

"Hell, no, you Irish damn' fool!" Cursing, Flat Nose spun back to glare at the trussed-up stock detective. "Between this four-eyed little polecat there and that sauerkraut- eatin' Swede, they've fixed me good."

"Look out, George, here comes snoopers from the train!" Warner yelled, untying his bay and swinging up into his saddle. "Light out or we'll be fightin' off half of Medicine Bow!"

Harry and the others saw the train conductor and several baggage men running toward them, carrying rifles. And another group of armed men were coming from the direction of the sheds.

"Hit the saddles!" Currie ordered. "Don't open up unless they start the ball!"

As they hurriedly mounted, the trussed-up lawmen, silent until now, began to shout for help.

Then came the cry of "Hold-up!" from the train men, and several bullets shrilled unpleasantly close to the riders as they whirled their mounts and headed out of town.

"Bass . . . Harry Bass! This won't be the last time!" Joe LeFors shouted after Harry, who yanked his sombrero to wave it in a sardonic farewell as they burst through the milling gang from the cattle pens.

There was a scattering of shots, returned in kind by Currie's men, and then they were pounding down the windswept road to the west.

Finally the rain that had been threatening swept across their path in gray tattered sheets and the last Harry saw of Medicine Bow was the town's false fronts and depot water tank bending and distorting in the clouds of whirling dust and driving rain.

"Holy damn!" Tom O'Day riding next to Harry through the murky, rain-lashed gloom, tugged his sombrero over his ears. "This sure ain't no kind of way to make a profit in the cattle game."

Chapter Seven

The long ride north to the Hole came off without any sight of Sheriff Jeff Carr's posse or Joe LeFors. It was as if the entire action had never taken place except that George Currie and his riders were returning without their anticipated riches. But not completely empty-handed.

When they'd unsaddled, thirty miles northwest of Medicine Bow, the first evening, the storm had blown over and the sky above the saw-toothed mountains rimming the Continental Divide was a gleaming mass of ruddy, flake gold in the late light.

"Take a good look at that there sunset." George Currie spoke up as they sat around the fire. "If that crooked Swede and his range dick pal had had their way, some of us'd never have lived long enough to see it."

"LeFors and old Jensen was in cahoots?" O'Day mumbled, still down in the mouth.

"Yeah. LeFors figgered we was goin' down to Medicine Bow, so he rode on ahead to powwow with that blamed Swede. Jensen would hold himself ready to go along with me, business-like but friendly. Then LeFors would up and spring his little trap along with that Jeff Carr, and they'd box us up. And Jensen had already figgered to get the herd at a rock bottom price, seein' it would be impounded stock."

"So we done the drive and got nothin' to show for our

work," gloomed O'Day, while the rest grinned wryly.

"Oh, we've got a little." Currie patted the inside of his shirt and turned to Harry. "It'd been a damn' sight worse if you hadn't gone for that little hop toad's gun. That was a brassy thing to do."

"Wasn't much." Harry shrugged it off. "I saw it was one of those Colt Lightnings . . . double actions. Those guns only work half the time."

"Yeah, not like the old thumb busters. But it still took sand. Anyway, you're one welcome addition to Hole-in-the-Wall Ranch." Currie unbuttoned his shirt and pulled out a handful of gold backs. "Guess there's about a thousand or so here. Yanked that damned Swede out from under his desk and cleaned out the slippery sidewinder's tin safe. Took him for every red cent in the place . . . even this." Currie fished out an expensive gold watch and chain from his vest pocket. "Figgered, if he wanted to play at the crook game, I'd raise his ante."

When Flat Nose's crew had finished toasting his own sand with a bottle of Old Crow, fetched by O'Day who'd detoured by the Monte Carlo on the way to the pens, they totted up the split—coming to something over $150 per man.

Harry, again winning the cut for first night guard, rode out to an overlooking bluff. Sitting on his black mare in the star-blazed moonlight and staring at the lonely, high mesas, he found himself pondering the same old puzzle—how he could ever come up with enough money to start that ranch he'd bragged to Jane about? When he was relieved by Elzy, he'd not come to any sort of an answer—except he could see the Hole-in-the-Wall bunch wasn't the sort to sit around feeling sorry for themselves. Somewhere along the line, they'd pull something that could pay off a lot more than a mere $1,000 and a gold watch! And he planned to be in any such game.

Hunt Down Harry Tracy

★ ★ ★ ★ ★

The return of the bunch to Hole-in-the-Wall wasn't that of any group of conquering heroes. Currie had pushed them to get into the Hole as soon as possible, as he retained a sneaking respect for the tracking prowess of Joe LeFors and wasn't taking any chances with the little lawman.

Next morning, after he'd breakfasted on half a pint of Crab Orchard and a plateful of ham and eggs, Currie went on record before the assembled gang members in the mess cabin. "They say that revenge is damn' sweet. And by the Lord, Harry, I'm going to take some revenge on those sons that nixed my deal at Medicine Bow . . . you see iffen I don't."

"You mean that sawed-off son-of-a-gun of a LeFors?" O'Day inquired, his eye upon the depleting pint.

"No, you Mick! I mean that gang of railroaders. Wouldn't have been no trouble handling those tin stars if the blue-bellied conductor and the others hadn't got it into their boneheads some sort of hold-up was going on and horned in."

"Well, just how d'you plan on gettin' the railroaders by the short hairs?" Matt Warner asked, winking at Harry.

"I saw that wink, Warner. I only need three good gun hands to make the thing tick, and you all can work out who. As for me, I intend to do some scoutin' and have things ciphered up in a week or so." With that Flat Nose arose stiffly from the rough table and stalked out, walking carefully.

"Bears out what I've said more'n once"—Warner grinned, beating O'Day to the bottle—"no one can think proper-like a-mixin' red-eye with ham and eggs so early in the day."

"Don't know." Elzy rubbed his chin thoughtfully, "George's also toting a big load of grief, and that can surely force a man into some serious thinking."

"But maybe George just don't care for my cookin' and it

makes him odd-like," said Bill Madden, who Sundance had appointed cook.

True to his word, George Currie saddled up and left the next day on his scouting expedition—and that was the last Hole-in-the-Wall saw of him for weeks.

The first word Harry or any of the others had of Flat Nose came from a drifter named Joe Walker. Walker, who hailed from the Green River area, had found himself *persona non grata* in that part of Utah following the shooting up of the town of Price after a drunk. Stopping off at Medicine Bow for another drink and supplies on his hasty trip north, he heard a blood and thunder tale of a recent raid on the railroad and stockyard. "Beat anything that Jesse James in his heyday would have pulled, they all say."

"Oh, give us some rest." Elzy laughed. "Wasn't more than some fuss at a school picnic."

"Would 'a' been plenty different if I was there," Sundance bragged, thumbs in his yellow suspenders.

"You give us a rest, too." Elzy flipped Sundance's galluses, and went on to fill in Walker on the actual event.

"Believe you, pardner, but take a look at this." Walker took out a folded newspaper and tossed it over.

Harry caught it, glanced at the front page, then read out loud:

OUTLAW GEORGE CURRIE
SEEN NEAR MEDICINE BOW

George Currie, head of the bunch that fought the forces of law and railroad officials some weeks ago during a bold robbery of the McCreary & Carey offices, has been seen near Medicine Bow.

Sheriff Jefferson D. Carr has several posses in the field seeking the outlaw gang captained by Currie and expects an early arrest of some or all of the brigands.

Noted stock detective Joseph R. LeFors has been retained by the Union Pacific Railroad to aid in running down the Currie gang, who are known to have stolen more than $5,000 at gunpoint from John Jensen. The representative of the McCreary & Carey offices had been empowered to purchase cattle from the aforesaid Currie for the supplying of beef to the U.P. section crews for the fall and winter.

"Five thousand?" Matt Warner exploded a fusillade of curses. "Flat Nose sure played us one hell of a three-card monte game. No wonder he lit a shuck outta here when he did . . . and ain't come back."

"Whoa, there," Elzy ordered. "You should know that skunk of a LeFors will lie anyone he could right into the ground."

Warner subsided growling, and Harry continued:

Officer LeFors has given a concise description of the bandits and informs us of a $200 standing reward for each member of the outlaw group—known by law officers as the Hole-in-the-Wall Gang. We print the following descriptions as a public service:

George Currie—About 5 feet 10 inches, weight 175 pounds, age 32 years, dark complexion, high cheek bones, flat forehead, flat pug nose, big hands and bones, stoops a little, long light mustache but probably clean shaven.

Matt Warner—About 5 feet 9 inches, weight 160 pounds, age 28 years, medium complexion, sharp features, dark blue eyes, long nose, small hands and feet, inclined to be bowlegged.

Elsworth Lay—About 6 feet tall, weight 180 pounds, age 27 years, ruddy complexion, blue-green eyes, dark brown hair, high forehead, square shoulders, clean shaven.

Harry Bass—About 5 feet 10 inches, 160 pounds, 22 years of age, medium complexion, blue eyes, brown hair, small mustache.

Harry Longabaugh—Known as The Kid Sundance, about 5 feet 10½ inches tall, light complexion, blue eyes, light hair, somewhat bowlegged, ragged mustache.

One other involved in crime—unknown description.

"Harry Longabaugh! My hind end! That fool LeFors thinks this here saw-toothed O'Day's me!" Sundance shouted, yanking at his own neatly trimmed mustache. "By gol', if I had that son of a buck in my sights for just one minute!"

"Easy, easy." Elzy laughed, grabbing Sundance's suspenders again, and hauled him back down onto the fireplace bench. "Could just as well have been Walt he thought was you. Remember, the paper says one of the bunch was unknown."

Sundance subsided to glare from O'Day to Matt Warner. " 'Sall right, all right." Sundance leaned back, squinting spitefully at Harry, who'd grinned at his hot-tempered outburst along with the others. " 'Sall right, Mister Harry Bass . . . Joe LeFors has got it in for you good 'n' proper they say. He won't forget you in a day of Sundays for rasslin' that old devil and grabbin' his shootin' iron from him in front of those tin stars and these here curly wolves."

Hunt Down Harry Tracy

★ ★ ★ ★ ★

During Flat Nose Currie's hiatus things jogged along as usual at the lonely hide-out. From time to time longriders rode in, including Tom McCarty who was on the scout from a bank robbery at Delta, Colorado. Once one of the most daring of bandits, the dark-featured McCarty was monosyllabic and morose, having lost his entire gang during the Delta fiasco. Harry and the others gave him a wide berth while he spent his time nursing a bottle and arguing with Matt Warner, his brother-in-law. When he rode out of the Hole a week later, Matt went with him. It would prove to be a bad move for Warner, for while McCarty seemed to have faded away into the limitless Northwest, Warner's hair-trigger disposition soon resulted in a shoot-out with Utah law officers and his capture.

Elzy Lay, Walt Punteney, and Tom O'Day, with little to do in the Hole and also tired of waiting for Flat Nose, rode out. But Sundance, having lost every dollar of his Casper hold-up to Harry in a poker game, could only bid the de-camping trio a profane farewell.

George Currie wearily rode back into the Hole on October 12th, having been gone nearly a month. The first thing he did upon painfully swinging down from his sweat-streaked mount was to inquire for Elzy Lay.

"Gone nigh two weeks," Harry said, helping Currie limp over to the split log settle in front of the bunkhouse.

"Damn! Just when I wanted him on hand the worst way."

Currie's usually deeply tanned features were pale beneath the trail dust. He addressed hovering Sundance and Bill Madden. "One of you git me a bottle of whiskey if you two tanks ain't polished 'em all off."

By the time Madden had returned with a bottle, Harry and Sundance were supporting Flat Nose, who was weaving on the bench, boot off and foot soaked with blood.

While Currie went to work on the Crab Orchard, Sundance and Harry bound up the injury, a bullet-creased ankle, and listened to Flat Nose's terse tale. "I ranged far and wide, I can tell you, just lookin' things over and cipherin' plans for any sort of a haul that'd repay us for that dirty deal we got from that Swede. Went far south as Tie Siding on the U.P. below Medicine Bow, far west as Rock Springs, and as far north as Malta, Montana. Finally hit pay dirt there. Got in cahoots with a railroad man nursin' a hefty grudge against the U.P." He took a long pull at the bottle, groaned with mingled satisfaction and pain, and went on. "It cost a bundle, but we'll take those infernal railroads for a real bonanza."

"Suppose it was part of that five thousand dollars we never got to see?" Sundance broke in scowling. "Don't think we don't know about that." And he tossed George the newspaper with the story of the Medicine Bow altercation and its perpetrators.

Currie glanced at the piece, ringed with a heavy lead pencil, and laughed painfully. "I swan, I see you were there, too, Kid Sundance."

Before Longabaugh could explode, Harry hastened to inquire into the proposed railroad raid, while Madden and an unusually quiet Sundance bent forward to listen.

"Just so, that paper shows you the way those yellow sheets blow things up. Wasn't more'n three thousand dollars. Now I admit holding out some, but I wanted enough to grease palms if I ran into the right sort of a set-up." Currie took another pull at the whiskey, wiped his mustache, and went on. "This yahoo of a railway express messenger was toting a big grudge for not getting paid when laid up. He was showin' off and hurt his back liftin' some sort of a trunk, but the railroad said he was just drunk on duty and wouldn't pay up."

"So what's he got for you?" Sundance inquired, reaching over to help himself to Flat Nose's whiskey bottle.

"A big gold shipment's coming over the U.P. to one of the West Coast Army Posts in less than a month. My pigeon'll let me know when he's sure of the date. He gets a quarter of what could be fifty thousand dollars, which he thinks'll make his back feel a lot better . . . and we get the rest, which'll be plenty." Currie leaned back and wiggled his bandaged foot.

Emboldened by the thought of so much money, Madden fingered his straggling mustache, grinning tentatively. "And how'd that little crease happen?"

"Fired at not ten miles from here." Currie grabbed the bottle back from Sundance. "It might have been that damn' dry-gulchin' Tom Horn, but I don't think he knew 'twas me. He's supposed to be workin' fer the cattlemen now. And I guess anyone comin' into the Hole these days is a prime target. The big cattle boys are shootin' to kill again, same as they done to pore old Nate Champion and Nick Rae years back. Next time I see Horn, I'll let him know I'm out of the maverickin' business. From now on it's just payrolls or trains."

Preparations went busily along each day for the trek up into Montana. Arms and ammunition were checked over, and the trio of grain-fed mounts, glossy coats shining in the late fall sunlight, were put through their paces with either Madden or Tom O'Day grooming them while various members of the bunch took them out for gallops down the north-ward trail through the valley.

The group rode out of the Hole on November 23rd, with the exception of George Currie whose leg had given him so much trouble he reluctantly deputized Sundance to ride in his place. Walt Punteney, who'd returned from a high lonesome over at Thermopolis, found himself left behind with Flat Nose as the last two inhabitants of Hole-in-the-Wall.

"My luck's gingered up as usual." Sundance crowed as they cantered northward, heading toward Buffalo, Sheridan, and the Montana line. "It's just as well old George stayed back. Him wanting to buy tickets and take on the train crew while we're ridin'. I say we pile timbers on the track and stop her that way."

"We'll do like George said and don't think different!" Bill Madden shouted over at Longabaugh. "Tip Gault tried to wreck an engine back in Nebrasky, but all he got was a batch of splinters when she driv right on through that woodpile. These engines nowadays weigh twenty tons, and you could smash 'em in one side and out the other of a brick house."

Harry, leading the pack horse and riding beside O'Day, nodded wordlessly when Sundance commenced a dissertation on the finer points of train raiding, beginning with the Reno brothers, for his own thoughts were far from his immediate surroundings.

Looking at the determined faces around him, then at the diamond points of light slipping down the shimmering surface of Crazy Woman Creek as they forded its broad reaches, Harry saw again the melting blue of the sky above Lake Michigan, the white gulls circling like angelic hosts, and the unforgettable smile of Janet Warrington.

"Said you'd better watch that there pack mare or you'll go for a long swim down river," Sundance bawled, and Harry came to himself barely in time to guide the horses up onto a sandbar and thence to the mossy north bank of the Crazy Woman.

It just wouldn't do to let the haunting face of the only woman he'd truly cared for come between himself and the business at hand. And what a business? Out-and-out robbery and freebooting. What would she think of such a life? Perhaps she'd turn away from him for good. But what were the odds? Hadn't she already turned away from him, for she'd never replied to a single letter he'd sent. Now, he'd go along with the bunch this time; his luck could change.

Chapter Eight

Currie's railroad raiders were near Malta, Montana by Monday, November 27th, having taken four easy riding days to travel up to the N.P. tracks. They'd passed west of Buffalo, and crossed the Montana line near the Crow reservation. Riding between the humpbacked ridge of Wolf Mountain and the looming blue bulwarks of the Big Horns to the west, they skirted the rolling bluffs along the Little Big Horn, passing near the site of the Custer fight and hit the old Bozeman Trail.

Fording the Big Horn River, they'd swung to the west, around Junction City, to take the rickety ferry across the Missouri, north of Smokey Butte. Just beyond Fort Peck, on November 26th, Bill Madden led the outfit up a blind cañon that was hidden from the main road, and there left Tom O'Day and the extra horses.

"Don't you go wanderin' off, Tom," Sundance told the lanky owlhoot as they all shook hands. "We'll be back in four days and you better have them beauties all ready to raise the dust."

"Git aboard, Longabaugh, and try to recollect I'm runnin' this here shebang," Bill Madden growled at Sundance, fingering his six-shooter. For as soon as they'd cleared the Hole, Madden had begun to shed the last vestige of his old lady image. No longer was he lowly cook to the

Currie gang, forever fidgeting that Flat Nose might throw a tantrum over the food. Now, once again, he was a bold freebooter as he'd been with the Tip Gault gang along the Oregon Trail in the 1880s, before a determined posse had drygulched Tip, and Madden had gone back to punching cattle, doing a little rustling on the side, and dreaming of those halcyon days of glory when he'd ridden beside the Bad Man from Bitter Creek.

Madden's drooping mustaches had seemed to stiffen and bristle with resolution and even pride as he'd led his little bunch northward to battle with the railroad.

The night of November 27th, Harry, Sundance, and Madden camped near Alakali Creek, five miles out of Malta. In the morning they rode into town, hitched before the Malta Café, and breakfasted. By the time they'd finished conducting business, they were met with a sober-faced Longabaugh hurrying toward them.

"Balloon's gone up." Sundance was peering over his shoulder.

"What?" Madden grabbed him by the elbow.

"Seen one of them gamblers I heisted at Casper."

"And?" Harry looked toward the saloon.

"He sure seemed to know me."

In five minutes Longabaugh was mounted and ready to ride toward the Milk River Bridge where Madden planned to stop Train No. 29 the next afternoon. "Camp out there and we'll join you after dark!" Madden called as the Kid hit a lope down the dirt road westward.

Madden took a tentative pull at his mustache and grinned at Harry. "That'll keep young Mister Know-All on ice while we wash the dirt outta our throats."

After they'd bought tickets for Great Falls at the depot,

they went on to Black's Saloon where Madden loudly ordered drinks for the house. "Step up gents and drink to a couple of top-rate cowmen from Manitoba!" Madden's munificence was a bit diminished by the fact the entire room contained just three people—a shabby cigar-chewing townsman, a sleek-looking gambler, and the fat barkeep.

"Decent of you, Mister . . . ?" As the seedy-looking citizen reached to grasp Madden's hand, his coat gapped revealing a badge and a pistol at his hip.

"Ah . . . name's Jones, and this here's Harry . . . O'Day."

Despite the hospitable urging of the gambler, Madden and Harry drank up and left the bar as soon as the barkeep and sheriff got into a heated argument over free silver.

"Damn! That blamed tin star looked me over like some long lost relation," Madden complained as they mounted their horses.

That night they made a fireless camp in a small valley near Milk River, and then prepared a good early breakfast in the near dawn, Madden directing an unusually subdued Sundance to act as cook.

Some time around 6:00 a.m., Sundance, with Madden's big-bored Henry jammed into his saddle scabbard, rode into town as far as the depot with Bill and Harry.

"Now, you take them two mounts back out to Milk River Bridge and watch fer us around seven," Bill Madden ordered Sundance. "Train should be here and on out that way by then accordin' to the ticket agent. We'll haul her down where that load of ties is stacked past the bridge."

When Sundance had ridden away with the extra horses, Harry and Bill stood on the lonely depot platform, coats buttoned down over gun belts, voicelessly watching a full moon slowly fade from a bright shimmering silver into a pale phantom of itself in the first gleams of pure golden light.

Then there came a faint moan off to the east. The moan became a full-throated bellow and within moments a tall black smoke plume drifted toward them as the Northern Pacific's crack Train No. 23 neared the still, sleeping town. Chuffing gruffly around a bend at the cattle pens, the big 4-4-0 pounded impressively into sight, pulling her string of varnished coaches to a clanking, begrudging, steam-spurting stop just past the small shabby station. A brass-buttoned conductor swung down importantly, looked up the nearly deserted platform, and, seeing only two nondescript passengers clambering up the steps of the first coach behind the baggage car, gave an imperious swing of his blue-sleeved arm as he waved engine and cars onward.

Harry and Bill had scarcely settled down into their fancy plush seats when the conductor, brass buttons flashing in the early morning light, stalked into the car.

"Here you be," Bill drawled, handing up the tickets. "But don't think we'll be on board long."

The conductor, a prim-looking young fellow with a yellow mustache, looked sternly down at Madden and the silent Tracy. "My good fellow these tickets will certainly entitle you to ride as far as. . . ." He broke off in midsentence as he discovered Madden's long-barreled Colt poking its murderous silver snout at his belt buckle.

"Like I said, we ain't plannin' on a far ride," Bill Madden declared, "so just throw up them pretty white hands."

By then both Harry and Madden were out in the aisle, six-shooters trained on both the conductor and the few sleepy-eyed passengers.

"Now, Mister Brass Buttons, I say those there tickets entitle us to take a good long look at what's ahead there in the baggage wagon."

Leaving the several open-mouthed passengers crouching

in their seats, Bill and Harry followed the conductor through the corridor into the express coach, where they found the messenger asleep upon a sack of mailbags. It was only a matter of moments to rouse and hog-tie that custodian of the Northern Pacific's treasure. Then, as Harry stood guard over the bulging-eyed messenger and stiffly attentive conductor, Madden slipped through the far door and over the coal tender.

Glancing out the barred window of the coach, Harry saw they were coasting to a halt near the Milk River Bridge, and caught a glimpse of Sundance running out from behind a pile of railroad ties, Madden's big Henry rifle in his hand. Then came the slam of the weapon as the Kid opened up on the engine. But even at a distance, Harry heard the bellowed curses of Bill and the fusillade stopped abruptly.

"Bring old Brass Buttons down here to give us a hand!" Madden shouted through the express car's open door.

Harry prodded the conductor onto the gravel right of way where Madden and the fireman were attempting to disconnect the express car from the engine's tender. Between them they managed to cut the air hose and, at a shout from Madden, the engineer, covered by Sundance, pulled his abbreviated train on across the trestle of the Milk River Bridge.

Back in the express car, Madden and Harry went through the contents of the mailbags, gleaning little, then turned their attention to the car's big steel safe, while Sundance, delegated as guard and look-out, glowered at the train crew and threw a shot across the bridge at the remaining six cars of No. 23 every so often to keep the passengers' heads where they belonged.

"No use tryin' to get into that there box," the hog-tied messenger volunteered. "She's a brand-new, all steel safe just put on this run, and nobody's got the combination." He grinned sourly. "You could look in that wart of a tin box in the corner."

"Nobody asked you." Harry scowled as he and Madden prized open a second, iron safe, near the door, to come up with a total of $50. Here was a fine affair, for no one, including Flat Nose, had thought to fetch along blasting powder. So, for all the riding and the ever-present danger from some trigger-happy passenger or trainman, they were as dirt poor as ever.

"Gol' damn that chuckleheaded Flat Nose!" Madden ranted, mustache bristling with fury. "Here's what we git for blowin' all that money on some lyin' sidewinder railroad snitch."

As Madden was vocally soliloquizing the advantages of returning to the coaches for a shake-down of the passengers, Sundance appeared at the express car doorway. "Come on! I just took a shot at a snooper in a horse 'n' buggy, and looks like the duffer galloped back to roust out the town." While he spoke, there came the rattle of small arms from the direction of Malta.

"Now that's the last straw . . . a damned posse!" Grabbing his rifle back from Longabaugh, Madden leaped from the car, followed by Harry. By the time a body of some dozen horsemen broke over a nearby ridge, George Currie's railroad raiders were retreating toward the northwest.

"How soon do we head for O'Day's remounts?" Sundance called as they put the steel to their horses, while, from back at Milk River, rifles commenced to bark and blue-whistlers slashed the air around their heads.

"We're north of the river and we got to keep on till we shake that damned bunch." Bill Madden snarled, sombrero brim and long mustaches flaring up in the wind of their passage. "And trust you to muck the deal . . . shootin' at some clodhopper 'stead of lettin' him go his way."

Harry spurred up, glancing over his shoulder at the on-coming knot of horsemen who seemed to be gaining with each stride of their mounts. Then Madden's big bay stumbled over a gopher hole, pitching rider and rifle headlong.

Sundance kept on without a backward look although Harry called to him. Seeing the Kid was intent on departing the area, he reined in and swung down in an attempt to help Madden up on his feet, but the old desperado was completely unconscious. While he struggled with the two horses and tugged at Madden, a bullet slammed into the ground at his feet and another shattered on a nearby rock, pieces of the lead slug splintering and screaming away with a banshee wail. That posse was right on top of them.

Madden was coming around, groaning and feeling his leg. "What in the name of . . . ?" Then he looked up. "Howdy, gents, looks like you finally caught up with us." He limped painfully to his feet, shrugging as he was dis-armed.

The posse, headed by the shabby-looking sheriff, a man named Orson Grimmett, got Harry and Madden re-mounted.

"Ain't we gonna take after that young polecat what was so free with that big-bored Henry?" one of the posse members asked.

"Hain't got a Chinaman's chance of comin' up with that rennygade," Grimmett replied, pulling the remnant of an unlighted cigar from his vest pocket. "He's probably halfway to Canady by now. A pair of birds in hand here's worth one in the bresh. We'll take these here two Canady cowmen along and show 'em some good old U.S. hospitality in jail."

"Y'stuck with me, pardner," Madden said as he and Harry were shoved into separate cells of the small, brick Malta jail, "and that's more than the Longabaugh Kid done."

"Guess he ran away to fight another day," Harry answered, sagging down on the straw tick covering his canvas cot. He didn't feel like talking. He was sure in one hell of a fix. There'd been talk about lynching from the saloon hangers-on around town. Although Currie's railroad raiders hadn't actually harmed anyone, and only Sundance had thrown any lead, there'd been so little action around Malta in the weeks since the last cattle drive the town was ready for any sort of excitement.

That night after a decent supper sent over from the local hotel, compliments of the gambler at Black's Saloon, Sheriff Grimmett dismissed the part-time jailer and paid Harry and Bill a visit.

"Don't you boys worry about any necktie party." The sheriff chewed down emphatically upon a new cigar. "I've wired the Great Falls marshal and he'll be here come midnight. And I got the doctor comin' over to look at your leg," he told Madden who'd complained of the result of his fall.

A bearded old doctor appeared within the hour and looked at Bill Madden's right leg. Shaking his head, he soon departed to the town's sole drugstore for some medical supplies. Returning, he soon had Madden's leg lashed with splints and bandaged tight as a mummy's. "Compound fracture of the fibula," the doctor told Grimmett. "Only way he'll go out of here's on a stretcher."

For a time, after the medico's departure, all was quiet. Grimmett snored in a chair in the corridor, Madden's Henry rifle balanced on his lap. Harry sat silently on his bunk, head in hands, trying to think of some way out of this predicament. He'd gone and risked everything to try for enough money to buy some little ranch for her—and now? He sank back on the crinkling straw mattress, then gradually became aware of Madden's painful groans battling discordantly with the sheriff's nasal efforts. Despite the rasping snarl of Grimmett's snores, the groans deepened and grew in hoarse volume to dominate the echoing corridor.

"What in tophet!" Grimmett came to in the middle of a half strangled snore, boots hitting the floor, Henry rifle clattering down on the boards.

Harry could hear Madden weakly begging for another slug of the bottled pain-killer the doctor had left with the sheriff. Bill's cell door cracked open and there came some muttered conversation—then silence.

"Harry, Harry Bass. Come to the door and git yourself a present." Madden's voice was so brisk and business-like that Harry leaped from the bunk. Grasping the bars, he peered down the lamp-lit corridor.

Bill hobbled painfully out into the hallway and with a wave of his hand tossed something that jingled as it hit just outside Harry's door. The keys to the cells!

Harry quickly let himself out, retrieving the Henry rifle from the floor, and got down to Madden's cell to find the sheriff snugly bound and gagged in a corner and Bill back on his bunk, grinning.

"Had enough extry windin' cloths 'round me to tie up a half dozen tin stars." He reached out for the Henry. "Here, I'll swap you Grimmett's pretty pearl-handled six-shooter I plucked outta his holster for that old pet of mine."

"Let's get out of here, Bill." Harry tried to help Madden up from the bunk, but the old outlaw waved him off.

"Nope. I wouldn't travel twenty rods on this leg, but you hit for the tall timber. Besides, someone's got to sit up with poor old Grimmett, all wrapped up tight like he is. So, in the meantime, I'll keep the peace until that Great Falls marshal gets here."

There wasn't much to say. He took Madden by the hand, then left him sitting on the bunk, twisting up his mustaches with determination, the Henry across his knees.

Once out in the moonless night, Harry found Grimmett's claybank mare still hitched and saddled behind the jail. Adjusting the stirrups, he swung up and slowly rode down a quiet side street until he came to the Havre-Wagner road, then, putting the spurs to the horse, turned due north for the Canadian line, just thirty miles away.

Tom O'Day, camping down at the blind cañon near Fort Peck, would soon figure out something had gone wrong and he'd have three top saddle horses for his trouble.

Chapter Nine

Harry spent several weeks above the Canadian line looking over the prospects, but found the cattle industry in about as poor condition in the Widow of Windsor's country as in the States.

Sitting one afternoon in the lobby of a small hotel at Willow Creek, he picked up a copy of the Saskatchewan *Elevator* and read that the province's Mounted Police were reported to be on the look-out for *several undesirables from the United States, thought to have been involved in a recent unsuccessful attempt upon the Northern Pacific.* That was enough. Harry paid his board bill, settled up at the local livery, and rode Black Beauty southward, crossing the Canadian line about four in the afternoon on the Turner, Wyoming road.

Eventually reaching Miles City, he continued along a route that took him to such towns as Casper and Cheyenne, for the roll of bills Madden had taken off Sheriff Grimmett came in handy. Bank-rolling that money with winnings from an occasional card game found Harry arriving at Denver on December 28th just as winter, unusually delayed, hit the West with a white fury that piled up drifts and blocked roads and rail lines for several weeks.

From December until well into late spring, Tracy whiled away his time at such gambling halls as the Inter-Ocean Club on Curtis and the Missouri and Chicken Coop, both on

Larimer. It was a good way to stay warm and out of the icy blasts of the vicious winter winds. He sometimes saw and played against such noted sports as the old con man, Lou Blonger, and Wyatt Earp, long gone from Arizona and dealing faro that winter at another of the Larimer establishments, the Arcade.

For quite a while luck went Harry's way, then, unaccountably, it turned and his winnings melted like the snows of the past winter. By mid-June he was living in a cheap, rented room on Larimer and scanning the want ads in the Denver papers. Too proud to brace any gambling acquaintance for a hand-out, Tracy picked up Black Beauty from the South Curtis livery on July 6th and rode out of town, his last dollars translated into a second-hand shotgun, ammunition, and a gunny sack crammed with tinned food.

Traveling leisurely along a lonesome, little-used trail that paralleled the Strawberry River, he augmented his Spartan diet of beans and coffee with game knocked down by his old double-barrel shotgun. It was rust-pitted with a chipped stock and not a patch on his lost Greener for looks, but on a trip of sixteen days he downed two deer, a stray mountain goat that had wandered far afield, and any number of prairie hens.

But his luck, which had seemingly changed, deserted him again just ten miles south of Provo, Utah, when Black Beauty stepped into a prairie dog hole and shattered her right forehoof an hour before sundown.

After reluctantly shooting his mare, Tracy walked five miles in the moonlight toward Provo, toting his saddle, gunny sack, and shotgun, and following the Provo-Springville Road. He was nearing a large, prosperous-looking farmhouse on a hill near the Provo Road when a storm, threatening for some time in the west with staggering splinters of lightning and muffled drumming, burst over the sky while slanting rain shafts, driven down by buffeting winds, rushed across the landscape. By the time Harry had gained the front yard of the place, he was as soaked as a drowned kitten. But not until he'd reached the porch did he realize there were no lights in the building.

He was debating a visit to the barn when the lightning's glare gave him a good look through the front windows, revealing empty rooms, barren of any furniture. Clearly the house was vacant.

Leaving the saddle on the porch and keeping in the shelter of the eaves, he edged around to the back door. It was locked as was the front door, but, spotting an unbolted kitchen window, he was soon inside.

The kitchen was vacant except for a table and several wooden chairs, but he found a stack of wood beside the cook stove and soon had a fire going. He scouted through the near empty house until he discovered an oil lamp in the pantry, and by its light ate the last of a sage hen shot the day before. After boiling up some coffee, he topped off his meal with a cigar, then looked around for some place to bed down.

Bringing in the saddle, he dried it off and, using it for a pillow and his overcoat for a blanket, he lay down on the kitchen floor near the warm range, listening lazily to the storm still raging across the roof. He drifted off into a comfortable sleep, unbroken by any dreams until—a boot in the ribs fetched him wide awake in bright daylight. A pair of Winchesters, barrels glinting in the morning sun, were leveled at his head, and the strangers holding them looked anything but friendly.

He roused up to find the shotgun kicked out of reach and his pearl-handled Colt thrust into the belt of one of the grim-faced strangers.

"Mister, you're under arrest for breaking and entering." The heavier of the two lawmen thrust out a double chin, as he waved Harry to his feet with the Winchester. "Good thing we rid out to my pore cousin's place this morning to feed his stock and spied smoke comin' from the chimbley."

"And you'll do time for this." His lanky companion shifted a wad of tobacco from one hollow cheek to the other for emphasis.

When he appeared in the Provo courtroom the following morning on the charge of forcible entry onto the premises of a Mr. Henry Smith, recently deceased, the additional charge of burglary added to his rap sheet, although the only things appropriated were stove wood and lamp oil.

Giving the name of Tom O'Day, Tracy was sentenced to a year in the Utah State Penitentiary at Sugarhouse, a section of southeastern Salt Lake City.

"Two months down and just ten more to go," Tracy's cell partner informed him as they sat in their narrow stone cell after lockup. Harry glanced over at Frank Lant, then at the smudged calendar tacked to the wall beside a *Police Gazette* page bright with Flora Dora girls, and extracted a block of wood and a homemade knife from under his straw tick.

"This here'll whittle down time a lot sooner than pulling leaves off that calendar."

"You carving out a key or something?" It was the first time Lant had seen the items.

"Something like that." Tracy jerked his head toward the next cell. "Brown and Edwards over there furnished this shiv and wood from the chair shop . . . so all you've got to do is come up with enough tinfoil . . . and I'll handle the rest."

Lant, a young Wyoming cowhand in on rustling charges and serving the last year of a three-year sentence, took a foil-wrapped pouch of chewing tobacco out of his hip pocket and held it up. "That's no trouble." He crammed a wad of loose-cut into his mouth and looked at Tracy thoughtfully. "If we try a break, which way'll you head?"

Tracy stared off through the lamp lit bars. "Up north to Hole-in-the-Wall, I guess, until the excitement dies down."

"I get you. But I'd say you should get down to Brown's Hole at the corner of Colorado and Wyomin'. That's the spot for fellows on the scout. Grapevine says this Cassidy has taken over the old Flat Nose Currie bunch, and more or less rules the roost at Brown's Hole."

"Cassidy? Where'd he come from?" Harry kept at his whittling with one ear cocked for any pussy-footing guards.

"He was in the Wyoming pen at Laramie on some trumped-up charge of horse theft, the way I heard it. After doing less than a year, he was pardoned off. He'd built up a gang, includin' Elzy Lay, Flat Nose Currie, Harvey Logan, Bill Carver, and that Sundance Kid. They've already pulled some slick bank jobs as far apart as Montpelier, Idaho and Castle Gate, Utah."

"Sundance?" Harry looked over from his whittling. "So the Kid's riding with Cassidy." He picked up the shavings, carefully hiding them away with his knife and wood block, and was peacefully lying on the bunk, hands behind his head, when a guard slipped past. "We could try to get down to Brown's Hole and I'd like to meet that Sundance."

After lights out, Tracy still lay motionlessly, ignoring Lant's snores, while reviewing the past weeks. He'd been determined at first to do his time, then put as much distance between Salt Lake City and himself as possible, but several work details taking him beyond the walls brought back the urge to move on.

While he and Lant were out dealing with ditches, drains,

and other works, employing the strong backs and limited intelligence common to most cowhands and housebreakers, their fellow prisoners in the next cell—Art Edwards, a forger, and Will Brown, an embezzler—were laboring in the wood shop as draftsman and timekeeper, respectively. Thus it was decided (over notes and whispered conferences at night) that the four would make a break, when things looked right—and Harry had an accurate facsimile of a six-shooter—hence his evening's devotion to the art of woodcarving.

Now with the half-finished model under his mattress, Harry lay enwrapped with his gray blanket and darker thoughts. Thinking over his younger days, he had to admit that, despite the warnings of his one-time Wisconsin idol (the feisty little timber boss, Mike Tracy) he'd gone and got himself trapped by the unexpected—and twice at that, not counting the Northern Pacific train robbery which was his own fault. The first was getting caught in that damned Little Rock jewelry shop and drawing a stretch at the Arkansas State Pen. He'd made some friends there, such as Jack Bennett, but instead of going straight upon his release, he'd let Bennett and that chuckleheaded Bill Pigeon sell him on bootlegging to the redskins. And now he'd fallen the second time. Trying to get out of a damned storm, he'd been railroaded again. No matter what he tried lately, he seemed bound to be dealt a losing hand. Bad blood? Could it be that old wive's tale? More than likely just bad luck. Looking at it one way, he should stay put, dig his ditches, and walk out a free man. But the more he'd brooded on things in general, the more he felt a growing urge to get his own innings.

And now, according to Lant, this cowboy Cassidy was another who'd got the dirty end of the stick and was getting even by collecting gold and yellow backs from society in general. Then his thoughts veered around to Janet Warrington. She hadn't seemed interested in keeping in touch, so that left her out—although, after he'd got things out of his system, he might make another try, perhaps on the West Coast.

As soon as that dummy pistol was finished, they'd go. In addition to Lant, Edwards and Brown wanted in on the escape. That might take some doing, but it shouldn't be too hard for a pair of rounders who'd made their living on the con.

Just two weeks later they were ready. There'd been several worrisome nights, for escape rumors, which always seemed to run in cycles, were circulating through the prison. Two shake-downs had taken place, but each time Brown or Edwards had got the word and the wooden pistol and actual knife had been slipped back into the shop.

On Monday morning, October 7, 1897, Tracy, foil-covered wooden six-gun under his prison jacket, was marched under guard out the front gate, followed by Lant—and Edwards and Brown. All were toting picks and shovels. Several days prior, the woodworking pair had begun kicking over the traces by refusing to do their jobs properly and gambling during working hours with the result that the warden had obligingly sent them out on the work detail to learn the error of their ways.

For an hour or so that brisk and frosty morning, the gang labored along a pipeline leading from the slums of Sugarhouse toward the prison, half a mile distant. One of the part-time guards, John Van Setter, cradling a double-barreled shotgun in his arm, leaned against the side of a small barn, puffing away on a cheap cigar while the frozen earth flew.

"Settle down there, boys, you'll fag yourselfs out before the day's half started." He chuckled and attempted to pass the time of day with one of the teamsters, heaving off a load of pipe. "They must be practicin' for the Klondike the way they're tacklin' that froze-up ground." Answering that he wouldn't be surprised, the teamster slapped the reins over his mule team and pulled away. The empty wagon rattled off down the street, while Van Setter fell to musing on the new gold strike in Alaska. His own brother had been one of the thousands flocking northward, and, as he chewed on the remnant of his cigar, he dwelt on the unpleasant fact that a wife and six children could surely be a ball and chain. He was nigh as much a prisoner as those four convicts slaving away in that trench.

He looked up at a shout to find one of the men, a broad-shouldered young fellow with a dark mustache named O'Day, pointing at one of the shovels. Van Setter hesitated, broke the shotgun, inspected the loads with an air of official interest, then cocked and locked the weapon before ambling over to the ditch. Although there were only four prisoners, it didn't pay to be careless.

"See, here, this shovel's bent like the devil." O'Day, the only man out of the ditch, indicated the damaged tool. "You want this work done, I'd say we need another."

"Told you boys to spare yourselfs and now you've gone and busted state property. Let me see that thing. Looks like it could be bent back." And Van Setter, scatter-gun held loosely in his left hand while reaching for the shovel, found himself staring at a silver six-shooter that had magically appeared just inches from his ample midriff. "Hey, now. Now watch that weepon!"

Tracy plucked the shotgun from the guard and waved the others out of the ditch. "Come on, work's done for the day. Hustle around that barn before someone spots us." He poked Van Setter with the shotgun. "You get around there with the boys. We need your monkey suit."

Once on the offside of the small barn, Van Setter was stripped of his coat, hat, and trousers and forced back into the bottom of the muddy ditch, while the three convicts legged it off down an alley lined with a string of sheds, barns, and shacks marking the southern limits of Sugarhouse.

Crouching in the bottom of the cold, muddy ditch in his red long johns, Van Setter anxiously watched the approach of the convict dressed in the guard's own uniform.

"Just stay there and keep your head down until I tell you to come up for air." That double-barreled weapon in the hands of the man called O'Day looked as large as a pair of field guns to the motionless guard. "I'll be watching from around that barn, so sit tight till I give you the word."

The guard cautiously emerged from the ditch an hour later, tense with the cold and apprehension. Approaching the barn, he found little to remind him of the escape save for a wooden pistol, covered with tinfoil, tossed on top of a small pile of convict clothing.

By the time he'd shivered into the coarse prison garb and headed on the run toward the prison, Tracy and his three "convicts" were parting company down near the railroad yards. He'd marched Lant, Brown, and Edwards through the streets without arousing much interest from onlookers, for the citizens of Salt Lake City and Sugarhouse were used to seeing groups of men in prison gray herded along from one street job to another.

Police and prison personnel fanned out in a hurried search for the fugitives throughout the day, but all came up with cold trails. The team of Brown and Edwards had successfully caught a side-door Pullman south, about 2:00 p.m., and were seen no more in Utah, while Tracy and Lant, helping themselves to a variety of work clothes from off a wash line, cut across lots to the Park City Road and managed a ride with a peddler north to Hoyville, explaining they were out looking for work in the area coal mines. The shotgun was kept bundled up in a blanket from the same clothesline that furnished their traveling clothes.

Sleeping overnight in a barn near Hoyville, they set off for the Wyoming line the next morning, and were able again to get a hitch, this time with a freight wagon all the way to Wahsatch, Utah. Holding onto the cash Tracy had found in the guard's pockets, nearly $20, they managed to get some eating money by splitting up a towering woodpile at a farm on the north side of town.

Again bunking down in a barn for the night and trudging on doggedly through the Bear River Valley the next day, they were close to Evanston, Wyoming at dusk. Here fortune managed a slight smile, when a local rancher, W. A. Evans and wife, out for a buggy ride in the mellow October evening, were stopped near a moonlit crossroad by two men, armed with a shotgun.

Moments later, Evans and his wife were returning afoot to their ranch three miles away while Tracy and Lant lashed the old, fat buggy mare down the Fort Bridger Road. With the advent of light, they hid out in a woods, letting the horse rest and catching themselves some needed sleep.

Rousing out at noon, they drove to Fort Bridger and purchased supplies with a good portion of Van Setter's $20, but left the horse and buggy concealed in some second growth north of the village limits. As they were about to enter a lunch room on Main Street, Tracy overheard several townspeople discussing the robbery of the Evanston rancher, the news having arrived over the telephone wires. Thankful the horse and rig had been left on the edge of town, he and Lant legged it back to the outskirts and were soon heading south on the

Burnt Fork-McKinnon Road, shotgun unbundled and lying between them.

Hurrying across the flat ranching country, they took a dirt road to pass by the village of McKinnon and were able to cross the Green River at Henry's Ford by day's end. That night as they camped in a cottonwood grove east of the river, they assessed their chances of reaching Brown's Hole.

Lant was set on getting back to the Powder Springs ranch where he'd begun cowboying nearly five years before. "Dandy bunch at Bender's Double-W spread. Old Dick Bender learned me all I know about movin' horses on the q.t. Sure helped me to a bundle of cash for a while."

"And then got you a stretch in the stone house to boot?"

"Ah, I got somewhat careless and tried to peddle a small herd to the railroad over at Rock Springs. But that damned Joe LeFors, he showed up and quizzed my hair brands. Got me sent up, he did."

"LeFors? He still around?" Tracy recalled the little, four-eyed bulldog of a man who'd tried to arrest George Currie's entire bunch at Medicine Bow—only to lose out when Tracy had got the drop on the meddlesome lawman.

"Yeah, and got a lifetime job as stock detective with the Cattleman's Association. That jasper's a real burr under the saddle."

"Well, let's hope we don't run into the likes of him on the way to the Hole. We've had ourselves enough commotion in the past few days to last a good while."

But that night as Harry lay staring into the orange eye of the small campfire, he wasn't sure he'd go out of his way to avoid trouble. In fact, it seemed he'd been courting excitement for years, even gone looking for it—peddling bootleg to the Indians, rustling stock with Currie's bunch, as well as taking on a train with Bill Madden and Sundance. It surely wasn't any way to walk the straight and narrow.

And he needn't have engineered the jail break when he'd less than nine months to serve. He seemed to have a growing urge to match his wits and nerve against the world in general. That was why he was heading for this Brown's Hole and its gang of wild men—George Currie, Elzy Lay, Walt Punteney, Matt Warner, this new fellow Cassidy, and even the unpredictable Sundance.

Chapter Ten

On Friday, October 11th, Tracy and Lant parted at the little hamlet of Powder Springs, twenty miles northeast of Brown's Hole. They'd swapped the buggy and horse at the local livery for a pair of broken-down cow ponies and two shabby saddles, giving the shotgun and their last $5 to sweeten the bargain.

When Lant rode off toward the Double-W, Harry headed his crow-bait mustang toward the Hole. Skirting the muddy stretch of Talamante Creek, he passed the humpbacked bulk of Look-Out Mountain, rode across the wind-swept barrens of the Owe-Yi-Kuts plateau, and at last came down through Irish Cañon into the vast valley near the Bassett Ranch.

Inquiring of a dark-haired young woman, who was hanging up some clothes, of the whereabouts of any of Cassidy's boys, she paused long enough to take a clothespin out of her mouth and reply that Robert and Elzy were to be found at Willow Creek, a good fifteen miles on up the valley. Tipping his battered Stetson, Tracy headed northwest up the wide, lushly green valley, thinking as he rode that settlers in the great Hole seemed at least resigned to strangers. It seemed that men on the scout were certainly tolerated, and that was the ticket. He might just look around for some land and try to make that pipe-dream ranch of his a reality.

About sunset he found Lay's cabin in a willow grove near a

branch of the Green. Once dismounted, he looked carefully about. A pole corral at the rear held a half dozen fine-looking horses, but there was no one in sight. On his left, the sun, descending behind the looming blue-gray bulk of Diamond Mountain, threw its tawny orange light across trees and buildings, and over the glittering length of a Sharps needle gun that had eased out, snake-like, from the cabin's nigh corner.

"Friend!" Harry kept his hands carefully before him, wishing for some sort of a weapon—even the vanished shotgun.

The big-bored rifle emerged along with the man holding the Sharps. "Friend? Well, by damn if you aren't." And Tom O'Day, long dark face crinkling into a half grin, lowered the needle gun and bawled out his discovery.

Other figures, in range garb, emerged, hands near their holsters. One was Elzy Lay and the other a stocky, broad-shouldered fellow with rumpled flaxen hair, whose keen blue eyes inspected Harry with the directness of a brace of pistols.

Greetings exchanged with Lay and O'Day, Harry was introduced to the blond stranger, who turned out to be Cassidy. After the buckskin had been let into the corral, all went inside the cabin.

Having arrived at supper time, Harry joined the threesome at the table. Following the meal, they wandered back out to sit along a split-log bench in front of the cabin. For a spell O'Day and Lay talked over events since the defeat of Currie's railroad raiders months past. While both seemed friendly enough, Harry felt an unspoken reserve. Cassidy wandered off into the nearby trees with a nod, smoking a cigarette and staying out of the conversation.

"I get a feeling I'm not as welcome here as I could be." Harry ground out his cigarette with his boot heel. "Guess you heard Bill Madden and I had ourselves one hell of a last stand before we got gobbled."

"Something like that," Elzy said, and glanced over at the dying sunset, reflectively chewing upon a match. "Surely rough all right."

"And pore old Bill's still doin' time up at the Great Falls stone hotel," O'Day muttered. "Seems you might have busted him out when you skipped . . . least that's what the Kid thinks."

"The Kid?" Harry sat up straight. "Well, Mister Sundance might have stuck around to help out himself instead of high-tailing it." He was beginning to understand his less than warm reception.

Before Lay or O'Day could reply, Cassidy sauntered back. "Time for another smoke?" he addressed Harry.

Together they strolled down the bank of the murmuring river until out of earshot. Then Cassidy turned his cool blue gaze on Harry. "I think you'd maybe ought to ride on." As Harry stared at him, he continued. "Know you've been a ring-tailed bearcat in the past. George Currie swears by you, and both Lay and O'Day pretty much back him up. But. . . ."

"But?" Harry had a feeling what was coming.

"Listen"—Cassidy clapped a friendly hand on Tracy's shoulder—"I'm trying to put together a bunch of top riders. And I sure don't need any sort of ruckus in the ranks."

Harry realized Sundance had been spreading some pretty tall tales to explain his own hasty retreat that had left his partners in the lurch. He felt a surge of angry resentment, then shrugged it off. "Last thing I want is trouble," he admitted.

Cassidy seemed to relax, and grinned for the first time. "This is sure a prime valley for cattle. More than one rancher around here got his start mavericking from those big, topheavy British ranches up in Sweetwater County. Folks like that are just ripe for the shearing."

There was more talk as Cassidy suggested several Brown's Hole ranchers Harry might visit to obtain possible grazing rights. And as they returned through the cool twilight haze, Cassidy mentioned a logical site for Harry—the former cabin of Matt Warner, across the Green, near the Crouse Ranch. "Matt just built himself that place at the foot of Diamond Mountain when he went all hot-headed and got himself three years in the Utah pen for a shooting scrape. So the spot's yours, if you want it."

In the morning, following a breakfast cooked up by Tom O'Day, Tracy got his mount from the corral and prepared to ride.

After helping saddle up, Elzy Lay put his hand on the buckskin's bridle and squinted up at Harry in the early light. "O'Day and me figure you got dealt a pretty poor hand here. But Butch is fretted about a set-to between you and Sundance. Guess he sees you're not one to get pushed much . . . while the Kid's getting spunkier all the time. So there's no telling what might happen when he rides back in here."

"Well, I'm riding myself, but not far . . . just across to the foot of Diamond Mountain to hang my hat. I'll be around this neck of the woods for a spell . . . if anyone wants to come calling." He shook Lay's hand, then turned his horse back down the river trail.

"The boys are split up pretty bad, and Flat Nose has gone back to Hole-in-the-Wall, but someone'll stop by!" Lay called after him.

Following Cassidy's directions, Tracy reached Warner's cabin on the mountain slope, cleaned it out, and hung up his meager possessions. By the time he'd ridden over to the

Hole's only general store at the western end of the valley, picked up supplies, and returned, he already found himself with a caller.

"Now what the devil happened to you?" Harry sat on a stump in the yard and looked over the dusty, woebegone specimen that was Frank Lant.

"Bottom fell out of everything," Lant answered while wearily piling off from a mount, even more bedraggled than himself. "That damned Double-W has been gobbled by some new-fangled British ranch combine, and old man Bender's gone and drunk himself to death in a Baggs saloon." He slumped to a seat upon another stump in the littered yard. "Now if that wasn't bad enough, I run into Joe LeFors. Joe claimed to have a dodger on me for a jail break, so he chased me all the way here. Guess he was leery of some ambush, for he pulled up short. But I was in such a tear that pore animal there and me slid halfway down Cold Spring Mountain."

"LeFors? He got a warrant for me, too?"

"Didn't stay around to ask." Lant rubbed his side and winced. "I did ask for you up the valley till I run into this Cassidy. He's the one sent me over here."

There was nothing to do but invite Lant to share the cabin. And over the next few days they had the place livable, as well as putting the rough pole barn out back into shape for the horses.

Paying a visit to the Crouse Ranch in the Green River bottom, Harry talked to Charley Crouse, a noted horse breeder, and, it was whispered, an accomplished horse thief. The gander-eyed Crouse readily gave permission to run any stock he might come by in the meadows between the Green and Crouse Creek, just east of the Utah-Colorado line—for a reasonable price.

Talking matters over with Lant, Harry decided to begin a

shoestring spread in the spring, when they'd be able to visit the many British-dominated cattle ranches northward while hunting out their strays.

But with the blustery winds of an increasingly bitter fall whistling over the barren reaches of Diamond Mountain and streaming across the vast valley to spin spider-web skeins of glistening ice along the creeks and fringes of the Green, Harry and Lant settled down to wait out the winter.

Their main problem was a pair of very empty wallets. Harry had charged a small amount of such groceries as flour, coffee, and baking soda at old John Jarvie's general store up the valley, giving Elzy Lay as his reference, but it seemed like slim pickings for the winter. They were also bereft of firearms, a decided detriment at such a time and place.

Things looked up somewhat around the 1st of December when Elzy rode over with a small buck deer he'd shot up on Cold Spring Mountain. Several bottles of Old Crow arrived with the deer and the three spent a rousing evening around the ruddy cheerfulness of the fireplace before Lay rode off into an early winter snowfall. In addition to the liquor and meat, Elzy had left a six-shooter, .44 carbine, and sufficient ammunition. "Now you can do your own hunting," he'd said, laughing, "but don't run up too steep a bill at old Jarvie's. It's certainly been quite a spell since any bankers have tossed their cash my way."

With enough to eat and a warm place to hole up, time slid along for Tracy and Lant until two days before Christmas.

Having just returned at supper time from a hunting trip into the reaches of the mountain, Harry was oiling up the Winchester and toasting his shins in front of the fire, while Lant was immersed in the contents of a mail-order catalog, borrowed from the general store, when there came a hail outside the cabin.

Both were on their feet, six-gun in Lant's fist and carbine at the ready in Tracy's arms.

"Lay?" Lant stared at Harry, peering out into the gloomy dusk from the edge of the window.

"Or . . . LeFors?" Harry said, and slipped across the room to blow out the kerosene lamp.

The voice sounded again, half muffled in the wind, but it had a familiar ring to it. Harry stepped back and flung the door open, then dropped the muzzle of the cocked Winchester. "I think we can expect some more drinking liquor for Christmas." He walked out into the yard and waved in Jack Bennett and a stranger.

"Well here I be . . . sort of that old bad penny." Jack Bennett shook Tracy's hand, then introduced the hulking, silent figure at his side. "And here's Pat Johnson, alias Swede Johnson, and maybe some other handles I ain't heard." He chuckled, but Johnson merely nodded and turned to see to the horses and pack mule.

True to Tracy's prediction, Bennett, like some lanky St. Nick, had fetched bottled presents in his pack, and the evening passed with cheerful exchanges of news. Bennett, particularly, was ready to talk to Harry about his immediate past. "Bumped inter Swede up at Rock Springs where he was peddlin' butchered beef to miners over on Zenobia Peak."

Johnson, about as noncommittal as Bennett was garrulous, managed a surly grin. "If Jack here ever keeps his own gab shut, we'll keep up the good work." Having rid himself of his longest speech of the evening, he went back to communing with the whiskey.

"Well, that's about right." Bennett chuckled. "The Swede's about as slick as they come. He's workin' as a hand at that Hoy Ranch over on Red Crick, north of the Wyoming line. He's goin' back there tomorrow and gittin' me a job, too. Sounds like a peaceful sort of spot to winter in . . . eh?"

When Bennett and Johnson left the next morning, Tracy breathed a sigh of relief. "Glad to see them on their way," he commented.

Lant agreed. "That Swede looks like someone itchin' to get into a wrangle."

"And old Jack Bennett's just unlucky enough to be right in the middle of it," Tracy grunted, poking up the embers in the fireplace. "I can't think much of a pair planning to steal beef off the spread they're working. That could lead to real trouble."

Throughout January and on to the end of February, Tracy had little news of Jack Bennett and his sour-faced companion, Johnson, except for a brief but telling item in a late issue of the Rout County *Sentinel*:

TROUBLE AT THE HOY RANCH
Warrant Sworn Out For Foreman

Valentine Hoy, who operates a ranch over the Wyoming line at Red Creek, swore out warrants last week for the arrest of his foreman, P. L. Johnson. The charge being theft of cattle from the Hoy establishment.

When Johnson learned of the warrants last Wednesday, an immediate altercation took place, with the foreman being said to have threatened Hoy with bodily violence.

Fearing for his life, Hoy and his wife packed up and left for safer quarters.

Johnson, who has taken over the ranch, told a reporter he'd signed a lease on the property several months ago and meant to stay.

"I knew there'd be trouble when Jack wound up with that Swede," Harry told Lant at supper. "That was a week ago, and who knows what's gone on since."

"Well, it ain't none of our business." Lant dished up his special dried-fruit pie. "We don't have to git ourselves mixed up in other folks' problems."

But Lant proved to be wrong next morning when a sober-faced Elzy Lay rode up with some disturbing news.

"You say there's a snooper in the valley asking questions?" Tracy asked as they sat around the fireplace.

"Yes, but he's not looking for Butch's boys. Got that from old Herb Bassett. This one's just interested in folks who've been moving around other people's cattle. He's probably from the Wyoming Cattlemen's Association."

"Stock detective? It's not LeFors?"

"No, he calls himself Tom Hix, but that might not be the right handle," Elzy said, and glanced at Lant. "Not to be nosey, but didn't you used to shift stock for old Bender?"

"Yeah, I did work for Bender, all right."

"Somehow Hix got a line on you . . . maybe from Joe LeFors, but this Hix has more sand than old Joe and he's come on into the Hole."

"He knows where we are?" Harry asked as he took Jack Bennett's last bottle from the rough mantle and poured out three shots.

"Not sure." Elzy lifted his glass to Tracy. "But it won't take him long to find out." He downed the liquor. "If you'll take some free advice, I'd leave here for a while."

After Lay had wished them luck and rode away, Lant turned to Tracy. "We might go across to Powder Springs. There's a few small ranches toward Baggs where we could hole up for a spell." He kicked at the frozen ground by the doorstep. "Of course, I don't think this Hix is looking for you."

Tracy poked Lant in the ribs. "I'll ride along. What'll I do for eats when the cook's off visiting?"

In the morning they loaded their equipment and victuals on the pack mule. As Harry was tossing dishwater upon the fire, Lant tore a page from the Kickapoo Indian Tonic calendar, nailed beside the fireplace. "Well, there goes old February, Eighteen Ninety-Eight, and now let's hope that March proves better for us."

With the last of their scant possessions lashed down upon the pack animal, along with some tinned food and Lant's cooking gear, they rode out of the dooryard and down through the pine grove.

When they rounded a turn in the rough trail at the slope's bottom, Lant glanced back at the empty cabin. "Easy come, and easy go, eh?" But his look belied the words. Tracy could see Lant didn't expect to return in the near future.

As for Tracy, he shrugged, keeping his mounting bitterness to himself. Whoever this Hix was, he remained a faceless symbol of the relentless forces of law and order. There was little reason to harass Lant. That cattle rustling charge didn't hold water in Colorado, and he was sure this Hix had no warrants for the Utah pen escape.

The day was mild and the thaw continued as they rode through the pine groves on into the bottoms and between the snow-sheeted walls of Ladore Cañon, eventually passing the Bassett Ranch on their way. One of the Bassett girls was in the yard hanging out washing, the sheets and clothing rippling and swaying in the soft, near spring-like air. Vigorous and full-bosomed, the young brunette waved a cheerful greeting to them as they trotted their mounts past.

Tipping their Stetsons, they put the horses to a gallop, heading eastward along Vermilion Creek. "Going to be

119

mighty glad to get to a town again," Lant said. "Seems an awful long time since I bedded me someone like that."

Tracy nodded silently, for his own thoughts had been weaving a similar daydream around about Miss Janet Warrington. And how that girl could fill a fellow's arms.

Splashing through the glittering shallows of a branch of the Vermilion an hour later, they passed southeast of the hulking white shoulder of the Owi-Yu-Kuts plateau and were within ten miles of Powder Springs when Lant pointed ahead. "I hope that ain't Hix."

Tracy, who'd been keeping an eye open for possible ambushes from some of the knife-like ravines and minor cañons they'd passed, peered off to the northwest toward the Look-Out Mountain and saw a rider silhouetted on a near ridge. From that distance it was impossible to determine who the horseback figure might be, but he was taking no chances. "Put the steel to 'em!" he shouted, and drove his mount onward.

Lant, leading the pack animal, thundered along behind. Within a minute they were across a small hogback and on down out of sight. There'd been no shots, but they continued their galloping dash through the slop of snow and mud until Tracy thrust up his hand as they pulled onto a fairly good road running eastward over the rolling hills.

"This is it. The road to Powder Springs," Lant informed Harry, leaning back in the saddle and rubbing the small of his back. "That was one hell of a ride, but maybe it was just some cowpoke out hunting stock."

"And maybe it wasn't." Tracy yanked off his hat and wiped at the sweat on his face. "But whether it was or not, let's push on for your ranches. We've traveled nigh thirty miles and the sun's lost its heat." Off to the west the day was commencing to die. The pale biscuit-size clouds of early morning were now little more than smears of burned ashes, while the mountains behind were rimmed with fading crimson.

Riding along the slushy track of a road, they dipped down into a shallow valley—and met two horsemen coming headlong at them through the dusk. As with one mind, Tracy and Lant turned off the road, Harry to the right, and Lant to the left with the pack mule. Before they could draw their weapons, one of the oncoming riders gave a shout and both reined up in a shower of frozen mud and slush.

"Hey! Ain't that Harry Bass?"

Harry recognized the voice of Jack Bennett and saw the other horseman to be Swede Johnson, both mere smudges in the dim twilight.

"Damn! Y'came near spooking our horses," Lant cursed, and jammed his saddle gun back into its holster, but Tracy chuckled.

"Yeah, and us to boot," Harry said, and guided his mount onto the rutted roadway. "Where in hell are you going? I thought you'd still be at that Hoy's ranch . . . or did he finally run you off?"

"Seen any law out here?" Swede Johnson asked, moving his big, raw-boned bay up to Tracy. "We're in a bit of a yank."

"Ain't seen hardly anyone today," Lant said, "but a fellow's back at the Hole looking for someone." He got his mount back on the track along with the pack animal.

"That feller at the Hole . . . he the law?" Jack Bennett asked, peering at them through the chilly darkness, then noticed the pack mule. "You-all on the move, too?"

"Not just sure who's back there," Tracy retorted, jerking his thumb over his shoulder. "Might be law, but we didn't stay around to see. But who's behind you?"

"Hell, we're in one devil of a fix," Bennett replied, and bent down to pat the neck of his heaving roan. "And we're just about damned sure who could be back there."

"That there Hoy?" Lant wanted to know.

"Worse'n any egg-suckin' Hoy," Bennett growled. "It's nobody but the Routt county sheriff. Swede had himself a mishap. Went and put a bullet through a kid out at the ranch."

"Shot a kid?" Tracy kneed his mount toward the silent Johnson. "Was it Hoy's?"

"Naw, a young un' named Willie Strang, an old prospector's kid from up valley," Johnson grunted. "Come around the ranch last week wantin' to cowboy some, so I took him on."

All the time the group had been talking, Tracy and Lant were glancing one way with Bennett and Johnson looking over their own shoulders to the west.

"Plumb mishap, that shooting," Bennett broke in. "Yesterday afternoon, Willie tipped a dipper of water outta Swede's hands and run for the barn."

"I pulled down on him just to scare him some, but the damned gun went off and the ball driv clean through the pore kid." Johnson cleared his throat and twisted around again to stare back into the frigid dark.

"So we saddled and rode, spendin' the rest of the day and night at the Ell Seven Ranch, but word come in that Neiman, the Routt county sheriff, was lookin' to serve that warrant the fool Hoy swore out," Bennett husked. "That and the fact we'd a killin' on our hands was more than enough to git us movin' again."

"Whyn't we head up toward Powder Springs?" Lant broke in. "There's an old run-down ranch house about three miles northeast of here where we could spend the night." He gave a short chuckle. "Safety in numbers, I'd say."

"And misery loves company," Tracy retorted dryly. "But why not? We'll stick together for a spell. And I don't take kindly to being rousted out by any tin stars . . . especially in such weather as this." As he'd spoken, the air was filling with great feathery flakes and a wind with a keen bite to it was commencing to drive snow into their faces.

Following Lant, the party pulled off the road, riding across the open range toward a dark line of hills, now barely discernible in the whirling snow—the location of the abandoned ranch house.

Chapter Eleven

In the morning, after a fair night's sleep upon the old ranch house floor, the fugitives put away a good breakfast, using Tracy's supplies, then set out on a southwest course to pass around Powder Wash before heading north on the horse thief trail toward Green River and parts beyond.

Jack Bennett rode back toward Powder Springs with the pack mule. Not being named in Hoy's warrant, he'd volunteered to go for supplies, then catch up with the party near the forks of the Green.

The snow, drifting considerably during the night, was hard upon the animals, so Tracy, Lant, and Johnson headed south for the West Boone Draw road where it curved leisurely in the direction of the Green River country.

Around noon as they were trotting their mounts along the road, Tracy spotted a buckboard coming up rapidly behind them from Powder Springs. "Looks like law to me," he told Lant and Johnson as they turned in their saddles to inspect the oncoming buggy. "And I think there's a rifle there."

Before they could spur their horses and turn off onto the slopes of a pine grove south, toward Douglas Mountain, the buckboard was near enough for them to see both men had weapons at the ready—although they failed to use them.

"Well, just let those honyockers try navigating these hills

with that rig," Lant said, chuckling as they urged their mounts up the tree-studded foothills.

"Not a Chinaman's chance, by hell," Johnson leered. But do y'think they gobbled Jack?"

Tracy reined in on the hillside to look back down the slope. "I don't think they ran into each other, but we've still got a problem getting back with him."

"And we're gonna need the pack mule before we do much traveling," drawled Lant, looking closely at Johnson. "Was that the law down there with the warrant?"

"Yeah, its old Neiman and his deputy, Farnham. Both deacons, along with Hoy, in the local church. Die-hards, too . . . once they fasten onto a body's tracks." Swede Johnson pulled out his saddle gun and inspected it thoughtfully. "They'll get rid of that fool buckboard before long and raise themselves a posse. We'd best be makin' tracks."

"We can't go off and leave Jack," Tracy said shortly. "We'll make tracks, but only as far as the Green."

After some discussion, it was agreed they'd ride up into the pine-clad mountain slopes and make a try at flanking any posses in the morning.

"That old rough floor of last night's surely going to look mighty good to me before long," Lant remarked as they urged their horses on up through the timber. "It's already about as cold as a lawman's heart."

"Before you get out of this, there may be enough hot work to keep you plenty warm," Tracy joshed his partner.

Discovering an adequate windbreak in the shape of a great outcropping of maroon-colored sandstone enclosed by a thick stand of pine and aspen, they spent the night there, huddled out of the wind—fireless and supperless.

Long before the first metallic gleam of a frigid dawn stained the star-powdered sky, they were carefully on the move. Descending the timberline at a right angle to the previous day's ascent, they eventually reached the roadway, two miles to the west.

"Eating snow ain't the best way to quench a fellow's thirst," Lant grumbled as they broke out of the underbrush and onto the road.

"No, and this don't seem to be the best way to dodge a posse," Tracy tersely commented, gesturing toward the West Boone Draw road where a dark body of horsemen was coming toward them.

Hurriedly guiding their mounts back into the trees, they waited. The six riders came abreast of them, hesitated, then rode on down the road to stop again and peer up into the tree-strewn slopes of the mountain.

"Don't think they saw us, but it looks like a hull damn' army," muttered Lant.

"And it's that gol-damned, Bible-thumping Hoy with 'em!" cursed Johnson.

"Well, they'll have to be slicker than most to stop us from circling around to pick up Jack at the Green," Tracy declared.

Keeping within the timber belt's shelter, the trio made its way around the base of the mountain, sometimes riding and sometimes trudging through the drifts.

Around three in the afternoon, Tracy and his companions gained a hogback overlooking the forks of the Green River within rifle shot of Ladore Cañon's yawning gulf. Although they'd passed near the Bassett Ranch on their westward swing, they hadn't caught sight of any pursuit. After dismounting and staking out the horses in a neighboring stand of aspen and pine, they went into camp in a great nest of granite boulders.

Settling down in the rock shelter and deeming themselves

far enough away from pursuit, they built a small fire, being careful to use only old wood to guard against much smoke. Then they waited for Jack Bennett and his supplies. Sitting nearly motionless, ears and eyes alert for either posse or Bennett, Tracy and the others became involuntary nature watchers, observing two mule deer and a small black bear move through the timber during the slow hours.

"That little buck could have made a dandy meal," Lant mourned. "My backbone's rubbing right against my belt buckle."

"I'm ready to settle for one of them fool picket pin squirrels," Swede Johnson growled. "And if one comes nigh enough, I'm gonna chunk a rock at him."

Tracy decided it was time to break out the emergency sack of flour he'd secreted in his saddlebag. And, with Lant installed against his wishes as camp cook, a passable meal was made of fire cake—flour mixed with snow and baked on a flat rock.

As the golden ball of the sun lost its warmth and gradually slid toward the violet-rimmed horizon, they edged nearer the orange and yellow petals of the small fire. While they waited for Bennett, they passed the time according to their natures. Lant pulled out a creased copy of Pawnee Bill's adventures, *Pawnee Bill's Best Shot*, and began to follow the printed trail of his dime novel hero, while Tracy and Johnson sat close to the flames, wiping their saddle guns and speculating upon Jack Bennett's whereabouts.

Twice before full dark closed in, Tracy walked to the top of the ridge, searching for sign of posse or Bennett, but saw neither.

Sleeping fitfully through the night, enwrapped in their horse blankets, they were awake at dawn. After baking up another batch of fire cakes and rendered desperate by the urgent need to thaw out their half-numbed condition, they built up the fire until it was a roaring tower of flame hurling thousands of fiery red-gold sparks toward the fading stars.

"If they don't see this," mumbled Lant, chomping stolidly upon some of his own blackened handiwork, "they won't see anything."

Tracy, silently debating leaving the warmth of the fire and climbing the ridge to scout the vicinity, grinned and held out his hands to the blaze. "Maybe Jack'll see it first, but, if he don't, then we'll give them a hot welcome. They've got to come up the cañon to get near us."

A rifle bullet, slamming into the ground at their feet, shattered the dawn—and Tracy's boast. Close upon the first shot came a fusillade. But the unseen riflemen were wide of their marks in the poor light.

"Get away from that fire and grab your guns!" Tracy yelled, sweeping up his carbine and plunging downhill through the underbrush, followed by Lant and Johnson.

Gaining the temporary safety of a scattering of boulders, thirty yards down the slope, Tracy and the others lay, panting and cursing the posse. But Harry was also quietly condemning himself for getting caught off guard. Once again he'd let himself be surprised—something his old friend and mentor of the logging days, Mike, had warned him against.

Despite growing daylight, the weather was bitterly cold, but there were no more shots or sounds from the ambushing enemy. Time wore on.

Close on noon, Johnson, Mackinaw turned up about his red ears, arose stiffly to look around. "Them bastards are gone off to git warm and leave us here on ice till they come back to start the war again."

Agreeing, Tracy and Lant got up, rifles in hand, to scan the sunny but frigid surroundings. Lant shook his head.

"Don't seem like Jack Bennett's about to put in any appearance."

"Yeah, he's had time enough to git here . . . if he was comin'," Swede Johnson declared, glaring half defiantly at Tracy.

Harry paused, undecided as to what course to pursue. Then: "I guess the only thing we can do is keep moving. If Jack shows up and we're not here, he'll know enough to hit the trail for Rock Springs."

"Yeah, he'll probably think we're already ahead of him," Johnson agreed. "And if we want to git out of this bottleneck before they come back and cork us up . . . we'd best move on."

With Tracy leading, they carefully made their way up to their abandoned camp only to find the invaders had appropriated their blankets, saddles, and, worst of all, the horses.

After staring about the empty campsite, Lant bent over to pull his small flour bag from under a bush. "Well, we've still got grub, even if Jack's went and lost himself and those pious bastards stole our horses."

"Much better they'd left the mounts," Johnson pronounced, scowling. "I'd surely rather have me a horse steak than them burned bricks you think's fit to eat."

A sudden crashing through the underbrush above them brought all three to their knees, rifles at the ready. Tracy, who'd caught a glimpse of the vanishing buck's white flag, spoke up with more determination than he actually felt. "That could just as well have been the posse, again. Swede's right. I vote we move out now."

Cautiously descending the snowy slopes, the trio made its way without further incident, down to the cañon floor, and set off west along the frozen expanse of the Green River.

They'd traveled several miles along the blinding, white

carpet of river ice when they found the Green entering a steeper cañon. There the frozen river opened, flowing onward so swiftly over submerged boulders that it boiled up, the drifting spray nearly blinding them with its chilly rainbows. On either side, the cañon walls vaulted to a height of several hundred feet. They'd wandered into a cul-de-sac and there was nothing to do but retrace their steps.

Hours later, half exhausted and nearly benumbed with cold, they were back upon the mountain where the sun was dying out in a nest of purple and iron gray bars.

Realizing they'd been forced again into Swede Johnson's bottle, Tracy decided to sit it out for one more night. The only alternative was a trek by foot across the wide reaches of Brown's Hole, or the vast stretch of open country to the east. Either way, they'd be fair game for anyone on horseback.

As they rested in the lee of a great upthrust of talus rock, Tracy spoke up. "There's no way out of here except back down toward Bassett's. Now I see it was a damn' fool idea to try and meet Jack here, but we still could have pulled it off if those bastards hadn't come around on some trail they knew and grabbed the horses." He gave a short dry laugh, then went on. "So we'll wait for 'em to come back, and then we'll do our own ambushing."

"Still want to fight?" Lant asked, face drawn with cold and something else, staring at Tracy, while Johnson moodily tugged at his long mustache and whistled tunelessly.

"I don't want to get into any running battle," Tracy replied, attempting to penetrate Lant's odd expression, "but this time we could get the drop on them and take their horses. That'd be a good joke."

There were no smiles, both shrugged, then began making plans for an evening fire. With Johnson off in the cedar groves for wood, Lant immediately approached Tracy.

"This here fight's not ours. We don't owe that Swede nothing. I don't feel like sticking my neck out for someone who'd plug a kid for a joke." Before Harry could frame a reply, Lant hurriedly continued. "That there damned posse ain't got a thing on us. Probably ain't even got a warrant . . . except for the Swede."

"Well, how'd you know this Hix, or whoever he is, isn't riding with that bunch looking for you?"

The return of Johnson with an armful of wood put an end to the argument, but Tracy now realized Lant was beginning to have second thoughts.

Johnson's wood proved to be poor stuff, and it took the combined efforts of the three fugitives to build a successful fire—that and half the pages of Lant's Pawnee Bill.

"Now don't fret yourself," Tracy told Frank while Lant grumbled away at his chore of baking. "You might be so busy tomorrow you won't have any time to read." Swede Johnson bared his uneven teeth in appreciation of Tracy's *bon mot,* but Lant turned aside to continue a muttered conversation with himself.

In an effort to keep a certain amount of peace in camp, Tracy divided the night hours into equal stretches of sentry duty, with the Swede taking the first four, followed by Lant, and then himself. There was little resentment from Johnson or Lant, for they'd experienced one ambush and weren't looking forward to another.

With little reason for concealment, the fire was kept burning brightly during the long dark hours. At the welcome end of another night, Tracy threw enough broken cedar branches upon the glowing coals to produce a thin ribbon of smoke visible for several miles. "Sort of like those old wandering Jews," he remarked as they gathered up their weapons in the semidark, "we had ourselves a pillar of fire last night, and now here's a cloud by day. We'll see if that doesn't fetch up those psalm singers."

After downing the remainder of Dave's cakes, which Tracy called hardtack, and the Swede declared to be dried dog bones, they cautiously worked their way up to the very top of the rimrock.

Settled down in the commanding position, a dish-shaped depression in the rocks, occupied the day before by the posse, they waited for full light.

Within an hour voices were heard at their abandoned campsite. "Swallowed the bait," Tracy whispered, grinning slightly. "Now let's see which way the cat jumps."

Although the sky was heavily overcast with the threat of more snow, Tracy could easily distinguish several forms including the stocky county sheriff and a lanky figure Johnson declared to be Valentine Hoy.

"Quiet, you damned fool," Tracy gritted at Lant who, in shifting his position at the bottom of the uneven depression, had let his rifle clatter against the stone wall.

The posse men, who'd been easing up from behind the great shattered chunks of talus, quickly dropped from sight. Some sort of a conference seemed under way.

Suddenly: "Johnson, throw out your guns and surrender. You know the law'll go easier with you if you do."

It was Val Hoy, the Swede whispered.

"Maybe we should take them up on that," Lant said, poking Tracy. "Swede'll come off all right . . . and we. . . ."

"And we . . . what?" Tracy asked, peering, in the growing light, at Lant's face, pale as the dirty snow rimming the rocky trench. "If we turn ourselves in . . . then what?"

"They'll give us a fair shake, that's what," Swede Johnson said, glaring at Tracy with bloodshot eyes, and attempted to get to his feet.

"Watch it, you fool." Tracy yanked the Swede down so hard Johnson grunted with the impact. "You want to dance on air? That's a posse."

"You haven't got a chance!" someone called. "Every trail's blocked from the mountain." It was a hard voice, speaking hard facts.

"That's the sheriff," Johnson muttered, getting out a soiled white handkerchief and tying it to his Winchester's barrel.

"Keep down, I tell you." And Harry shoved the Swede again with such force that Johnson's rifle, dropping to the bottom of the trench, exploded the round in its chamber.

There was instant answering fire from the posse. Bullets whined and cracked against the rocks about the fugitives, buzzing away with the venom of aroused hornets.

Harry motioned Lant and Johnson to keep their heads down, waited until the posse's fusillade had spluttered off to a halt—then quickly raised up to get off a shot. "That's to let 'em know we're still here," he grunted, purposely keeping his Winchester's muzzle pointed in the Swede's direction. "Still here, and no white flags."

There was no response from either Lant or Johnson, both clutching their rifles and staring tensely from Tracy to each other.

Quiet fell over the mountain slope, then Valentine Hoy's grating voice was heard again. "This ain't goin' to drag on! You-all and that Swede don't come out peaceable, you'll get what Bennett got!"

Tracy looked from Johnson to Lant, then cupped his hands. "What about Jack Bennett? Where's he?"

"Decorating a tree!" came Hoy's nasal reply. "And that's gonna happen to you ungodly whore sons if you don't come out prompt!"

Kneeling in the shallow rock depression, Tracy turned to Lant and Johnson. "Hear that? That's what you'd be walking into." Then to Hoy: "What's the idea? Jack Bennett wasn't wanted!" Tracy jacked a shell into his rifle's chamber and waited.

"Bastard stole my beef along with that murderin' Swede!" Hoy shouted. "And he was tryin' to tote back a load of grub for your bunch!"

A gleam of sunlight momentarily breaking through the overcast streamed broadly across the Owl-Yu-Kuts plateau to gild the rocky face of Douglas Mountain with glaring gold, making it difficult for the fugitives to see the posse. Squinting cautiously above the lip of the talus rock, Tracy could faintly discern several figures, now standing boldly upright down in the old camp.

"Watch it, dammit," Lant warned. "You're telling us to stay down, but you'll get plugged." He grabbed at Tracy as the latter arose, Winchester at the ready. Johnson crouched, motionless, watching with glittering eyes.

"Hoy!" Tracy's voice rang across the mountain top. "It's you and me! You hung my friend and now you'll pay!"

In the sun sparkle, Tracy could dimly make out the stocky Routt county sheriff tugging at the lanky posse man, apparently arguing with him. But Hoy broke loose and lifted his rifle.

Two shots cracked out. One took deadly effect. As he jumped for the hole, Tracy saw Hoy stagger and fall in a heap.

Instantly the posse's guns roared. Bullets shrilled and exploded against the boulders, blasting knife-sharp splinters and dust over the rimrock's defenders.

"Hell! You blew Val Hoy into Kingdom Come and now we'll die for sure," Johnson growled, crouching on his hands and knees like some animal seeking a deeper burrow. "They've stretched pore Jack's neck and we're next."

"Told you we oughta made terms with them," Lant mumbled, wiping a streak of blood from his forehead, where a rock splinter had sliced his sombrero to part his hair.

"Didn't you hear that son-of-a-bitch?" Tracy snapped. "They lynched Jack Bennett . . . and for no more than trying to bring us supplies."

There was no reply.

As time slipped away, Tracy, Lant, and Johnson eyed each other often. It seemed they'd little or nothing to say to each other, although Tracy could tell from Lant's lethargy that he viewed the situation as hopeless. As for Johnson, he'd withdrawn completely, sitting with his hands clasped over his knees staring up at the increasingly cloudy sky.

Throughout the remainder of the gray day, there was little noise from the posse, a fact that grew increasingly apparent to Tracy. At last he mentioned it to the silent pair beside him.

"I may be wrong, but I think those fellows are commencing to find they've bit off more than they want to chew. They don't dare come up here without inviting a bullet . . . like Hoy . . . and they haven't got sand enough to sit it out through the night, even with a fire."

"What are you getting at?" Lant asked, roused up somewhat, while Johnson abandoned his sky watch.

"I figure they're going to let us get out into the open, then make a try at running us down."

Tracy's estimate of the situation proved correct. Before the cold night swept in over the huge valley and ridges, the fugitives caught sounds of the departing posse.

Waiting until near dark, Tracy, followed by Lant, made his way quietly down the slope to discover the remnants of an expiring fire, half a sack of feed, and a patch of blood-splotched snow.

"That took the starch out of them, all right," Tracy told Lant to buck him up as they clambered back to confer with Johnson, cautiously awaiting them on the rimrock. "Hoy's surely out of action, dead or wounded. Too bad . . . but he had his chance at me."

"And, besides, he helped lynch old Jack," the rejuvenated Johnson snarled, brandishing his rifle and cursing the posse.

"Well, let's get down off this damned rattrap of a mountain while there's a chance," Tracy said, breaking in upon the flow of Johnson's war-like vituperation. "We can stay here and starve or take a chance on a shot at some deer. If we move fast before daylight, we might get some distance . . . more than they're counting on. I'd like to try for some horses, either at a ranch or maybe the Ladore-Snake River stage."

They moved down the trail the posse had broken through the cedars and underbrush. The cold was intense again, but no snow seemed to be forthcoming as the overcast began to unravel and shred apart. By the time they'd stumbled out onto the bottoms, the silver bangle of a new moon gave them enough light to strike the northeast trail toward the Sparks Ranch on Talamante Creek. Lant was now sanguine enough to believe they'd obtain shelter and food at one of the sheep camps near Powder Wash, before making their way on to a friendly ranch.

Two days later Tracy, Lant, and Johnson were sitting in the low-ceilinged living room of Herb Bassett's ranch house, under guard and the curious eyes of more than sixty ranchers, posse members, and mere gawkers.

The past forty-eight hours had brought them nothing but

more hardships and disappointments, despite Tracy's stubborn resolve to shake off pursuit.

After descending the mountain they had trekked twenty miles through the night, across the valley's many plateaus and low cedar ridges to Sparks's ranch on Talamantes Creek. There they'd hoped to raid the horse corral, but it was after daylight when they got there and they'd been forced to take cover in one of the ranch's haystacks. The arrival of one section of the posse under Farnham had completely thwarted their attempt and they spent the rest of the day in the stack.

On the following morning they were able to get away in the dawn and reach the nearest Davenport sheep ranch at the Talamante forks. When the shepherd left for the other camp, Tracy had downed one of the sheep with a rock and they'd hurriedly hacked off enough mutton to carry away.

Their attack upon the sheep camp was their undoing, for the nearly starving men were crouched in a small arroyo near Powder Wash, roasting the meat, when their fire gave them away to a posse that had been scouting their trail.

On being ordered to surrender, Tracy picked up his rifle and ran for the wash, but Johnson immediately threw up his hands. Lant soon followed suit, although he was fired on by a posse member as he came up out of the wash.

After some time, Tracy, realizing the impossibility of getting out of the trap, his boots nearly falling off his feet and bereft of enough firepower to stand off six men, surrendered. And was fired on by Deputy Sheriff Farnham.

And now, as they sat in the Bassett ranch house in the late afternoon, friendless and guarded by half a dozen posse men, Ladore, Colorado Justice of the Peace J. S. Hoy, brother of the dead Val Hoy, interrogated the prisoners. It was a long, slow, and generally unrewarding process for the lawmen, with Johnson sullen, Lant vague with apprehension, and Tracy noncommittal. Only once did Tracy's steely nerve break with exhaustion and frustrated anger—when the justice of the peace stiffly inquired: "Which of you men killed my brother?"

"Well, it must have been one of us here, wasn't it?" Tracy stared back at the sober-visaged Hoy, knowing full well this particular Justice wouldn't lift a finger if the crowd within the house and those gathered around the barns were to take the law into their own hands—as Hoy's brother and others had done with Bennett.

With the cold, wintry day gradually coming to its end, the coal-oil lamp, hanging overhead, was lit and Justice Hoy, scribbling away at his papers in the yellow pool of light, at last cleared his throat to read the findings:

Office of the Justice of the Peace
Ladore, Colorado, March 5, 1898
On the above date, F. L. Johnson, Frank Lant, and Harry Bass were brought before me by the sheriff of Routt County charged with the killing of Valentine S. Hoy on the afternoon of March 1, 1898. I examined the three prisoners, also examining Sheriff Charles Neiman, E. A. Farnham, and James McKnight.

To me the evidence taken and the circumstances surrounding the killing of Valentine S. Hoy was sufficient to bind the prisoners over to the district court without bail, and they were accordingly remanded to the custody of the sheriff to be confined to the county jail until the decision so rendered by due course of law, except in the case of P. L. Johnson, who was turned over to the custody of Deputy United States Marshal Charles Laney, who claimed Johnson on a writ of requisition from the Governor of Wyoming. The Mittimus remanding Lant and Tracy to the county jail contains the names of four principal witnesses in the prosecution, to wit: Charles Nieman, E. A. Farnham, James McKnight, and J. S. Hoy.

When Hoy ceased, the room buzzed with comments, and many less than veiled threats toward the prisoners. Vernal posse members were the most outspoken, for they'd ridden many miles on the 4th to get in on the capture—and were now urging the quick formation of a necktie party. This action was quietly denied by the stern-faced Sheriff Neiman, who herded Tracy, Lant, and Johnson into a storeroom off the kitchen to put them under guard of Farnham and a rancher named Rouff.

When Josie Bassett, the same girl Tracy and Lant had greeted on the way from their cabin on March 1st, brought in their supper—three dishes of beef stew and coffee—Tracy arose and bowed. "I don't know which I'd rather see after all those sour faces out there, Miss Bassett . . . you or your food." Lant and Johnson merely nodded and took their plates.

"Blarney ain't goin' to save you from the hangman," Farnham grunted, while Rouff chuckled.

"Well, gents"—Harry looked up from his food—"after this fine, hot grub, all I ask is a good horse, twenty-five yards' head start, and you'd never see me again."

Going out for his own supper and leaving Rouff and another rancher with the prisoners, Farnham returned in a half hour to report the arrival of Utah officers demanding that Tracy and Lant be turned over to them for their escape from the Utah Penitentiary. "But those Jays won't win out, for Neiman and the old Justice are dead set on takin' your scalps for Val Hoy's shooting. So tomorrow, while Johnson's going to Wyoming for that other killing, you lucky devils'll be on your way to Hahn's Peak."

Farnham's sardonic prediction proved correct, for Tracy and Lant were rousted out in the early morning by Sheriff Neiman, apprehensive of an overt lynch attempt from the dozens of ranchers still camped upon the Bassett property.

Then the two prisoners were quietly taken in cuffs to the small log jail at Hahn's Peak, fifty miles east of Brown's Hole.

Chapter Twelve

Sitting on their plank bunks in the Hahn's Peak jail, spooning up the noon meal of slumgullion, Tracy voiced one of their mutual thoughts. "We've been here for three days and I still say it beats starving in the rocks or decorating some tree like poor Jack Bennett."

Lant shrugged somberly, cleaned up his plate, then flung himself back down on his hard bunk.

"And you might as well stop looking so peckish," Tracy told him. "We walked out of that Utah stone pile, didn't we? After we get our second wind and I have a few things sorted out, you watch our dust."

Sitting back up, Lant reached for their copy of the March 7th Denver News and waved it at Tracy.

"Old man Hoy's guff? Well, twenty-three to him!" Tracy spoke of a letter in the issue of the 7th written by the justice of the peace for Ladore—something being discussed throughout the village, and beyond.

"That old devil won't give up till he sticks our necks into some noose legally, or fires up a bunch of lynchers," Lant said, uneasily watching Tracy looking through the paper.

Although understanding Lant's concern, Tracy silently blamed both Lant and Johnson for their capture and imprisonment.

After a wry glance at his cell mate, he re-read the outburst, which ranted against the riff-raff wintering in such robbers' roosts as Brown's Hole and demanding action against them up to and including a reward of $1,000 each for the capture of members of the various bands.

Tracy tossed the paper back to Lant with a prophetic comment. "Shouldn't wonder if such talk won't cost Mister Justice Hoy a little trouble in the long run."

Four days later, when the deputy sheriff fetched in their inevitable slumgullion and coffee, he brought along another issue of the Denver paper, with a small item ringed in pencil on the front page. "Your crooked pals at the Hole ain't helpin' your case any. Looks like they're goin' at it so strong, the first jury picked will bury you both ten feet deep." He tossed down the Denver *News* and went back out, whistling as he slammed the cell door.

MOUNTAIN OUTLAWS' RAMPAGE

Sweetwater County—Our Green River correspondent has reported the Hoy Ranch and a number of JS cattle camps were raided yesterday by an armed band of unknown riders.

Cabins were burned, supplies destroyed, and cattle and horses run off.

It is thought this outrage was committed by members of one of the gangs now infesting the western end of Brown's Hole, with the view of answering with violence the letter that Justice of the Peace J. S. Hoy had recently published in this paper.

"Hoy seems to have riled up Butch's bunch." Tracy laughed. "That might take the old J.P.'s mind off of us."

Lant shook his head. "That tin star, Farnham, says this could get the public yelling for someone to make a public example of . . . and we're mighty handy."

"Then I guess it's about time we said good bye to this hotel-de-gink," Tracy replied, thumbing on through the paper in search of news about the Spaniards. Ever since the story of the sinking of the *Maine* had come into the Hole, that subject had furnished a good share of the daily gossip around the general store, together with the never-ending debates over the advantages of sheep raising opposed to cattle production.

March 23rd arrived with still no indication of when their case would come to trial. By early evening Lant was already asleep and muttering in his bunk, but Tracy lay wide awake. Their part-time guard, an out-of-work bartender, who'd come on at nine, was already comfortably dozing in his corridor chair.

A thaw had set in after dark and the *tap-tapping* of the melting ice and snow dripping from the eaves drummed monotonously outside the little log jailhouse. For a while Tracy tried to ignore the sounds as they forced their way into his thoughts, but finally gave it up and began to listen. There was something not quite right about such common sounds—something not exactly natural. Then he had it. Someone outside the cell's one window was tapping against the cracked pane. Someone out there wanted him.

Peering through the washed-out yellow of the jail's coal-oil lamp, Tracy found the guard slumbered on, indifferent to sounds—natural or unnatural.

Slipping softly to the window on stockinged feet, he stared into the night and made out the shadowy shape of a horseman near the jail's wall. The little jail on a lonely lane, a block from the village's main street, was an isolated island in the wind-swept night. There wasn't much chance of his visitor being

143

spotted, unless he was the first of a band of lynchers. Considering this—Tracy moved away just as the horseman guided his mount back up to the window.

There came the insistent tapping again, and Harry, peering out, recognized Elzy Lay, who waved him closer and held up a slim package.

There was no way the bundle could come through the bars unless the glass was knocked out. Looking over his shoulder at the drowsing guard, Harry wrapped a bandanna around his fist and gave the pane a quick *thump*. The glass split apart, one piece falling into the snow. It was the matter of a moment to shove the other section after the first as the out-of-work bartender snored away.

Raising a gloved finger to his lips, Elzy shoved the paper wrapped bundle through the bars. Then before Tracy could respond, Lay turned his horse and, with a shadowy wave, was off down the lane. Gone in the night.

Squinting hard in the dim, yellow lamplight, Tracy eventually made out the message: *The boys all think you could use a little hand, so we're sending this with our best. Even Sundance says hello. Butch and I think you might want to head for a warmer clime, and we feel you might try the WS Ranch down at Alma, New Mex Territory. As they take in traveling men, we'll probably join you after some railroad work this summer. Good luck from the boys!*

The note pleased Harry nearly as much as the six-shooter. He'd always felt men of the caliber of Lay, Warner, O'Day, and even feisty old Bill Madden were his kind. Cassidy was a new type, a meticulous, level-headed chieftain who brooked no disturbance in the gang he was carefully assembling. Sundance, on the other hand, was just a wild, young hothead, destined to ride for many a fall, and the newest members, Logan and Kilpatric, were unknown to Tracy.

Hunt Down Harry Tracy

Mulling things over as he waited out the long hours until dawn, Tracy came to the decision Lant wasn't cut out for the sort of life they'd been leading. The more Tracy thought of the past, the more he was convinced that he and Lant would have to come to a parting of the ways somewhere down the road.

Morning finally arrived while the night guard awoke to be replaced by the sardonic deputy sheriff. And Tracy was waiting for him.

Two minutes after Ethan Allan Farnham swaggered up to their cell he was lying unconscious on the floor, tied tightly as a steer on branding day. Shoving the unexpected six-shooter into Farnham's belly, Tracy had removed his keys, then belted the white-faced deputy alongside the head with the Colt's barrel. After ripping up a blanket, Tracy and Lant bound the inanimate deputy, rolled him into the cell's corner, and then hurriedly rifled his pockets of a gratifying $95.

"Must have been in some card game," Lant offered as they split the roll.

"Wherever he came by it, it's only part payment for his shot at me after I had my props up," Tracy grunted.

Aware the jail would soon be visited by either Sheriff Neiman, who sometimes checked on the prisoners, or by another of the part-time deputies, Tracy and Lant assembled their outer gear. Taking the pair of six-shooters, along with the deputy's gun belt, they carefully reconnoitered the outside.

Finding the village's shadowy streets still empty, Harry and Lant slipped up a block and entered one of the liveries, without disturbing the sleep of the stable hand who remained dead to the world on a cot at the rear of the barn.

Exercising his expertise as a practicing horse thief, Lant chose the animals and got them quietly from their stalls, as

Harry fetched saddles and bridles from a store room. Then with Harry mounted upon the sheriff's own chestnut, and Lant straddling a wall-eyed bay, they put steel to their mounts and left jail and village behind as the sun commenced to burn away the night mists over the mountain of Hahn's Peak.

Within two hours Lant's prestige as an authority upon horses was being challenged by an irate Tracy. First the sheriff's mount developed a pulled tendon in the right forefoot. This slowed their southern flight down to a walk near the Elk River-Mad Creek forks, ten miles south of Hahn's Peak. Then, almost immediately, Lant's mare threw a rear shoe.

Rather than risk more ill luck, Tracy and Lant turned the horses into a fenced field, near the settlement of Elk Creek above Steamboat Springs, and, taking cover behind a small barn, waited for the imminent arrival of the Hahn's Peak-Steamboat Springs stage.

Within thirty minutes Harry discovered further reason to curse Lant's choice in horses. Hailing the oncoming coach, they found themselves staring into a scatter-gun's twin barrels, held by the stage's sole passenger—Sheriff Neiman.

"Hell! Who'd have thought anybody from Hahn's Peak would be up this early," was Tracy's only comment at the turn of events. Lant had nothing to add as they were both cuffed, thrust into the coach, and relentlessly watched by the sheriff on their return to the little, log jailhouse.

The following morning, March 25, 1898, Harry and Lant were put aboard another stage by an exasperated Neiman, and taken, under guard, to Aspen, in rugged Pitkin County, eighty miles south in the high Rockies.

Unfortunately for Neiman's strategy of placing his unruly prisoners in what he thought to be a more secure jail, their Aspen stay was even briefer than that at Hahn's Peak. Within two weeks, Harry, who was developing a finely honed ability for split-second moves, overpowered a careless guard at supper and freed both himself and Lant, making little noise in the process.

Once again on the loose, with the guard securely gagged and trussed up in their vacated cell, the determined Tracy led Lant down the darkened side streets of the small, mountain town and into another livery. There they surprised the owner, who was just closing his place for the night.

"I'll take my own this time," Tracy told Lant. "I want to be sure of putting plenty of distance between here and wherever."

Consequently Harry chose a clean-limbed bay with a big chest indicating staying power, despite a lively eye that spoke of spirit—the sort of horse he should have had when they'd skedaddled from Hahn's Peak. Lant picked out a chestnut that had the appearance of a goer.

After buttoning up his heavy Mackinaw and pulling on some gloves rummaged from the tack room, Tracy spoke. "I'm going to try for that WS Ranch in New Mexico. It's long past time to clear out of this territory. What do you say?"

Lant straightened from tightening a cinch and rubbed the small of his back. "I'm getting mighty tired of these jailhouse bunks and I'd like to ride for Wyoming. I ain't known around there yet. And the papers have been full about some Wyoming rancher called Torrey who's raising himself a cavalry troop to whip the Spaniards. Calls it Torrey's Rough Riders. So I guess I'll give it a try."

"I'd have thought you'd had enough rough riding to last for a damned long time," Tracy snorted. "I know I have. But that's up to you." He was relieved Lant was going off on his own. Lant was a good enough fellow, but the time had come to ride different trails. Powder Wash had proved that.

Leading their horses out into the crystalline night with a ready eye on the quiet street, they shook hands, then swung up into their saddles, Lant tugging down his Stetson and securing the buttons on his long overcoat.

Before long they were out in the open country, under the brittle stars and a glowing half moon, Lant heading north on the Carbondale road, while Harry galloped his big bay on a route leading through towering Independence Pass and westward.

Now that he was on the move, he'd take the Union Pacific at the nearest station and ride the cars all the way to the West Coast. There'd be no WS Ranch in New Mexico Territory after all, for he was through with longriders and gun play.

He was ready for a new life.

Chapter Thirteen

Four days later Harry was walking the streets of Seattle, taking in the sights. Part seaport, part frontier town, it differed from any place he'd ever known. Although founded in 1851, it was a far Western boom town whose boom came from timber, instead of gold. The continuing boom was evident in the piles of raw lumber towering up on the many docks that ran out into the glittering blue and silver bay. Sitting upon its seven hills like a lesser Rome, Seattle climbed toward the "respectable" neighborhoods from the bay with its cheap hotels, lodging houses, and saloons stretching from Seneca to Jackson on the north and Second on the east.

From his arrival on Friday until Sunday, Harry lodged at a fairly respectable rooming house on Frontier and spent his evenings at the Horseshoe Saloon at Columbia and Front Streets.

Harry played in several modest poker games, yet refrained from plunging heavily. But on Saturday night he sat in a game with a hodge-podge of players, including a miner just back from the Klondike, several lumbermen, a ship's captain, and a rather sporty young fellow dressed in a flashy checked suit and red necktie.

By closing time he'd scooped in over $300, including some of the young swell's money. Bidding the grumbling group a good night, he walked out of the Horseshoe into a foggy morning, for the mist had rolled in from the bay and sound. Carefully navigating from street lamp to street lamp, he came to Frontier at last. He heard footsteps behind him as he turned the corner but thought little of it until something swished dangerously close to his head.

"Hey! Where'd that come from?" It sounded like the young swell in the checkered suit—for Tracy spun, cat-like, pulling his Smith & Wesson from under his coat in one motion.

"Introduce yourself or I'll let daylight through your pretty vest." Tracy shoved the long silver barrel under his assailant's long nose.

"Hell, I was playing cards with you not ten minutes ago."

The swell's hands were reaching for the dim stars, blackjack still clutched in one of them. "Name's Dave . . . Dave Merrill. Wasn't about to. . . ."

"No, you were just going to tap me out and take back your cash. I ought to slam you right now . . . then see what's on the end of that gold watch chain." Tracy cocked the pistol and jammed it into the other's midriff. "Now get out of here before my finger slips. And from now on be damned sure you know how to pussy-foot up on someone before you try it. You could get yourself shot dead."

Harry stood grinning by the street lamp as he watched the fellow vanish off into the fog, then turned back toward his rooming house, patting the comforting roll of bills in his coat pocket. If the pickings in Seattle were this good, he just might settle down for the rest of the year and gamble for a living. It was always easier work at a card table than on the end of an axe or a cross-cut. Besides, it would be cold out in the lumber camps before too long, while spring would come around as always.

On the following morning, Monday, after dressing, Tracy

took up his Winchester, still tucked away in the slicker, and the six-shooter, which had been under his pillow, then departed the rooming house. He had breakfast and a few drinks at the Horseshoe, and was staring at the bottom of his empty glass and mulling things over when he heard a familiar voice at his elbow. Harry glanced up to see the hatchet-faced Dave Merrill, now wearing a rather seedy, dark suit, grinning down at him.

"Could I sit? I been hunting you."

Tracy waved him to a seat.

"Seattle's one peach of a town," Merrill said, "but it's dog eat dog every day of the week. And that's why I come looking for you." He leaned across the table after signaling the barkeep for a bottle. When the whiskey arrived, and was paid for, he continued. "I figure you for a fellow that wants ready cash and don't care much how he gets the sponduliks."

"You're taking one hell of a lot for granted," Tracy gritted, pouring himself another shot. "Just what makes you so sure of yourself . . . or me?"

Merrill, who'd attempted to catch up with Harry's drinking, was becoming somewhat intoxicated—and loud. "Hell's fire, I can always pick a fellow who knows how to play his cards." He grinned lopsidedly at such wit. "And I know you're heeled. While you sure ain't no sort of law."

Tracy, aware the other's voice was carrying around the saloon, grasped Merrill's wrist before the younger man could lift the glass again. "Let's get out of here and take ourselves some air."

When Tracy stepped back out through the batwings of the saloon that autumn morning of 1898 with Dave Merrill, he walked away from a part of his life that was over. He found Merrill to have been a fellow escapee, in this instance from a California prison. The fellow was a new type of hardcase to

Tracy—this time of city streets and second stories. According to his talk, Merrill was an accomplished burglar and stick-up artist.

And Tracy was also a different man from the wandering cowhand who'd left the high plains seeking the anonymous safety of the Northwest's logging camps. While Cassidy's gang might still be riding high, wide, and handsome, the growing web of telephone lines and improving road systems across the West was beginning to spell the end of all wild bunches everywhere.

As he sat in another saloon near Merrill's rooming house at Third and Main, Tracy came to a decision that this hawk-faced young fellow could be the right sort. He seemed to have plenty of sand as well as a sardonic lack of respect for the law, together with a working knowledge of the Pacific coast's towns and cities.

Always a self-sufficient loner, Tracy had sometimes still felt the need for a partner, someone to watch the other's back. Never one for much self-analyzing in a determined day-to-day existence, he was forever seeking that particular person who might replace his unforgotten friend and confidant of the past, Mike Tracy of the Wisconsin logging camps—the man who'd been a combination left-handed brother and foster father to him.

Learning from Merrill that word was commencing to circulate around the city's Tenderloin of his suspected skill with the pasteboards, Harry realized that form of income was finished as far as Seattle was concerned.

"Don't need to fiddle around with slick decks, anyway," Merrill informed Tracy. "You can use that persuader under your coat." Merrill took a murderous-looking slungshot from a pocket and rapped it on the edge of their table. "Generally use this here with mighty good results."

"Except on me." Tracy was watching the bartender who seemed overly interested in their conversation. When he turned the bar over to a fellow bottle-pusher and eased out a side door, Harry yanked Merrill up and they exited themselves.

"Guess I talk a bit too much sometimes," Merrill offered as they made their way up Third to Dave's rooming house. Harry merely nodded.

They decided to leave Seattle when Merrill admitted there was an outstanding warrant on him for housebreaking. Harry thereupon picked Portland, Oregon, after learning Merrill had a mother and a sister in that city. Portland would also be nearer to some of the lumber camps.

Chapter Fourteen

Tracy and Merrill arrived in Portland on Friday, October 10, 1898. They'd ridden the day coaches for three days, not wishing to spend the cash on Pullman berths.

When they reached the Merrill home, a small white frame house badly in need of paint, at First and Market Street near the Union Pacific tracks, Dave had gone ahead to knock on the door. "I'll tell 'em we tried our luck at Seattle, and then came here so you could look into the timber business. Lumberman and rancher from back East, that's you."

Tracy expected to see a female version of her lantern-jawed brother when he was introduced to Mollie Merrill. But he was relieved to shake hands with a pretty, curvesome young woman, whose reddish-amber hair reminded him of the long gone Pearly Mae from American Falls.

Mrs. Merrill had obviously been as good-looking at one time as her daughter. Harry figured Dave's father must have been an older version of his lanky son, for a framed photo of a long-faced man in a stringy beard scowled down on the group as they sat at dinner.

"And exactly what business are you in, Mister Tracy?" Mrs. Merrill asked, peering over her glasses.

"As Dave said, I'm checking on prospects in the lumber business." Tracy grinned slightly, for he could feel the pressure of a foot upon his—and he knew it wasn't Dave at the far end of the table or his mother at the other.

Mrs. Merrill hesitated. "Then you might be able to find David some sort of a job. He'll be all right once he settles down and gives up his fancy ideas of living on air. That's brought trouble before." She passed more biscuits to Harry. "Yes, your coming here could be a good sign."

Mollie, across the table, smiled warmly. "Well, I think Mister Tracy will be good for all of us."

For the next several weeks, Mollie Merrill's estimate of their new boarder seemed correct. Harry squired his friend's sister to some of the entertainment spots about the town. Together they attended the Orpheum, seeing blonde Ada Lewis in *Reily and the 400,* a play poking fun at the stuffy world of society. They also took in *A Trip to Chinatown with its Tong War* on stage at the Belasco, but the flickering Edison Vitascope at the Forest Theater proved to be the highlight of their almost nightly outings—until Harry learned Mollie Merrill's name happened to be Mrs. William Deffenbaugh.

Married in early spring to a San Francisco hardware drummer, she'd returned home in late summer. "And I'm going to get a divorce mighty soon, you can bet," she told Tracy as she nestled warmly against him in the streetcar on their way home from another visit to the Vitascope.

During the day, Mollie worked at a millinery shop, while Harry and Dave prowled the streets, ostensibly looking over the lumber trade.

In order to please his mother, Dave would start the evening with Harry and Mollie, but invariably dropped out somewhere at one saloon or another to await their return. His friend and sister, if they didn't take in some show, usually wound up at one of the town's cheap hotels.

These rendezvous began soon after Tracy received an answer to the letter he'd written Janet Warrington upon arriving in town. The first word he'd had from Chicago in two years was short and anything but sweet. Dated two weeks after he'd written, it was signed by Janet's mother:

October 24, 1898
Mister H. Tracy,

I see I must, finally, communicate with you so you will know certain facts and stop trying to get in touch with my unfortunate daughter.

For your information, Janet has been confined to a local hospital for several months with consumption. However, she has responded to her treatments quite well and should be completely out of danger within the next year or so.

A fine young man here has taken a decided interest in her case, and has kindly helped defray much of the expenses.

So please don't attempt to write any further as Janet now knows you are certainly not the right sort.

Mrs. Warrington

That fine young man had to be that son-of-a-bitch Ogden Palmer, but if that was the way it went, then to the devil with her! Somehow he felt sold, played for a sucker. Janet herself could have written if she'd cared one snap for him. But he had the means at hand of revenging himself upon such women—Mollie Merrill.

Thus, almost every evening they could possibly get away from the seedy respectability of the Merrill bungalow, Harry and Mollie checked in to the Pacific Arms, behind the Portland City Hall.

Although Harry had remained true to the memory of Janet

Warrington in the past, with the exception of several casual dalliances along the way, he threw that memory away the first time he shut the hotel room behind Mollie and himself. Passionate as her red hair proclaimed her to be, Mollie Merrill turned out to be an extremely demanding bed partner. But it was just such demands that Tracy delighted to fulfill.

One evening, as the trio walked home through the misty fall night, Dave, who'd been unusually silent since joining them in front of the Sterling Saloon, dropped back, tugging Harry by the elbow.

"We got to make some sort of a move . . . soon."

When Harry inquired, under his breath, what Merrill was talking about, Dave waved his sister on. "I'm about out of cash and I don't guess you've got much left yourself . . . the way you been tossing it around on her."

Seeing Mollie waiting ahead by a street light, Harry stopped and lit a cigarette. "What's on your mind?"

"This." Turning sideways away from his sister, Merrill opened his coat and Tracy saw the cold glint of a six-shooter in Dave's shoulder holster. "We up and turn midnight bankers . . . cash in our pistols."

Dave was right. They couldn't loaf around Portland much longer. He'd been eyed more than once by police as he sat on a park bench in the plaza. It was nothing more than the cursory glance any yard bull would give a tourist or a bum, but it set his teeth on edge. He should be doing something more than hanging about saloons or wandering the streets and harbor. He was also low on money, for, as Dave pointed out, he'd been tossing around considerable cash, spending over $50 on Christmas presents for the Merrills. And those shows and evenings with Mollie at the hotel weren't free. So he began to listen to Merrill, as it was Dave's town, while he was a mere visitor.

W. R. Garwood

Winter was coming and he didn't feel like heading out to the lumber camps. The more he listened to Dave rattle on about easy pickings, the more he saw it as a way to get his hands on ready cash. One part of him was for the idea—a six-gun jammed straight into a city dweller's face would do the trick. And yet the other side scorned such penny-ante tricks. Would the Hole-in-the-Wall boys make raises by hoisting saloonkeepers? No—they'd raid across the high plains, taking their chances there—even fighting off posses if it came to that—then go their way.

Well, he'd fought more than one posse himself, and rode with some of the best of them, but this was just about 1899, with changing times. He'd go along with Dave for the time being and get enough cash together for a stake.

One fall night while they sat over a bottle in a Curtis Street wine parlor, Harry learned that Mollie's erstwhile husband, William Deffenbaugh, the hardware drummer, had turned up at her place of employment that morning.

"I told him it was all over and I was getting a divorce for him walking out on me." She emptied the glass again and poked it over. "Gimme another."

Harry had to chuckle. After she downed her refilled glass, he spoke up. "Well, let's not keep him nor your mother waiting." He pulled out a wedding band from his vest. "Won this in a game the other day." He took her left hand and slipped on the ring. "Now let's go tell them we're married."

"But we ain't yet."

"No, and you're not divorced yet, either." Tracy tossed $1 on the table, got her up and out the door. For a girl she could sure put it away. "So, we tell your mother and this here Deffenbaugh, if he comes around, that we're hitched."

"But we really will be, won't we?" She clung to his arm as

158

they stood in a doorway out of the foggy night air, waiting for the streetcar.

"Just as soon as you can tie a can to that fellow. Then we'll get spliced legally. But in the meantime, we'll go through the motions as if we already are, eh?"

There was some tall explaining to do the following morning at breakfast when they broke the news to Mollie's mother. Dave was already wise to the charade, having been tipped off the previous night, and he assured Mrs. Merrill he'd seen the legal papers of divorce at the courthouse. "And I was witness and best man all rolled into one." Merrill chuckled, forking more griddlecakes onto his plate.

"I must say it was a mighty fast thing." Still bemused at the sudden news, Mrs. Merrill frowned at her frying pan as she poured out more batter. "I only hope you're not too hasty, the both of you." Looking over at the bridegroom, Mrs. Merrill wagged her head. "And Mollie's the only one with a job, as it is."

"That won't last," Harry spoke up after a wink from Dave. "I've a job coming up on the waterfront. Head night watchman for a shipping company. Pays well and I'll hold it down until my job as foreman with that lumber company comes along in the spring."

"So you see"—Mollie beamed—"Harry will bring in enough money, along with mine, so we can get out and look for a place of our own."

A discussion followed in which it was decided the newly-weds would begin housekeeping over near Central. With Mollie taking the morning off, they left in high spirits. Mrs. Merrill, more easy in her mind, called after them: "Now come home early all of you, and I'll have a cake fixed up." Then she paused. "But what if Mister Deffenbaugh calls around?"

"Tell him twenty-three skidoo!" Dave shouted back as he, his sister, and Tracy went up the street, laughing.

Three nights later, with Harry and Mollie sharing a two-room furnished flat on Fifth at Central, there came a knock at the door.

"That'd be Dave," Harry told Mollie, who was washing dishes at the sink. "Had him come along to see if I can't find him a job at the docks, too." Taking up his dinner pail and pulling on a heavy coat over his rough work clothes, Tracy opened the door.

Similarly garbed, Dave waited while Harry kissed his bride, then the pair went down the two flights of creaking stairs.

"She tumble?" Dave pulled a six-shooter from his Mackinaw pocket and looked it over in the dim flare of a street light.

"Why should she? She thinks I'm a regular magician to get her washout of a brother to work." Tracy tugged a broad-brimmed hat down over his eyes. "Here's the second night we've been out. Now where'll we go sucker hunting?"

By four in the morning they'd nearly $200 apiece, having braced two saloonkeepers, three late-closing groceries, as well as several pairs of strollers.

For the next month, from January 7 until February 8, 1899, Tracy and Merrill prowled south Portland's cold streets night after night in a two-man crime wave. In addition to the Acorn and Delta Saloons, they'd even braced the owners of several livery stables. But after throwing down on the conductor of an empty Second Avenue streetcar in early February, Tracy was all for calling a halt to their nightly campaign for a spell.

"Here's about where I get off," he panted as they ran across backyards, vaulting board fences and sliding through wet alleys. "Don't mind such shenanigans on horseback, but be damned if I want to keep at such high hurdles. It's dangerous. One or the other of us is bound to get stove up. Besides, we've got ourselves damned nigh a thousand dollars. Enough to lay off for a while."

Merrill agreed, and, splitting up, they parted for the night, Tracy to return to the welcome warmth of Mollie's bed and Merrill to go home to his mother's.

By now the Portland papers were trumpeting demands for the arrest and conviction of what they were terming the False Face Bandits.

Harry was puzzled where the news hacks had come up with such an appellation, for neither he nor Dave had worn more than bandannas over their faces during the robberies. He finally decided it just made better copy for the breakfast readers. With the papers splashing their escapades in bold headlines, Harry found a certain wry satisfaction in reading the flamboyant details, but felt little pleasure in such actions. It was a pure tinhorn game no matter how one looked at it.

As the weeks passed, Tracy and Mollie successfully kept up the appearance of newlyweds. Even Mrs. Merrill began to look on Harry as a second son, and he took particular pains to fetch over a well-filled bag of groceries when he and Mollie came visiting.

On an early winter morning in 1899, as Mollie readied herself for work, Harry lay abed watching her pin on her new hat and slip into her plush cape with the brown-bear fur collar.

"The girls down at the store surely think I married myself a real sport when I wear this cape you bought me." She stopped at the hall door before leaving. "I'm glad you quit that old night job for a while. Now maybe we can go out some again."

Tracy assured her they would as he rolled back over on the

161

creaking brass bedstead. By the time the door closed he was again thinking of leaving town. The weather had started to break and February was coming in warm for that time of year. He'd no qualms over deserting Mollie Merrill, or Dave for that matter. He knew they'd cramp his style in time. He was stretching his luck hanging around town, and with nearly $500 in his kick, he'd plenty of cash to travel. He recalled what Elzy Lay had said about that WS Ranch in New Mexico. A perfect hide-out with just enough riding and roping to keep a fellow's hand in the game. In spite of everything, he still hankered after the old range life.

Tracy's resolve to pull out grew stronger when Mollie returned that night to report her ex-husband had been seen hanging around the front of her store.

"I don't know what he's up to . . . but Goldie Garrett said she saw him gassing with a policeman over on Sutter when she went to lunch."

"Probably asking directions to the nearest knock shop." Tracy grinned at her over his meal. But that decided him to talk to Dave in the morning.

He and Mollie made an evening of it after supper, taking in a stereopticon lecture show at McGonigal's Hall that featured the Spanish-American War and the Philippine Campaign, then spent another hour over a bottle at their favorite wine room.

Catching the streetcar home about midnight, Tracy saw it carried the same conductor he and Dave had braced the week before, taking $50 in the process. When he and Mollie had seated themselves, Harry kept his hand near the .38 Colt Lightning in its shoulder holster, but the gander-eyed railway official turned away after a puzzled half glance at the neat, mustached young man in the blue serge suit and curl-brimmed derby. To Harry it just demonstrated what a difference a bandanna and a six-shooter made—an impression that blotted out just about everything else.

The following morning, February 9, 1899, Tracy got around soon after Mollie had gone to work and took the streetcar to the Merrill house. He hadn't been able to get his mind off Deffenbaugh. That fellow might try to make trouble as he was bound to discover that Harry hadn't married Mollie—nor was there any divorce. Walking up to Dave's front door, he found himself wondering if the jilted drummer might have spilled the beans to Mrs. Merrill.

He hadn't long to find out, for the door opened and Harry was staring into the face of a stocky stranger who wore a baggy green suit, a boiled derby, and a professionally grim expression. He had all the appearance of a city gumshoe.

"Sorry, guess I've the wrong address." Harry backed off the step and turned for the street.

"Lookin' for who? Maybe I can help." The man with the bulldog face came out onto the porch, closing the door behind him.

"A friend, but I see I'm a couple of blocks off." Tracy gave the fellow a wave and headed down the street with businesslike purpose. Damned if the police hadn't grabbed Dave. The bulls were probably knee-deep inside that house. That did it! It was the railroad depot for him, and as soon as he could get there. It was *adiós* to Dave. What could he do for him now? It was also good bye to Mollie and her featherbed. But that was the way it went.

Glancing over his shoulder as he crossed the next street, Tracy's eyes narrowed at the sight of the same gumshoe sauntering behind him. The fellow was now joined by a big harness bull. It seemed they were merely satisfied to keep him in sight, but Harry was determined to shake them. He could smell a pinch in the making.

Crossing the street and hurrying purposefully up the first alley he spotted, he came out a block from the depot. But instead of heading toward the station, Tracy walked the other way and entered a neighborhood billiard hall.

After a quick glance out the door, which told him the pair had rounded the block and were strolling down toward the building, Harry went into the washroom at the rear of the smoky hall and shut the door behind himself. There was a window halfway up the rear wall, and it was only the matter of a moment to open it and clamber out onto the alley.

Landing on his feet in the littered passageway, Tracy walked back toward the depot, pulling the .38 from his shoulder holster and sticking it into his right-hand coat pocket. He mingled with the pedestrians heading toward the depot. He'd nearly reached the main entrance when he recognized the same patrolman who'd been with the plain-clothes man. This officer had stationed himself by the depot doorway and was scanning the faces of the hurrying crowds. When he saw Tracy coming toward the building, he lifted his basswood nightstick and waved it in the air over his round-topped helmet.

Halting, Harry spun back in time to see the detective trotting toward him. Leaping out into the busy street between a mail hack and a pair of freight drays, he dashed across the Union Pacific tracks and was able to clamber up into the cab of an engine just pulling out. There came the *clang* of a steel-jacketed pistol slug against the metal cab, and the echoing bark of the pursuing detective's weapon.

With a threatening wave of the .38 Colt Lightning at the startled engineer and fireman, Tracy ordered them to heave on the coal and fired two shots at the Portland lawman. By now the train had picked up speed and was rocking and creaking its way out through the rail yards.

But as they reached the junction at Sixth, the engine began to slow down, and the engineer had to tell his unwanted passenger that it was out of his hands, for someone in the coaches behind had yanked the emergency cord.

Seeing the cards were stacked against him, Harry shrugged and leaped down from the coasting engine. He had to get uptown and lose himself in the crowds. Jogging across several back yards, he had to grin wryly at his fix—what was it that old king had yelled? His kingdom for a saddle horse? About then Harry would have given almost anything he'd ever owned for a good mount and time enough to get out of this unlucky town.

As he ran, he could hear shouts over on the next street, and, as he whirled around to head back in the opposite direction, a fat-gutted old man in yellow suspenders and a red undershirt burst out the back of one of the houses and fired a shotgun point-blank at him. Fortunately the paunchy dry-gulcher had used birdshot, which flew high, knocking Harry's roll-brim derby into the bushes and putting several stinging pellets into his right shoulder. For a split second Tracy halted, pistol in hand, debating putting a .38 slug into the old devil, then dashed onward. It wouldn't amount to a hill of beans if he'd up and shot the interfering fool or not. But that shot and his hesitation had given the police time enough—for when Tracy ran out into the street, he crashed headlong into the gumshoe.

Fifteen minutes later, handcuffed and seated in the back of a patrol wagon, Harry was heading downtown to the court-house. In another hour he'd been booked on suspicion of armed robbery and was occupying a cell—with Dave Merrill!

"So you had to cave in like a white-livered four-flusher and sign a confession for them," Tracy gritted as he lay back on his straw mattress, staring across at a silent Merrill, who sat on his own bunk, head in hands. "Spilled everything like some egg-sucking kid caught stealing chickens. That dough-faced cop, Weiner, showed me your yellow-bellied drivel. Wanted me to sign a sheet of my own. Said it would go better for me . . . the same as you . . . Jesse James, Junior, I don't think."

"Aw hell, Harry. You don't know what they put me through. Punchin' and kickin' me where it don't show. Said they'd got so much guff from the ward heelers they'd be glad to beat the stuffin' out of me, unless I came across."

Tracy sat up on his bunk. "I guess I can't blame you too much. You just haven't got what it takes." His brow furrowed and he leaned close to the long-faced Merrill. "Well, sit tight. I've been in worse spots than this sardine can. Confess and blow all you want to, but I'm standing pat. They can't convict me, because I won't admit a single thing, even if they pound on me with everything they've got."

But Harry was wrong, for although the police left him strictly alone, both he and Dave were hauled into the Portland District Court and convicted within the week. Dave's confession had seen to that.

Mollie had been called as a witness, and, although her testimony failed to clear Tracy and her brother, it also did not betray them. After a final word with the pair in court, surrounded by their police guards, Mollie left with the grim-faced Mrs. Merrill. That was the last Harry was to see of breezy red-headed Mollie Merrill Deffenbaugh, for she left Portland shortly after the two-day trial concluded. And he was to learn later she'd caught a southbound passenger train with no one else than Deffenbaugh himself.

The following week, while Tracy and Merrill were still held awaiting sentencing, something happened that turned Tracy's troubled world completely upside-down. A note was smuggled into his cell from Janet Warrington:

Hunt Down Harry Tracy

Dear Harry,

At last I've found you. I didn't know where you'd gone until I read a piece in the Chicago paper about your troubles here in Portland. Then I found out my mother had been stopping your letters. And so I never knew what had happened to you in all this time. I left the day after I read the story. And I don't care what they say you've done, and I'll do anything I can to help you get free.

I'll write again soon. The guard that brought this can be trusted I think—for I'm paying him enough.

Love,
Janet

"Here's the key to the cell doors," Tracy told Merrill, and went on to inform him something of his past in Chicago.

"What happens when she finds out about you and Mollie?"

"Don't worry. She came out fast enough when she found where I was, didn't she?" He patted the note with a finger. "She's just what the doctor ordered."

Then began an exchange of notes over the next week between Tracy and Janet, who, it appeared, was staying at a hotel over on Walnut. He read some of the missives to Dave, but left out the more intimate details. All the messages were delivered by the guard who was well paid by the girl.

"You certainly got a way with the ladies," Dave commented after listening to one of the notes. "Wish I had some filly like that waitin' to have my brand slapped on her hide."

"She's already got mine," Tracy absently retorted as he penciled another reply to Janet, one that was to set up the planned break out.

The following night when he was taken to the adjoining washroom, Harry managed to find the pistol that Janet had smuggled in behind a washstand. While the guard who brought in the notes looked the other way, Tracy was able to stuff the .38 Smith & Wesson into his shirt.

With lights out, he fetched the weapon from under his mattress and displayed it for the uneasy Merrill.

"Now, what'll you do with that . . . get us shot full of holes?" Dave wanted to know. "Those guards are armed to the teeth . . . that Ferrell, in particular. Wouldn't it be better to just take our medicine and get it over with?"

"Don't bother your head about Ferrell. He's the one that sneaked in the notes and gun. He'll be meek as a lamb when I throw down on him."

The following morning, March 21, 1899, it was a plain case of the double-cross, for, when Harry and Dave were ready to go into court, Ferrell rattled his keys on the bars and waved them out.

As Tracy stepped from the cell followed by the apprehensive Merrill, Harry jammed the Smith & Wesson into the guard's side, and ordered him to open the bullpen door, but the big, beefy Irishman balked, shaking his head. "I'll blow a window through your brisket," Tracy snarled, suddenly enraged by the turn of events.

"Go on and shoot," Ferrell growled back. "Y'ain't gittin' outta here except in the paddy wagon."

While Tracy considered the next move, the deputy sheriff, Tom Jordan, came through the far end of the corridor, saw what was happening, and pulled his own pistol.

Not wanting to bring on a shoot-out, Jordan and Ferrell were on him, slamming him onto the cold stone flooring, then it was just a matter of moments till Tracy was cuffed and shoved along down the stairs to the adjacent courtroom by the rumpled, cursing officers. Another guard brought up the rear with the white-faced Dave.

"You won't get away with this, you yellow sneak," Harry muttered to Ferrell as the big guard stood grinning at his side as they faced the puzzled judge.

"Won't I? Well, if you don't want your twist gettin' herself tossed into a cell, you better just clam up and take your medicine," Ferrell retorted out of the side of his beefy face.

Realizing that the guard, guilty though he might be of aiding and abetting an escape attempt, would have the ear of the authorities, Harry tightened his jaw. With Janet on the outside—next time would be different. As he stood in the packed courtroom, he vowed silently to himself and to the pale-faced beauty in the audience, who was Janet Warrington, that he'd get free no matter what. They'd never kept him under lock and key for very long, and they wouldn't now.

Then the judge, a mutton-chopped, red-faced old gentleman, had his own say. "I'd intended sentencing you to fifteen years, but, after what has just transpired, I'll add another five. The sentence of this court is that you be confined to Salem Penitentiary for the next twenty years. And at hard labor!"

Dave Merrill received thirteen years at hard labor.

Three days later the ponderous, iron gates of the Salem Pen creaked shut behind Harry Tracy and Dave Merrill. It looked like the end of the road.

Chapter Fifteen

Once the huge, forbidding doors of the Oregon Penitentiary clanged shut behind the two new prisoners, Dave Merrill, No. 4088 and Harry Tracy, No. 4089, on March 22, 1899, Tracy began to plot an escape.

He told himself, as he lay on his bunk in the cell with Merrill, that he had to scheme his way out. He fell asleep night after night swearing to himself it wasn't going to be a case of the Sugar House all over again. They weren't going to keep him locked up that long.

After the first week they were assigned jobs in the prison foundry where the work was hot, noisy, and monotonous. Dave was placed on a team that handled the pouring of the molten metal into the forms. Harry, having admitted to working around the lumber camps, was assigned the job of carpenter, building forms and boxing up the finished products—cast-iron stoves.

After a month, they were eligible to receive visitors every other Sunday, meeting guests in a room off the prison mess hall under the watchful gaze of guards. Dave's mother came when she could, but pointedly had nothing to do with Tracy—the man she'd publicly declared to be the rascal who'd led her industrious son astray. Nevertheless, both Tracy and Merrill shared her food boxes and newspapers.

One Sunday, after Dave returned to their cell from a visit

with his mother, one he never looked forward to with much enthusiasm, he brought the usual box of edibles, some old magazines—and a piece of disturbing news.

"Guess who's the new guard on our cell-block?"

"Who, as if I care one tinker's damn?"

"Just thought you might be interested. It's your pal, Ferrell."

Through some sardonic quirk of fate, the man who'd been instrumental in thwarting Tracy's bid for freedom at the county jail had been transferred to the state prison's guard detail.

Although Tracy saw Ferrell from time to time, there was no indication the security officer recognized the man he'd bamboozled. In fact, it seemed Ferrell went out of his way to avoid Harry in foundry and mess hall, at least at first.

Ferrell was the least of his worries as Tracy wasn't sure Janet Warrington would ever show up at the prison. Immediately after the trial he'd received a short note. Reading between the lines, he saw she'd been thinking of the smuggled gun and was afraid Ferrell might still involve her in some kind of trouble. *I can't help you Harry in any sort of situation,* she'd written. There was little else except that she was returning to her home in Chicago for a while, but planned coming back to Salem in the future. After that there was nothing but silence. No letter from Chicago or anywhere else.

Then late in June, 1899, Janet returned. Tracy should have been overjoyed to see her again, except that the guard on duty was Ferrell. There was no way of knowing at the time how it had happened, but Tracy was later told by a guard named Girard, who had the original visitor's quarters duty, that Ferrell had suggested switching jobs. Thinking it over, Harry surmised Ferrell must have been aware of the visit from scanning office file sheets and cut himself in for some reason.

That reason would become apparent in time.

Noticing Ferrell in the room with several other lounging guards, Janet sat down hesitantly across from Harry at one of the rough tables. "What's he doing here?"

"That's not much of a greeting," he told the pale-faced girl. "Forget that jay and tell me where you've been. I never thought I'd see you again. No letter . . . no nothing."

"Harry." Janet held out her hands, but Ferrell snapped an order for them to keep apart. She flushed and dropped her hands in her lap. "I wanted to come before this . . . but. . . ." She hesitated. "I had to go home. Mother's been ailing . . . and. . . ." She smiled slightly. "And you might as well know I've had a touch of consumption. That's why mother was able to stop your letters. I was in a sanatorium outside Chicago."

Tracy stared at Janet. She was the same beautiful girl he'd known—yet there was something different about her. Her face was as beautiful as ever, but strangely thinner and there were faint shadows under her eyes.

"Gee, kid, you still look good to me. I can't wait to get my hands on you again. . . ." Seeing her odd expression, he turned to find Ferrell hovering at their elbow.

When Tracy had stared Ferrell down and the guard reluctantly backed away, Janet went on. "I'm better now. Mother's doctor thinks I was really just run-down." Her face lit up with a flash of the old devil-may-care Janet he remembered so well. "Really, I'm as full of the Old Nick as ever. You'll find out."

"Time's up!" Ferrell, who'd been exchanging ironic glances with his fellow guards, pulled out a whistle and blew it lustily.

After a brief smile, Janet left with the other visitors. It was plain to Harry she meant to keep away from Ferrell. As he walked back to the cell-block along with the other prisoners, he cursed the beefy guard for interfering. If Janet failed to return, it might be one hell of a long time before he could get any plan into the works. But Janet had said she'd see him again—that much he took back to the cell.

Late that night as they lay on their bunks after lights out, Dave grumbled: "Some folks have all the luck. Only one who comes around to see me is Maw . . . and she ain't been here for near on three weeks. While you just up and pick yourself the fanciest peach in the orchard. But what're you goin' to do about it? Y'said once she was the key to outside, but nothin' come outta that smuggled gun. All we got was just extra time for it." He rolled toward the wall. "Thinkin' it over, I ain't sure she's such good luck. Good-lookin', I guess, but good luck?"

There followed a long, wearisome wait. It wasn't that Janet had stopped coming to the prison, for the week after her last visit she'd moved to Salem, rented a room some miles from the prison, and found herself a job, both tending to trade and working after-hours as a seamstress in a women's dress shop. But the wages were relatively low, so she wasn't going to be able to build much of a bank roll in the near future, although she thought she possibly could eventually amass about half of the $600 Harry needed to make his scheme work.

At first she'd been hesitant to become involved in another escape scheme, but Harry managed to convince her—when Ferrell was not attending the Sunday visits—that his unfortunate circumstances had come about by a mistaken but sincere desire to raise enough money to purchase a homestead for the both of them. It was something he'd told himself so often—that he began to believe it.

So the months dragged by with maddening slowness into the year of 1901. From time to time the Seattle papers printed some word of the fate of his old saddle partners. The first to take a fall was his friend, Elzy Lay. Lay had obviously followed his own advice and drifted to New Mexico where he'd been involved in a train robbery, then been captured and sentenced in October of 1899 to an indefinite term in the New Mexican pen. The next to go was Flat Nose George Currie, shot by a sheriff's posse on Utah's Green River in April of 1900. But some of Cassidy's bunch evened up the score a month later by dry-gulching, in turn, Utah Sheriff Tyler, responsible for Currie's end.

Cassidy's gang continued to make news in the late summer of 1900, stopping a Union Pacific flyer at Tipton, Wyoming and relieving it of $50,000, and then raiding a Winnemucca, Nevada bank, getting over $30,000 in the haul.

Having little contact with the world beyond the walls, Harry and Dave doggedly worked on in the foundry's inferno when they might have requested transfers to other duties, but Tracy felt it to be the best place to put his plan into action at the right time.

The foundry was situated at the far end of the prison grounds, nearly backing upon the west wall. Beyond that lay several hundred yards of brushy ground, bounded by Mill Creek, a small-size stream. The banks of that watercourse were lined with willows and offered a fair amount of cover once a fugitive made it across the distance between creek and prison. Although one of the guard towers commanded that area, it was the only place for the break. Tracy realized that tower would have to be knocked out before they could get to the creek in one piece, but he never mentioned it to Merrill.

He did discuss some of the problems with Dave but held back on the exact time and method of obtaining firearms, for he'd begun to mistrust his partner, something he'd never done with Lant. Lant might have been lacking some sand, but he was the sort to stick by a man all the way.

Matters could have come to a head in the fall of 1901. Janet had succumbed to Tracy's arguments and managed to have another pistol smuggled into the prison through a trusty who went outside the walls for supplies. The weapon, a Colt Bisley .44, came in past the guards in a barrel of flour. Tracy was able to get his hands on it when he was ordered to the prison kitchen to repair some shelving. Concealing the weapon in the foundry under a pile of lumber, he was baffled to discover it missing the following day.

"Your bunky seems kinda friendly with that there Ferrell," Ingram, a wizened lifer from the foundry side-mouthed as they lock-stepped to supper.

"Friendly?"

"Saw him talkin' to that bugger when you was gone for more nails yesterday."

"Thanks," was all Tracy had replied, for he already had a good idea of that conversation. Dave was getting a bit loco. He wasn't the kind to do easy time. And Harry wouldn't have taken any bets that Dave hadn't tipped off the flabby-faced Ferrell—currying favor if nothing else.

But the gun was gone and, perhaps, just as well. One lonely six-shooter wasn't going to have much impact on the guards in that watchtower with their complement of high-powered Krag Jorgensen rifles. He needed rifles himself and ample ammunition.

Although upset at the discovery of the pistol, Janet remained willing to help in any way she could. She repeatedly told Harry that fact each time on visiting days. But the money just wasn't all there yet. There was just one place to get that vitally necessary other half of the $600.

Dave's mother. Harry went to work on Merrill, saying

nothing about the vanished six-gun, for it was possible Dave could have spilled the beans just to avoid another confrontation with the brass buttons. Another reason to get the rest of the money from the Merrill household was the fact that it would tie up Dave completely. He wouldn't be able to sing sad songs to his mother—or anyone else. Tracy wasn't taking any more chances.

Night following night, after the lights were out, they debated the escape, arguments varying little, Harry pressing Dave with the inescapable facts of a long, grinding life in prison as balanced against a few minutes of bold action, backed up with sufficient firepower.

Merrill, having lost his hardcase outlook, began arguing for doing time and working toward an earlier release through good behavior. But Tracy scoffed at such talk and played on Merrill's fear of growing prematurely old and ill from the foundry's grinding labor. "You want to grow a hump toting pig iron or go stir crazy pulling leaves off your calendar?"

It took weeks but at last, one night in late January of 1902, Tracy's one-man debate eventually paid off and he had worn down Merrill to the point where he agreed to apply to his mother for funds. Dave was to assure his mother the money would strictly go toward bribing guards—greasing officials' palms and opening certain doors.

"Maybe there won't be any fireworks," Harry mused from his bunk, now satisfied with the possibility of an early break. "Ferrell must have found that pistol in the lumber pile after all." He glanced over at the motionless form of Dave, but his partner remained silent. "Think he did?"

"Don't know. Damn it, how'd I know?"

"No matter. If Ferrell found that weapon and still didn't blow, why then he just might be the one to give us a hand. If we paid him a pretty hefty figure and promised to double the amount after we're out . . . he might go for it."

"But he's the one that fouled up your other play. Could you trust him again?"

"Think we could . . . if the money's right. Didn't pay enough last time. That was Janet's fault. Now that I know Ferrell for a money-hungry crook, I can play him on the line like a grub-grabbing bass. We'll give him just enough, like I said, and hold out the rest till we're out."

"You'll still give him what you promise?" Merrill raised up from his somnolent position, galvanized in spite of himself.

"I'll play fair with the bastard, if he plays fair with me."

The following Sunday Dave's mother came to the visiting hour. Harry and Janet watched Merrill out of the corner of their eyes as they held their own meeting in the guard-haunted room, together with several score of couples.

"She's shaking her head," Janet reported as Harry kept on the look-out for Ferrell, who was patrolling the crowded room with the other guards.

"She won't shake long . . . Dave'll get to her. And when she contacts you, as I've said, you'll be told where to send the cash."

Harry was right. When the visiting hour was over and the prisoners were back in their cells, Dave reported that his mother would see the money was sent to Janet. "She kicked up a real fuss until I told her your lady friend was putting up the rest of the cash and that she'd see there'd be no rough stuff . . . just money spent in the right places."

"Knew you'd cut the mustard." Harry clapped Dave on his bony shoulder, and then threw himself onto his bunk and took up the Sunday comics. "Now we'll get busy on the rest of our scheme."

"Like I said, Ma don't cotton to you at all, but she thinks

177

Miss Warrington is real lady-like and it's a damn' good thing she does or we'd whistle for that money. She's still sore at you plenty for me doin' this damned stretch and all this under the table shenanigans to git back out and she wants to know where I'll land when we go over the wall."

Tracy glanced up from his perusal of the antics of the Katzenjammer Kids. "Why I guess we'll head out toward Hole-in-the-Wall. Seems healthier back there than down in New Mexico, though it's not too safe for sheriffs. Cassidy's riding high, wide, and handsome these days, but he might think about taking on some replacements at that."

Dave was silent for a moment, then he went on. "That wasn't what I had in mind. Thought, maybe, we could get up across the line to Canada. Maybe as far as the Yukon Territory. I ain't cut out for your Wild Bunch sort. I'd rather lose myself in the great outdoors till they forget all about Mister Dave Merrill."

Harry turned to the doings of Happy Hooligan. "I'd say they'll have a little trouble getting us out of their minds when we leave this hell-hole."

"But won't that six hundred do the trick, greasin' palms . . . Ferrell's in particular?" Dave sat up, nervously rubbing his hands on his knees.

"Could be," Tracy answered noncommittally. Tossing down the paper, he fished under his bunk, extracted a cigar box, pulled out paper and pencil and began to write a note. "This has got to go out tomorrow noon with Bub Wright. He's getting released at twelve."

Here was the pay-off of those quiet conversations he'd had over the months with Bub Wright. A short-timer, in for his artistry with a pen and happy to discuss the finer points of forgery, Wright thought a few weapons could be spirited into the prison foundry. He was also happy to deal with Harry's lady love, eyed by most cons on visiting days. She'd pay as much as need be, although Harry hoped the combined $300 of Mrs. Merrill's along with Janet's $300 would be more than enough.

Squinting in the dull yellow glare of the single electric bulb in the cell's ceiling, Tracy wrote: *It will be just a short time now before we're together again, but you must help right now. The bearer of this is a friend of mine. Give him the $300 and he'll get things fixed. Don't mention this to anyone, or I'll have to serve out a much longer sentence. Contact Mrs. Merrill and tell her to have $300 ready, then Dave will be free soon.*

The following day, after the note was passed hand by hand to Wright at breakfast, before that trusty was released, Tracy approached Ferrell. The burly Irishman had recently been appointed head guard at the foundry, another odd turn of events, but one Tracy was ready to use to his advantage.

"Got a minute, Ferrell?" Harry had paused on his way to the foundry tool shed.

"A few." Ferrell grimaced slightly, his heavy bulldog jowls wrinkling with the effort to smile. He leaned on his Winchester and spat at Tracy's foot, the amber stream barely missing the scuffed boot. "Got a few, but you got plenty more'n me."

"Could be." Tracy moved his foot back. "Let's not talk time though . . . how'd dollars sound?"

"Keep a-talkin', I'm listenin'." Ferrell glanced over his shoulder.

"I know you found something some while back, and I'm not faulting you, for you kept it to yourself . . . something you didn't do when we were sentenced damn near three years ago. But then you didn't get much money for your efforts back then, eh?"

"I remember something like that. But whatever you say I found, was it you who lost it?"

"You know damned well I did." Harry had to hold himself in. "I guess you didn't see much profit in that, either, but now. . . ."

"I'm still listenin', but I'm not hearin' exactly what I'd like to hear, get me?"

"You want to hear something? How does three hundred dollars sound?"

For the first time Ferrell grinned widely, gold tooth gleaming in the blaze of the foundry fires. "Sounds pretty interestin'. What would I have to do to see that sort of figger?"

Tracy stopped and, bending over his portable tool box, inspected several hammers until a group of convicts, including Dave Merrill, staggered past bearing a crate to the landing dock. "I'll see you get the first hundred when our little party starts. We'll let you know a day in advance about that and where to pick up the other two hundred afterwards. All you have to do is look the other way and keep the guards busy. Maybe kick up a rumpus somewhere away from the back wall. Could be you might see a riot starting, or anything to keep your friends with the guns busy elsewhere."

"You're talking my language now." The beefy guard nodded. "I'm certain we can do a nice piece of business." He grinned again, his wide mouth splitting from ear to ear. "Y'know, I was thinkin' straight when I came over to this place. And I had you figgered right. You're the kind that gets his way, sooner or later. And I'll make a nice piece of change for bein' helpful. Right?"

For the next fourteen days Tracy and Merrill went about their daily chores as if passing time had no more meaning to them than to the rest of their 700 sullenly hopeless fellows.

Only two others behind the walls watched the calendar with any sense of immediacy—Ferrell and that little scrawny lifer, Frank Ingram.

The guard stayed away from Harry and Dave, never even acknowledging their existence by a nod or a word. But Ingram, a fidgety, little ground squirrel of a man had just too much of the Paul Pry in his make-up not to sidle up to Tracy and mutter a question. "What you got goin' with the guards?"

"What the devil are you talking about?" Harry looked to see if anyone had heard or even read Ingram's lips in the chattering roar of the machinery.

"I see a lot." Ingram's smirk revealed a snaggling series of teeth, mostly missing. "You braced that big son-of-a-gun, Ferrell, two weeks back, and, before you broke apart, he was grinnin' like an egg-suckin' dog, and you didn't look half so sour as usual. So . . . I figger you've got some sort of graft goin'."

"Well, when the time comes, you can make up your mind if you want to be cut in on our little graft. Now button up your flannel mouth or you might get it shut permanently." Tracy strode off with his tool box, leaving the little convict scratching his receding chin.

On Sunday, June 1, 1902, Dave Merrill's mother came to the prison during visiting day. Although Harry had expected Janet also to come with information regarding the progress of their secretive negotiations for arms and ammunition, she failed to appear and he had to rely on Merrill for news.

"Maw says she gave the money to Bub Wright when your gal friend sent him to see her. The money's gone and she just hopes it gets to us. Told her I was sure it would, and she left, hopin' I'd be out of here mighty soon. Told her we'd likely head for the Canadian line, and then let her know what we're up to." He tossed a bundle of week-old papers onto a bunk.

"She said somethin' else that Bub Wright told her. Your Miss Warrington's been under the weather lately."

"Under the weather?"

"Yeah, Bub thinks she'd workin' herself into a good case of consumption."

"So that's why she's not been up." Harry was relieved and apprehensive at the same time. "Well, she has been putting in a lot of hours at some damned sweatshop. When I'm out, I'll get her out of here."

"How you gonna do that? Take her along?"

"We'll manage." But he wondered how. That was one aspect of the escape he'd not solved.

"Bub Wright told Maw something else. Told her to tell us to watch for a box marked with a big blue circle that's due to be shipped into the foundry tomorrow morning. She thought the money would be in it."

Tracy sprang up and walked the narrow length of the cell. He was still pacing like a trapped panther when the lights out bell rang. At last he threw himself full length upon his bunk, chuckling. "A box with a blue circle! That's where they'll hide our persuaders and ammunition along with the money." He then proceeded to fill in his partner with further details of the escape plan as it was now too late for Dave to back out. His mother's money had effectively involved him. "You keep your eyes open. That box should arrive at the foundry before we eat breakfast . . . along with three hundred to grease Ferrell's palm. So when I say frog, you jump high and wide."

"But how do we get out of the foundry?"

"A ladder, you bonehead. We'll use the ladders in the foundry shed, and things will go smooth as new butter, providing. . . ."

"Providing what?" Now Dave was up and pacing the cell.

"Providing that sawed-off Ingram keeps his nose out of

things, and providing you keep your pecker up . . . and, most of all, providing Ferrell keeps his end of the bargain. That's a lot of providings, but we'll still win ace, jack, and game."

Chapter Sixteen

Aware of the upcoming break that depended on the arrival of the packing case, neither slept much during the early hours of the night. And when Tracy and Merrill at last fell into an uneasy slumber, Dave kept Harry awake with his mutterings.

Tracy resolutely willed himself to slumber, but it was very late before he slept, as he was unable to stop thinking of Janet. If she were sick, what could he do? He couldn't reach her after the escape—there'd be too many bulls watching her place. Perhaps he could slip back in a month or so, but first he had to get out himself. And mulling over such thoughts, despite Merrill's groans, he let the darkness sweep him away.

At last the interminably long night was finished and both were dressed and ready for breakfast at the 6:00 a.m. whistle. When the cell doors opened, they lined up with the other convicts in their block and were marched to their morning meal in the mess hall by one of the better-liked guards, Fred Girard.

"Where's your pal?" Dave asked, staring around the room through half-lidded eyes. "He should be here, shouldn't he?"

"Pass the coffee. He won't fall down on this one. He likes money too much."

But when the prisoners departed for the foundry it was the good-natured Girard who led them to another day's labor. There they found Ferrell and two other guards already on duty. According to prison regulation, none of the guards was armed, merely carrying heavy wooden clubs to keep the men in line.

"Now we'll see how those damned Irish shillelaghs stand up against honest to God weapons," Harry muttered to Dave while they watched the others shuffle to their appointed tasks.

Going over to the small packing case marked *Foundry*, which sat on the floor near the large pattern cases, Harry saw Ferrell watching. Casually prying open the case with a crowbar, he caught a glimpse of the blue barrels of two .30-30 Winchesters, a pair of Colt six-shooters, and a soiled white envelope in the straw packing. Closing the case door, he hurriedly tore open the envelope to find a single $100 bill and a short note:

Tracy,

The weapons cost more than we thought. Good luck!

"Let's see that!" It was Girard, the friendly guard, but he was smiling no longer. "You cons can't pass notes around like a bunch of schoolgirls." Tapping the long, locust wood club in his hand, he advanced on Tracy.

"Hold on Fred." Ferrell thrust himself between Harry and Girard. "Just remembered you got a call from the warden's office. Better check on it. I'll handle this." When Girard began making his way out through the echoing building, Ferrell shouldered Harry into the shelter of a pillar and stuck out his hand. "All right, let's take a look here."

Harry handed over the money. "We're a bit short, but you'll get the whole two hundred from a friend as soon as we're over the wall and out of sight."

"OK, you and your pal start the ball while I make us a little hullabaloo." Slapping Tracy on the shoulder, Ferrell began to follow Girard, now nearing the foundry door.

Harry sprang back to the packing case and tore it open. As he did so, Dave Merrill came running across the floor.

"Here!" Tracy thrust a Colt pistol at Dave, and then tossed over a Winchester.

"Look out!" Dave shouted, dropping to his knees, clutching the .30-30 to his chest.

A pistol bullet slammed into the wall, spewing splinters about Tracy's head. The six-gun barked again and Tracy dived down beside Merrill, jacking another shell into his Winchester.

"Where'd Ferrell get a gun?" Dave gasped, pressing flat against the greasy flooring. "Guess your fix didn't stay fixed."

"It will now." Tracy sighted down on Ferrell as the hulking guard tried a dash from one pillar to another. The crash of the Winchester was echoed by Dave's weapon. Ferrell threw out his arms and folded up with a bullet in the head, dropping the pistol.

In less than ten seconds the entire foundry was a seething madhouse. As he fished out the extra ammunition boxes and stuffed them into his shirt, Tracy saw Girard whirl around and start back.

"That's right, Fred! Come over here and we'll take you for a walk!" Tracy waved his rifle at the guard. But Girard, having seen Ferrell's body, dashed for the door.

"Come back!" Harry sighted down on the fleeing guard, but, as he squeezed off a shot, the Winchester's barrel was knocked up, the weapon discharging into the foundry ceiling.

"Damn it, Ingram, what in hell are you doing?" Tracy yanked the Winchester away from the little convict's grasp. "I ought to blow a window through you, too!"

"Harry!" Dave tugged at Tracy's arm. "What's wrong? And what'll we do now?"

"We leave . . . with Mister Ingram, here, for good measure. Nobody'll fire on us with a pal of the screws along." He grinned mirthlessly at the pale, shaken Ingram. "Right, Frank? You wanted in on our little graft, and now here's your chance."

As Ingram backed off, vigorously shaking his head, Tracy gritted: "I thought so. Come on, Dave, head for the tool shed out back. We'll get a ladder and it's off and away for us." He stared around at the now silent foundry. "Anyone want along on this party? No? Then get out of the way!"

Running through the foundry, Winchesters at the ready, they reached the back door with no opposition, the entire group of prisoners milling silently about, now that the guards were out of action—one dead and one on his way to alarm the rest of the prison.

"Bunch of sheep!" Tracy shouted at Dave as they burst into the tool shed and began to tug out the sixteen-foot ladder. "No more guts than a flock of woolies."

But several sudden rifle reports, snapping from the east wall tower, gave deadly proof of a growing opposition to the escape. "Watch out!" Tracy shoved Dave and the ladder down and, lifting his Winchester, sent shot after shot at the watchtower as fast as he could jack the .30-30 shells into the chamber. Glass crashed in the tower windows as his bullets thudded into the masonry and ricocheted like insane wasps. "Got those bindle stiffs all right." He pointed at the tower where a pair of blue coats—Tiffany and Ross—finding the fusillade too hot were already dropping off the outside wall.

"Give it to the damned place, Dave, there may be another screw in there." Then as the wild-eyed Merrill, crouching behind a stack of crates fired off a series of shots, knocking out a guard named Jones on the north wall, Tracy, lunging forward with the ladder, slammed it against the rear wall, climbed it, and waved up Dave.

Once they were on top of the four-foot-wide barrier, Harry lowered the ladder on the other side and, with a final volley in the foundry's direction, he and Merrill scrambled down. But the moment they'd leaped to the ground, they came under heavy fire from another guard and the deputy warden, both shooting from the far guard tower.

Dashing around a projection of the wall, the leaden fingers of the law clawing at them, smashing against the granite barrier and slamming into the turf, Tracy and Merrill stumbled over Tiffany and Ross, the pair of guards they'd driven from the east watchtower. Both officers had flattened themselves against the wall, waiting out the small but deadly war—Tiffany with a shoulder wound and Ross in a white-faced panic.

"Get 'em up and toss over those pistols." Tracy took their two Colts, thrusting them into his belt, and then poked the muzzle of the .30-30 at them. "Now we'll take a run across the rifle range."

The four jogged over the rolling ground toward a small bridge spanning Mill Creek, Tracy and Merrill halting from time to time to snap back shots at the clustering figures atop the south wall. Despite the whine and crackle of the returned fire from the prison, Tracy, Merrill, and their two captives reached the bridge.

As Harry tossed Merrill a box of Winchester shells, Tiffany made a successful grab for Tracy's six-shooter, got it, and was cocking the Colt when Harry leaped backwards. The double crash of six-shooter and Winchester slammed out— then the guard crumpled with a .30-30 slug in the ribs. Tumbling from the bridge, he carried Ross with him into the water.

Not stopping to check on either guard, Tracy and Merrill pounded over the echoing planks and along the creekbank for sixty yards till they reached some bushes. Pausing for a breather, they held a hurried consultation, then jogged on half a mile and struck a heavier growth, affording better cover.

Panting in the dense thicket, they heard the mournful *clang* of the prison bell tolling out its brazen call for help.

"Superintendent Lee's probably burning up the wires yelling for the sheriff and even the militia." Tracy laughed shortly. "I'd say we finally tossed a little action into that old devil's life."

"Didn't think we'd have to start the Battle of Cuba again." Merrill rubbed his heaving sides and groaned with the effort of the run.

Regaining their wind, they ran on down the creekbank to a stand of timber and, although both fugitive's bellies were complaining, burrowed deeply into the underbrush to wait for the night.

When the sun at last went down in a golden cloud bank and the mellow mauve of twilight spread out over field and woods, Tracy and Merrill, Winchesters under their arms, strolled out of their hiding place and made directly for Salem's outskirts. Dave had protested any such a move, but Harry scoffed at him. "We'll look like a pair of quail hunters in the dusk, and, besides, I intend to get a square meal before that old sun comes up again. Three years is a hell of a long time to wait for a civilian meal."

Now with full dark, there was little need to keep to the alleys and byways, and they'd progressed well into the suburbs before they came across a J. W. Roberts standing at his front gate. Taking the cool air in his shirt sleeves, Roberts was filled with that benign good will usually following a hearty supper and was inclined to pass the time of evening with anyone, including two rough-looking men approaching with rifles.

Within two minutes that householder stood shivering in his blue, ribbed union suit and congress gaiters, while Harry struggled into the captured clothing, addressing his companion-in-arms with an ironic promise. "Don't look so dry, Dave, we'll get you a change pretty soon."

The victim of their clothes heist, clutching arms about himself, began to trot toward his front door, but halted dead in his tracks at the arresting sound of a cocking pistol. "A word of advice!" Harry called after him. "Don't get in touch with the police before morning. We just might be in the neighborhood again."

Cutting over to the next block, they spotted a pair of overalls and a coat hanging upon a back yard line. While Harry waited, Dave clambered the board fence and carried out his own raid. Once Merrill had donned the rustled garments, they continued on their way and were lucky to find a livery stable owned by a saloonkeeper, LeBranch, just three blocks away. Although already closed for the night, its lock was easily forced. After hesitating at the stable door, Harry set Dave on look-out while he slipped into the warm, hay-scented darkness. There he selected two mounts in the dim light entering the barn window from a nearby street lamp, as well as picking out riding gear.

Carefully closing the stable door, they mounted up and rode quietly down the deserted street toward the northeast.

As they turned a corner near the livery, they passed another citizen of Salem, also lounging on his front gate. Tracy waved casually to him, then put the whip to his mount, Dave racking along beside him. "Probably wonders what we're doing with some of LeBranch's nags," Merrill said to Tracy.

"I let him see my rifle, so let's hope he thinks we're part of some posse."

At the mention of posse, Merrill lashed his bay mare and passed Tracy. Not to be outdone, Harry whipped up his black stallion and together they loped down the dusty road leading out of Salem in the direction of the small village of Gervais, fifteen miles away.

By four in the morning, as the moon was setting, they saw the light of a small cabin a mile east of that hamlet. Pulling up to rest their heaving horses, they could plainly see a man in trousers and undershirt busily cooking breakfast.

"Damn, I've got to have something to eat," Dave grumbled. "It's been nigh twenty-four hours since our last meal, and drinks of water in creeks don't count for nothin'."

Harry agreeing, they knocked on the cabin door and asked for food, explaining they were loggers off on a hunting trip and would be happy to pay for their meal.

The cabin's owner, a woodchopper named August King, was more than willing to share his meal of griddlecakes, side meat, and coffee with these early morning visitors, refusing to take any payment. Although they discussed local events, Tracy supplying some of the subjects gleaned from second-hand prison papers, it was obvious the old woodsman was unaware of any prison escape.

They parted at daybreak, and rode toward a densely wooded area mentioned by King, after telling him they planned a look at the local timber in passing.

Fortified by the hearty meal, Tracy and Merrill spent the daylight hours in the green depths of the woods. Several times during the day they heard the *chunk-chunk* of axes, but, as the sounds never increased, they ignored them. One thing they couldn't ignore was the condition of their horses. Although Harry had tried, the stock in trade at the LeBranch livery was wanting when it came to mounts with sufficient bottom to keep up a grueling pace.

"We've run these spavined crow-baits into the ground, and now what do we do?" Dave wondered aloud fretfully as the day wore along.

A lover of horseflesh, Harry was unable to abandon mounts in the timber. "We'll stake them out where someone can find them. And then we go into that burg and rustle up some more."

At twilight Tracy and Merrill rode their used-up mounts near the village and left them saddled in a farmer's field. Then, carrying their rifles as inconspicuously as possible, the pair walked up the town's main street without arousing any particular interest from the few folks met.

Sauntering along Gervais' three blocks of houses and stores, they stood in the lee of a barn debating taking supper in a café or walking over the S. P. tracks to await the possible arrival of a freight. They were still discussing this when they heard the approach of a horse and buggy. A rig with two men creaked slowly past as Tracy and Merrill walked along in the shadows, listening to their conversation.

"Hear that?" Tracy muttered. "That pair's been out hunting us."

"Posse?" Dave came to a halt, but Harry grabbed his arm and yanked him around.

"Yes, posse. Let's not disappoint them."

Before Merrill could reply, Tracy jog trotted down the sandy path paralleling the road and stepped in front of the buggy. "Looking for someone?" He levered a shell into the Winchester, then waved it silently toward the street. The astounded posse men, a Dr. White and a merchant named Dupis, recognized the menacing pantomime. They also understood Merrill's pistol pointing at them and handed over their arms, a shotgun and a Remington .38 Russian pistol before climbing out.

"Congratulations, gents!" Tracy clambered into the buggy, followed by Merrill. "Oh, put your hands down, we're not holding it against you fellows, but you should have better sense than playing second-fiddle to some boneheaded lawmen."

Wheeling the rig around in the sandy roadway, Harry gave the silent posse men a wave and, slapping the reins over the horse's back, left Gervais and its posse men at a fast clip that took the fugitives along a road to the southwest.

When two miles south of the village, Harry turned the buggy into a wood lot and there they bunked down for the night, Merrill wrapped in his overcoat and Tracy using a blanket found in the buggy.

When daylight filtered through the trees, they discovered they were within a few miles of the woodcutter's cabin where they had eaten the day before and, throwing the harness onto the horse, drove there without meeting anyone on the way.

King was still abed, and, as there was no time to wait, Harry walked into the small shack and awakened the woodsman. "Sorry to roll you out, old man, but we've been caught a bit short and need some supplies."

While King was rummaging in his pie safe for bread and some canned goods, Dave Merrill appropriated a pair of trousers.

"You boys got to be the jailbirds that flew the coop over to Salem," King ventured. Lighting up a cob pipe and taking himself to the room's one chair, he sat down in his union suit and puffed away with apparent unconcern. "Sure foxed me with that lumbermen guff."

"I've been one in my time, all right," Tracy answered, stuffing the bread and tinned food into a flour sack. "You've got plenty of grit, old fellow, but don't let it go to your head. Keep quiet about this."

"If you want to stay healthy," Merrill added, pants in one hand, six-shooter in the other.

"That old reprobate'll hustle for town before we're a mile off," Merrill complained as they left the cabin. "And you can bet that pair from last night'll have the township out after us to boot."

"Two can play those games," Harry answered. "While they're fumbling around for us, we'll watch for them. I've outguessed a lot better posses than these hay shakers . . . and I'll show you how."

Demonstrating his expertise, Tracy left horse and buggy in the King dooryard, and they struck out on foot, southward, by-passing the roads, despite Merrill's protests at leaving their conveyance behind.

"They're bound to start blocking the byways, so we're better off hoofing it for the time being."

After they'd trekked several miles through the fields and woods, Harry turned back on a more westerly course. "That old man saw us heading south, so we'll lie up in the woods until dark, then take our chances in another direction."

Several times during that day they heard the baying of hounds and distant shouts of what might have been posses, but no one came their way. Dining on the bread and canned goods, including tinned peaches, they slaked their thirsts at a small rivulet coursing its crystalline way through the nearby underbrush and passed a portion of the day in slumber, with one at a time on guard.

Late in the afternoon Merrill had become so uneasy that his restlessness eventually influenced the normally self-possessed Tracy into agreeing to move out before nightfall.

"All right, we'll cut across the fields north of these woods and see if we can't fort up somewhere and have some fun with those fellows out there."

Tracy and the still apprehensive Merrill, weapons at the ready, slipped through the trees, listening for the sound of approaching danger, but everything was still except for a mounting wind rippling the grass of the fields and flaring the bushes at the timber's edge.

Moving down into a gully that slashed diagonally across the field, they emerged onto higher ground commanding a wide range of view to the south, east, and west.

"Here, move a few of those rocks and some of the dead wood by that fallen tree," Tracy said, "and we'll hunker down and see what happens. I've a hunch there's folks nearby."

Tracy, despite himself, was glad to be out of the woods, and Merrill now seemed more like himself as he helped throw up a breastworks. Then Dave had a sobering thought. "What happens if they come from the north behind us?"

"We'll take our chances. When you've dealt with posses, you'll find they generally do just about what you want. See if I'm not right."

Tracy's hunch proved correct, for near dusk several armed men in rough hunting garb appeared south of them with a pair of dogs on leashes.

Tracy nudged Merrill who'd been facing the north with rifle cocked and ready. "Here's company come calling."

They crouched behind their makeshift barricade, waiting. The posse men slowly advanced across the open space until they suddenly halted upon discovering the barrier. Then one signaled with his rifle to unseen reinforcements beyond the fugitive's line of sight. Presently two more men appeared up out of the gully and the group huddled in conference, their hounds backing and tugging at the leashes and wrapping themselves around their owners' legs.

"Damned dogs are sure enough hog-tyin' 'em." Merrill moved about restlessly, cursing to himself. "Why don't we jump 'em now before they get untangled?"

"There'll be more where that bunch came from," Harry cautioned. "Let's hold on a bit and see if they come where we can really burn their britches." He grinned at Dave. "But I'm glad you've got your dander up at last, for you'll surely have some blue whistlers singeing your whiskers before we're shut of this damned country."

But as he spoke, the knot of posse men, rifles, dogs and all, began to ease back down the hill toward the gully.

Tracy squeezed off a shot that kicked up a cloud of sand and gravel at the gully's lip, the echoes racketing around the fields. "Let's see if that little invitation fetches anyone back to the party." He looked over at Merrill to find him upon hands and knees, staring through a gap in the barricade. "Oh, hell! Give 'em a couple more, Dave."

But the fusillade Merrill pumped down the slope brought no more results than Tracy's single shot. There came the rasping cry of a disturbed jay and the faraway yelp of some dog, then again the lonely soughing of the evening wind.

"Not much fight in that bunch," Tracy commented, lying back full-length and relaxing. "I think they've gone on to raise up another couple dozen to help. I say we move on to the northwest come dark, but still staying off the roads."

While the moon floated like a battered silver dollar through the starlit night, Harry and Dave trudged across the fields and wood lots until they came to a group of farm buildings. Searching along the back of the barn, they discovered a door ajar. Slipping in, they were able to burrow down into a pile of hay and there slept, rifles in hand.

Awakened in the dim, pink dawn light by the fussy *cluck* and *cackle* of barnyard fowls, they edged out and headed up a lane that led toward the village of Monitor, arriving there in broad daylight.

Knocking at the door of a house on the outskirts, they took breakfast with an uneasy family that eyed the uninvited visitors with silent alarm, but was eventually put somewhat at ease by their guests' scrupulously polite behavior. Breakfast over, the fugitives departed.

Thus the next week went, hiding out in the timber during the day and traveling the empty roads at night. Continually attempting to work their way northwest, they'd appear at some lonely farm or ranch house in the early hours of the morning to demand a meal. Although there were, at times, a force of nearly 250 militiamen, deputy sheriffs, constables, city marshals, detectives, and armed citizenry in their wake, Tracy and Merrill easily stayed ahead of such sprawling mobs that were often more of a danger to each other than their elusive quarry.

By the time the fugitives, ever bearing northwest, crossed both Marion and Clackamas Counties, they'd left the settled portion of the state behind and now ranged through one of the loneliest sections of Oregon. Here the terrain became constantly more impassable so that the militia companies were soon ordered home. The army of civilian manhunters, always a day or two behind Tracy and Merrill, also began to dwindle until it was at last decided to abandon the chase completely.

Without being fully aware of the extent of the posses on their trail, Tracy had amply demonstrated to both partner and pursuers that he'd been master of the situation from the very beginning of the break.

Chapter Seventeen

With little access to farms or ranches in the wilderness country near Mount Hood, Tracy and Merrill had no trouble subsisting on game, although short of other edibles. Both were good shots, but Harry was more apt to wing a pheasant or sage hen than Dave, who did manage to bring down a ten-point buck.

At last, tiring of the time wasted lazing along, for they'd covered little more than 100 miles since the break out despite all their twisting and turning, they veered back toward the winding Columbia, reaching the Randall Ranch near New Era, where they invited themselves in for a meal, then commandeered another team and buggy. Randall, eyeing the fugitive's weapons, made no objections whatever. Thus outfitted, they came to Portland, passing through the center of town without arousing the least attention in a region becoming used to armed posse men. From there they traveled to the Columbia Slough Road, leaving the buggy with a note, requesting its return to W. G. Randall.

At noon that Sunday they walked down to the slough's edge, having noticed a pair of fishermen. The teenage anglers were suddenly aware of two rough-looking men on the bank with rifles.

"We'd like to get over the river to Washington," Harry informed the gaping young fishermen—George Sunderland and Walter Burlingaim—when they'd hastily rowed ashore.

Hunt Down Harry Tracy

Although neither of the teenagers was able to accommodate the fugitives, much as they protested they'd like to, they admitted having a friend nearby. They led Tracy and Merrill to the summer cabin of a W. W. Paddock, and together all walked back to the river landing and were rowed across to the state of Washington.

"You can bet those young devils'll just about bust their galluses gettin' to the law," Dave grumbled as they stood on the high bank of the great Columbia, watching the progress of the boat back across the vast, diamond-sparkled river.

"Now, what do you care?" Harry poked Dave in the ribs. "We've had ourselves a pretty dull time, laying out in the hills. It's all been about as flat as being back in the pen itself. So it might stir up your blood to have a little hot work again." Slapping Merrill on the back, Tracy led off to the north.

That evening, as they lay in a small pine grove near the Fort Plain Road, they heard the nearby commotion of a group of men that had ridden up the pike and were fanning out across the fields. From where they crouched, Harry and Dave could hear some of the posse's careless talk.

"They think they've got us penned up?" Tracy whispered. "Then it's time to be going. And we'd better steal a couple of horses to teach them a lesson."

"Sounds like half of Washington state's out there," Merrill cursed softly. "I was right about those younkers at the river. How are we gettin' out of this without a fight?"

"By being lighter on our feet than those clodhoppers. Come on and follow up close."

Emerging from the grove's shadowy depths, they saw a dark mass of men that seemed more interested in warming themselves at a good-size fire than in beating the bushes, although three or four silhouettes were moving along the road.

"Lucky they haven't got dogs," Harry muttered as he and

Dave slipped across the road, south of the main body of lawmen, making for the safety of a dense woods beyond. Guided by the golden orange gleam of a crackling fire pulsing the night with ruddy splashes, Tracy and Merrill entered the inky depths of a huge track of timber.

"Now damn 'em, let 'em come," Dave gritted as they trudged slowly into the forest. Turning to glare back toward the still visible fire glow, his eyes glittered. "Damn 'em."

"That's the stuff." Tracy chuckled. "You've got to admit this is better than being cooped up like animals. And if they want to hunt us down like animals, we'll make them feel our teeth . . . if they get too close."

Next day they made their way across the country without trouble, catching several hours of sleep in the early part of the morning and eventually coming out of the timber some miles from the river at the run-down spread of an old German rancher, Henry Tiede. After inviting themselves in, and finding him alone, they informed Tiede they were officers seeking the fugitives and needed horses, having lost theirs crossing the river. But they found the rancher to be aware of their identity.

"As you wish, Mister Tracy." The older man philosophically bustled around setting the table, while Merrill went out to the barn to inspect the animals.

"How'd you know us?" Tracy slumped into one of the split-bottomed rockers as he watched Tiede fry up bacon and slice potatoes, obviously left over from the previous meal.

"From dee papers." Tiede jerked a thumb at a stack of newspapers lying on another chair. "Tells about you pooty gute, I'd say." He grinned slyly. "Undt don't make any anchels of you, eider."

Merrill, who'd returned to report he'd selected a pair of mounts, glared at Tiede. "Keep your trap shut, you old

Dutchman!" He waved his Colt under Tiede's nose. "We don't need any such talk!"

"Easy, Dave." Harry reached over and pulled Merrill's arm back. "Take a gander at yourself in that mirror and you'll see you don't look like any sort of angel, nor me, either." He fingered the shaggy stubble on his chin, then reached for the newspapers.

Merrill subsided, muttering as he went back out to saddle up the horses. He returned while Tracy was still thumbing through the papers. "Say, Dave . . . look at this." Harry held up the front page of *The Oregonian*, date lined June 11th. "Here's both our handsome mugs right on the front page."

Momentarily forgetting Tiede's joshing, Merrill leaned over Tracy's shoulder, eagerly scanning the story. "That picture of you don't show your mustache, and by thunder they've even got our descriptions from the damned pen. Look there. Five hundred dollars cold cash for each of our hides." He stared at the old man calmly placing food on the kitchen table. "One thousand berries, eh? And I'll bet you'd like a chance at collecting it."

"Sit down, chents," the old rancher said, waving them to the table. "Sit down undt eat before it cold gets."

Merrill reluctantly followed Tracy to the table but continued to read out the reward descriptions as they ate:

$1,000 REWARD

FOR THE CAPTURE

DEAD OR ALIVE

OF

HARRY TRACY

AND

DAVID MERRILL

Or $500 each, who escaped from the Oregon State
Penitentiary on the morning of June 9, 1902

Following is a description of each:

HARRY TRACY—Age 27 years, height 5 feet 9
inches, weight 160 pounds, complexion medium, hair
light brown, eyes blue, medium build, but well set up,
cut scar second joint left thumb, cut scar second
knuckle right forefinger, other scars on legs and shoulders.

DAVID MERRILL—Age 31 years, height 5 feet 10
inches, weight 147 pounds, complexion medium,
brown hair, gray eyes, medium build, slightly stoop
shouldered, several scars on knuckles.

Both men are heavily armed and extremely dangerous. Caution is recommended in approaching either.

If apprehended report to:

J.D. LEE
Superintendent Oregon State Penitentiary

"Caution? Damned right," commented Harry as he
wolfed down the food. "And a thousand bucks, eh? Pass the
potatoes."

"It's not a thousand any more. It says here that on June
Thirteenth, those bloodsuckers raised the ante to three thou-
sand dollars." Merrill set down his coffee cup and stared from
Teide to Tracy. "No wonder they's a confounded army on
our trail." Then another idea struck him. "Say, I'll bet Jesse
James never had that kind of money on his head."

"And yet they plugged him," Tracy dryly retorted.
"Hustle up and finish. We can't impose on this kind gent's
hospitality. But as you say, he could have ideas about cashing
us in . . . eh, old-timer?" He dug the bewhiskered elderly
German in his ample midriff.

Hunt Down Harry Tracy

The meal over, Tracy requested a razor from Teide and, after washing up at the sink, proceeded to shave, sparing the dark mustache he'd grown since the escape. "Now you, Dave. We've got to spruce up a bit . . . can't go traipsing around looking like the devil. Mister Tiede, here, pointed that out."

While Merrill was shaving, Tracy packed food for the trail. After gathering up a side of bacon, canned goods, and a small frying pan, he escorted Tiede into the small bedroom, and rummaged through the old man's clothing. When Dave joined them, Harry shucked his worn garments and got into new underwear, socks, boots, and trousers, then Merrill followed his example.

"Sorry to repay your hospitality by riding off with your stock and your duds," Harry told the phlegmatic rancher. "But we've got to keep moving, and also pay heed to our looks, seeing we're now worth three thousand dollars on the hoof."

"And you stretch out on that there bed and be damned quick!" Merrill pulled his six-gun and poked Tiede. "What's up?" he asked when he found Tracy staring at him. Then: "If we don't tie up the old goat, he'll be spreadin' the news like those other Paul Reveres. I'd like a little less rumpus on my travels . . . wouldn't you?" At Tracy's shrug, Merrill went back into the kitchen, returning with a length of clothesline.

"Putt I'll be starvedt soon," Tiede pleaded as they finished roping him to his rickety, brass bedstead. "My hired handt iss in Vancouver undt wond't be pack for anozer day."

After reassuring Tiede that the first person they met would be told of their host's predicament, Tracy and Merrill went out to the horses with their supplies.

Now changing his strategy, Tracy headed northwest on a route keeping them near the Vancouver Pike, reasoning they needed to get as far as they could before the state of Washington began sending out their posses. Riding through the fields but keeping the pike in view, they made such good time they reached the Salmon River bridge by dark. Here they unsaddled and camped in a hemlock grove until midnight, eating and reading their newspapers by the light of a small, carefully concealed campfire.

Going down to the river about one o'clock in the morning to get water in a pair of quart beer bottles carried in lieu of canteens, they were suddenly fired on—the placid surface of the moon-tinged river exploding into twin geysers.

"Damned posse!" Both leaped back from the shoreline and dashed for the shadows, but the ambushing rifles cracked out again and Dave stumbled and fell, his water bottle slipping back down the riverbank. "Bastards!"

"Come on." Tracy grabbed his partner's arm only to have Merrill curse with pain. "They crease you?" he asked as he got Dave to his feet, and then they jogged back across the bridge. By the time they'd flanked the unseen foe, they halted at their campsite about 100 yards from the bridge, and there Tracy helped bind up the wound in Merrill's right arm, using strips of a shirt taken from his saddlebag.

"Damn it, I knew those devils would get me sooner or later." Merrill leaned against a tree trunk, then slumped to a sitting position, holding his wrist in his left hand.

"Why, hell, you aren't going to let a little crease keep us from some sport with those jays?" Satisfied Merrill's wound didn't appear serious, Tracy scouted down the road, returning in a few minutes to report having sighted two lone figures across the river. "Come on, let's find their rig or horses, move 'em, and then lay for the chumps when they start scratching gravel."

The horse and buggy were discovered around a bend in

the roadway, and, helping Dave into the seat, Tracy drove the rig quietly several hundred yards, then tied up the horses again. Slipping off into the surrounding woods within easy distance of their own mounts, they waited, Merrill still favoring his wounded arm and grinding his teeth.

When the two posse men, Bert Biesecker and Luther Davidson of Vancouver, found they'd been outmaneuvered, they began a hasty search for their property.

Eventually discovering the rig, they were just untying the horse when they were fired on—one bullet ripping through Biesecker's coat and searing his shoulder. Others grazed the horse as the amateur lawmen leaped headlong into their buggy and whipped up the frantic animal. Stung by bullets and urged on by the lash, the horse thundered away, while Tracy leaned against a tree, holding his sides with glee, joined by Merrill, although Dave's laughter was punctuated with painful curses.

"Wish we'd 'a' killed 'em both, the infernal rattlers," Merrill gritted. "Firin' at our backs like that."

"No use shooting any more than we have to." Tracy helped Dave into the saddle, then swung aboard his own mount. "We've enough of a hornet's nest kicked over right now. Live and let live . . . but, if they crowd us too hard, then we'll scrap. That's the way to keep them off balance."

They put twenty miles between the river and themselves despite Dave's wound, before they swung into another woods for the night.

On Saturday June 28th, following a hasty breakfast on the remains of the food taken from the old rancher, they traveled along smaller county roads, by-passing the town of Ridgefield by a good distance.

Now in Cowlitz County, the small ranches and farms that had sprung up began to peter out again, and they counted themselves lucky to come across a lonely farmhouse, five miles southeast of the village of Chehalis. Merrill, worried about his injury, had opted for visiting a doctor, but Tracy was able to talk him out of it—for the time being.

Swinging down from their saddles, they cautiously examined the shabby house and outbuildings, but no one seemed about. Rifles at the ready, they drifted up to the back door, hesitated, then tried the knob. The door opened easily.

"Make yourself at home," Tracy told Merrill. "I'll get the horses out of sight." When he'd returned from watering the animals at a tank near the barn, then tying them in the stalls and shaking down some alfalfa, he found Dave sitting at the kitchen table.

"Enough of this and I won't care if school keeps or not." Dave raised a nearly full bottle of Old Crow Whiskey and took another belt. "Ain't nobody around as far I can see. Found this here in that pie safe."

After searching the house and taking several suits of underwear and some shirts from the bedroom bureau, Tracy cleaned the bullet wound in Merrill's arm and rebound it. The missile, possibly from a small-caliber Stevens .25-25, had passed through a fleshy part of the shoulder and had not bled to any extent. Then Harry built up a fire in the wood cook stove, heated water, and shaved, using a razor discovered on a shelf.

Considering Dave's plight as he cleaned up, Harry was of two minds. While the wound was growing inflamed, his partner had ceased to complain of any pain. And as far as visiting a doctor, they could be sticking their heads into a pair of nooses if the sawbones couldn't be trusted. He decided to wait a few days.

Rummaging the kitchen, he turned up enough victuals to prepare a decent dinner of beans, side meat, and coffee. Dave needed all the Arbuckle's he could get down as the whiskey had dealt him a tremendous wallop. Before they left the place, Tracy was able to find some cash amounting to a roll of $25 in the Seth Thomas clock on the sideboard. He also obtained pencil and paper and wrote a note thanking their absent hosts for the whiskey, clothing, food, and cash, adding a postscript regarding the plight of the German rancher, Tiede.

They rode onward, with Merrill swaying in the saddle from a combination of injury, fatigue, and Old Crow. Crossing the rolling countryside of Lewis County, they fetched up in another pine woods at evening.

Day after day following the prison break, the weather had been warm and pleasant, but now as they unsaddled in a secluded grove, the sun, slanting down into a red featherbed of clouds, began to darken. Rumbling thunder rolled toward them, and winds sweeping in from the west began to push and press through the treetops.

The following night was eight hours of damp misery as Tracy and Merrill huddled over a small fire that barely held its own in the lashing wind and rain. Merrill insisted on finishing up the whiskey, and Tracy, cold and miserably wet, was only too glad of several jolts of Old Crow himself. Around dawn Harry awoke from a sodden doze to find Dave saddling his horse. There was a wild, drawn look on Merrill's long face as he stared down at Tracy.

"Now where do you think you're off to?" Tracy asked.

"I think it's damn well time we split up." Merrill reeled, barely saving himself from falling by grabbing at the saddle horn. Giving a groan, he struck the horse, which jerked and plunged. "Damn it to hell, we've got to get out of this. Maybe we ought to give up."

By now Harry was aware that Dave was filled with fever and just about out of his head. "Come on, you're right."

Helping Merrill onto his horse, Tracy got his own mount ready, and, with Dave hunched over the saddle, they emerged from the timber and rode off across country.

Although now well into Washington, the landscape was very much like that of Oregon—low-lying hills cut by ravines and covered in many areas by tracts of timber as well as scrub fir.

By dusk they'd ridden into Skamana County, but Dave was all in. By a stroke of luck they came across a small sparkling stream in a secluded valley, and went into camp. Tracy settled Merrill down upon a blanket, and did what he could to dress the wound, now badly festered. After unsaddling the horses and watering them at the rivulet, he grained them by hand. Then he got a small fire going, boiled up some coffee, and roasted some side meat, but Merrill lay shivering, head rolling from side to side, unaware of the fire's welcome heat for much brighter flames were burning through his emaciated figure. Watching him, Harry felt Merrill could be dying.

Springing up, Tracy paced back and forth past the fire, six steps one way and six the other, over and over—the distance from wall to wall in a prison cell. Out of one cage and still locked in another.

At last he sank back onto a fallen tree trunk, sipping at the hot Arbuckle's, munching a chunk of side meat while resting and trying to think. Listening to the growing night wind, he caught the distant baying of hounds somewhere to the west. Posse! That word was never far from the back of his mind. Listening and looking over the Winchester and pistols, he thought the sounds were nearing. Beyond the firelight's wavering shadows the horses stamped and moved about restlessly. They'd also heard the sounds.

"Dogs." Merrill roused up from his stupor. "Damned hounds! I hear 'em, why can't you?" He glared at Tracy.

"Hell, let's get ready for 'em." Staggering to his feet, Merrill pulled his six-shooter and, before Harry could stop him, fired a shot. The unexpected slam of the heavy .44 banged and clattered across the little valley while the horses plunged at their stake ropes.

"Damn it!" Tracy made a grab at Merrill's pistol, then dived for the ground as the gun exploded again, shattering the ringing silence. "Damn it, Dave, you'll have the whole National Guard down on our necks."

But there was no reply as Merrill had fallen, just missing the fire while knocking the coffee pot into the sputtering flames. Rolling him over, Tracy saw that Dave was unconscious.

Listening intently, he found the hounds' baying becoming stronger. There was no doubt but that hunters—or posse men—were heading across the hills toward the camp. Gentling the horses, Tracy kicked out the fire. Dropping to his knees, he saw Dave was still breathing, but with a tell-tale rattle in his throat. It didn't seem as though Merrill would last the night. Harry cursed his refusal to get Dave to a doctor as he sat with a blanket wrapped about his shoulders, Winchester across his knees, waiting.

The belling of the hounds continued to swell through the windy night, and just as he was about to make his way out through the underbrush toward the oncoming body of men, the baying swung away to the south and was soon swallowed in the mounting wind rush. Seemingly the posse, if posse it were, had misread the gunshots and thought it came from another compass point—even possibly from another posse.

Completely bushed by the past days and the previous night in particular, Tracy slept the slumber of a drugged man. He was awakened well into the morning by the strident rusty-hinge cries of a pair of belted kingfishers fluttering along the nearby stream.

Getting stiffly to his feet, he found Merrill to be sleeping the sleep that has no awakening. Dave had succumbed to the virulent poison of the half-tended wound. It was a pure fluke that a young and active man should cash in from such a relatively minor injury, but Tracy told himself that was the way the cards were sometimes dealt. He himself had also awakened to another bitter fact. Merrill's horse had taken the second of those wild shots in the right foreleg and now hobbled about on three legs.

Looking over his own mount, he found the big bay in sound condition but in need of watering. Leaving Dave where he lay, he took his own horse down to the brook, staked him out where he could graze, then returned to Merrill's mount. There was just one thing to do, and, drawing his Colt, he shot the suffering brute between the eyes. As the horse went down onto its forelegs and then rolled onto its side, he again heard the sound of dogs off to the east. That damned bunch, whatever it was and wherever it came from, still had hounds afield.

Packing the cooking gear and rolling up the saddle blanket and tugging Merrill's out from under him, he stood silently debating. And all the while the baying song of the hounds drifted nearer. He searched Merrill, taking what few dollars he had as well as his two six-shooters. These he placed in Merrill's blanket and strapped them to the bay, together with the rest of the gear. Dave's Winchester was a problem, so, taking it by the barrel, he heaved it far out into the underbrush.

By now the clamoring pack seemed just over the next rise. There was no time to bury Dave—even if he had a spade or shovel. He'd have to leave him. Looking down at Merrill's drawn face for the last time, a thought came to him. *No. You bloodsucking bounty skunks, you aren't going to cash in on poor Dave. Damned if I don't go you one better. I'll raise you and see you.* Rolling the stiffening figure of Merrill over onto its face and placing his own pistol in the cold hand, Tracy took deliberate aim and shot Dave between the shoulder blades.

Running back to the bay, he swung up, muttering: "Now you bastards try and prove you got him. I'll tell someone we had a row and I won. A damned duel . . . that's what."

Sitting the bay for a moment and looking back at Merrill, Tracy saw the first of the posse's pack come belling over the hill. There was still no sign of riders, but they'd be coming. Spurring up, he racked away north from the little valley. But it seemed damned strange to have no one beside him. Alone.

Chapter Eighteen

On July 2nd, two days following Dave Merrill's death in the Sakamana County forest, Harry rode into the seaport town of Olympia at daybreak with an idea that had come to him on the all-night ride. He would dodge the blundering posses by taking a boat up Puget Sound to Seattle.

Tying his mount near a row of waterfront warehouses, Winchester in hand, he walked down to the only place of business that seemed open—the Capital City Oyster Company. As he started to enter the building, he remembered the two six-shooters in his bedroll on the horse, but stopped in his tracks at the sight of a city patrolman strolling up the street, idly twirling a nightstick. Shrugging, Harry walked on into the noisy room to find the cook busily preparing breakfast for five sailors. Announcing his name, he went on to inform the slack-jawed captain of the Capital City launch that he and his crew would be busy for the day. Following a breakfast of flapjacks and sour belly with the silent bunch and with the cook tied to his flour barrel, the cruise north began when the big gas launch cast-off from its battered pier at 8:00 a.m. and headed out into the choppy water of the great Sound.

Ten long hours later, Captain Clark of the N&S dropped anchor off lonely Meadow Point several miles beyond the busy Seattle harbor and the incredible voyage was over. In addition to train robbery, rustling, and prison escape, Tracy had added piracy to his outlaw accomplishments—something that not even Butch Cassidy or Flat Nose George Currie ever achieved.

Leaving captain and crew snugly tied up to the point where they were bound to untangle each other within the next few hours, Tracy trudged toward Ballard, thinking over the voyage.

Without his six-shooters, abandoned with the horse at the appearance of the city patrolman, his tales of the Rocky Mountain West had kept crew and captain in their place as much as the Winchester. Curious concerning their captor and loving a salty yarn as do all sailors, they'd listened, open-mouthed, to stories of prison breaks, train robberies, and rustling. Then, realizing he faced the perfect audience, he'd told them the tale of a forest duel with his partner—beating him to the draw and killing him with one shot.

Tracy chuckled, thinking of that bare-faced lie, while knowing that it would all be in every paper within a day or two—the falling out, the argument, the challenge, then six-guns at ten paces and the rest. Now let those damned bounty hunters claim they'd laid Dave Merrill low.

A sudden clatter of hoof beats rattled from behind, jolting him out of his musing. But having rounded a bend in the Ballard Road, he was able to dive into the roadside bushes before the oncoming riders swept past in the dusk. Posse men! Tracy had been able to spot the glitter of rifles and shotguns as the six riders pelted on down the road. So Captain Clark had managed to stir up the countryside, and lawmen were, again, ranging the highways.

Off through the dim starlight he saw the faint, amber pinpoints of lamplight in a house. As he approached the place, other buildings took on hazy, bulking form and he was soon nearing a barn and some scattered sheds. Although he heard

213

the sound of one dog, it seemed to be in the distance, a single hound and probably at another farm.

He discovered a water trough at a corner of the barn and, plunging his hands into the depths, drank and cleared his head. Thirst quenched, he investigated the rear of the buildings and found a loose window. Sliding it open, he clambered through, moving past some stabled cows and horses, and ascended a ladder into the loft where he burrowed down into the sweet-smelling hay. There was still a chance of some posse men prowling the night, and, although still hungry, Harry decided to catch some sleep before bracing the farmer.

For a time he lay staring out the loft window at the stars, thinking again of his father, then his fumbling half-brother Ervie, but at last he fell asleep, wondering about Janet and when they might ever meet again.

Morning came before Harry was ready for it. He'd not slept very well, his night filled with a hodge-podge of dreams. He was unable to remember most, but he vaguely recalled a ghostly figure that could have been his father, who tried to warn of shadowy dangers—dangers no longer solid and real in the bright morning light. Clambering out of the haymow, he washed at the water trough and was about to go up to the house for breakfast when he spotted several saddled horses tied at the rear of the farmhouse. Company!

As he turned to leave, he saw what seemed to be a smokehouse. With an eye on the horses, he broke the lock on the stone structure and found it contained a dozen well-cured hams, as well as several chunks of side meat, all neatly hung from hooks on the beamed ceiling. Here was the answer to his present need for rations.

Tracy was shortly beating a retreat across the fields with a ham and a slab of side meat in a grain sack slung over his shoulder, Winchester in the other hand.

Hunt Down Harry Tracy

Although morning had broken with a mellow sun, promising a warm and pleasant day, clouds were drifting in from the coast, changing minute by minute from mild, dove gray to a rolling leaden wrack, slashed by the sharp, jagged teeth of lightning. Thunder was colliding with thunder in slamming bangs. By the time he reached the S. P. tracks and was following it toward the town of Bothell, intent upon catching a freight, the rain swept in with a rush. Jogging along the wet ties and cursing the weather, he came upon a sturdy-looking log shack in a ravine just twenty feet from the rail line.

For the rest of the morning the rain lashed across fields, woods, and the one room hut where Harry sat out the storm. Once inside, he'd discovered a rusty, pot-bellied stove with enough dry wood to make a decent fire. The only furniture was a three-legged chair and a battered table in no better condition. Apparently the building was used occasionally by railroad section hands.

Having roasted a portion of the ham, Tracy lounged on the creaking chair and scanned the papers by the light of a single window. Among the sheets were a few dailies less than a week old. One Seattle paper carried several stories concerned with the attempts of various posses to net the fugitives, headlines and sub-heads fairly bristling with black type:

TRACY HAS ELUDED A PACK OF HOUNDS
AND ENCIRCLING SHERIFFS' POSSES!
VANISHED AS IF BY SUBTLEST MAGIC
EVERY TIME HE HAS BEEN IN REACH!

There was more. Parts of the accompanying stories claimed he'd been aided by outside help. There was still no mention of the discovery of Dave's body, but he was sure Captain Clark and his oystermen would spread word of the duel.

Occupying himself with the papers and keeping the stove going, Tracy kept an ear cocked for the whistle of an approaching freight. He'd seen a water tank not 200 yards down the track, and knew there was a good possibility of a train stopping sometime during the afternoon.

Around 3:00 p.m., when the rain began to slacken, he heard no welcome sound of a train whistle—but footfalls and muffled voices. Posse! His temper anything but equable after scanning the ink-slingers purple prose regarding a mad dog on the run, Tracy glared out the cabin window and saw four figures approaching.

Moving to avoid being penned in the shack, he grabbed his provision sack and rifle, and threw open the door. There was the *crack* of several weapons and splinters exploded from the hut as bullets ricocheted away.

Dropping behind a stump, Harry pumped out a half dozen shots at the bastards who'd fired without warning. One man went down and a second seemed to reel in his tracks. While the gunfire's echoes bounded and reverberated across the countryside, Tracy could hear the crashing of shrubs and bushes to his left. Someone was plunging through the undergrowth at the bottom of the railroad cutting in a try to outflank him. Then came the blasting of a heavy rifle from one of the posse men, now down behind the right of way and shooting over the rails at Tracy.

He again answered their fire with another volley and heard curses and a confusion of voices but the noise in the underbrush stopped and Harry knew the man was retreating. For several minutes Tracy lay behind his stump, waiting, but the life had seemed to have gone out of the ambushers—and with good reason. Deputy Sheriffs Raymond and Williams, both of Bothell, lay stone dead on the rain-soaked battlefield, while Karl Anderson, an investigative newsman, was wounded. Despite the furious gunfire of the ambushing lawmen, Tracy hadn't suffered a scratch.

Not lingering for any reinforcements to appear or for the arrival of some freight, Harry picked up his grain sack and Winchester and slipped off into the wet woods along the tracks.

At 5:00 p.m. he was on the main road within rifle shot of Bothell, where he stopped a horseman named Vincent, returning from the village to his farm. Posing as a deputy upon Tracy's trail, Harry seized the horse for government business and rode it till it pulled up lame near the Louis Jackson farm six miles onward.

Finding the farmer in the barnyard, Harry dismounted and disclosed his actual identity. "I'm Tracy. Hitch up that rig there fast. I'm in a hurry to keep moving. You folks are damned unfriendly in these parts."

Telling Jackson he meant to reach Seattle and fade away into the crowds till the hue and cry died down again, Tracy's luck held as horse and wagon with its occupants actually passed a pair of posse men standing on the Richman Beach Road, rifles at the ready.

"You did fine." Harry grinned at the sober-faced farmer. "If you hadn't, I might have booted you out to join those other chumps back there."

As it was now close to dark, Tracy directed Jackson to pull into a farmyard, near the village of Woodland Park. They knocked on the front door of the Van Horn place at 9:00 p.m., Tracy requesting supper from an apprehensive Mrs. Van Horn, whose husband was away in Seattle. Once he'd eaten a good meal together with his uneasy companion,

Jackson, and the Van Horn's elderly hired man, O'Reily, Tracy relapsed into a casual mood, discussing the weather, the country he'd traveled through, and even the prison break.

When Jackson hesitantly mentioned the growing amount of the reward, now risen to $5,500, due to the governor adding $2,500, Harry leaned back in his chair, faithful Winchester at his side, and smiled slightly. "They've got to get their hands on me before that sort of money can be any use to them." Pausing, his expression became bleak, eyes darkening. The sudden change surprised Jackson and the old hired hand, and actually startled Mrs. Van Horn.

"Blood money," Tracy declared with a withdrawn expression. "Blood money, pure and simple." He grinned coldly, and Mrs. Van Horn found that more frightening than if he'd merely scowled. "Well, there's some bounty-hunting devils that won't be around to collect." Then as the astounded Jackson, gaping Irishman, and open-mouthed woman listened, Tracy recounted the recent fight at Bothell in a few terse words. This done, he politely requested another cup of coffee.

Mrs. Van Horn now felt this soft-spoken young fellow was more dangerous than any tiger she'd seen at the circus or zoo—mild-mannered, and even lazily relaxed but ready to spring on the instant into ferocious action—and he frightened her more than all the rumors and tall tales in the papers. This was one person who more than lived up to his fearsome reputation.

A God-fearing church woman, Mrs. Van Horn felt it her duty to thwart this tigerish man before there were any more posse men's widows. It was while pouring coffee and trying to stop the trembling of her hand, she suppressed an unbidden thought—the reward. But she told her secret self that even a portion of it would go a long way toward purchasing needed farm machinery and a new roof. Laying out the meal, she'd been allowed to roam from dining room to kitchen and back. Her chance presently came with the late arrival of the Freemont butcher boy delivering a package. Once he'd heard of the dangerous guest inside the house, the lad led his horse down the dusky lane, scrambled aboard the patient old plug, and lashed it into town where, like a modern-day Paul Revere, he pulled up before the office of Sheriff John Cudihee with his explosive news.

Cudihee, a hard-featured Civil War veteran, facing a fall reëlection bid and with an eye forever cocked on free publicity, had just returned from viewing the two casualties of the afternoon. Electrified by the butcher boy's bulletin, he hurriedly rounded up a makeshift posse. This doughty trio of volunteers was composed of a local policeman, E. E. Breese, Neil Fawley, an old hard-rock miner, and J. I. McKnight, a businessman with a penchant for Wild West dime novels. The sheriff saw them mounted upon livery stable stock, and then led them on the gallop three miles out to the Van Horn place.

Cudihee had already gone on record in the local paper as declaring that if ever the chance came his way to pound nails into Tracy's coffin, he was just the man—this despite the fact that several bodies of militia, plus a dozen independent posses had scarcely crossed Tracy's trail, let alone confronted him. But that was before that afternoon's fire fight at Bothell.

Arriving at the Van Horn farm, they dismounted where Cudihee stationed his three volunteers in a semicircular position across the lane from the house, while he got himself behind a tree in the front yard.

The makeshift law team had barely settled into its places when Tracy, again having thanked his hostess, emerged into the moonlight, walking between Jackson and the hired hand.

As usual, Tracy was relaxed, joshing old O'Reily that he was due to take a ride with them.

But as Mrs. Van Horn had sensed, Tracy was never more dangerous than when apparently at ease.

The patrolman, Breese, upon seeing three figures emerge from the farm house, and not realizing that one of the strolling silhouettes was the man they were stalking, inquired if they'd seen Tracy. Getting a negative answer as the trio walked on toward the hitched wagon, but seeing moonlight glinting off a rifle barrel, Breese realized his mistake and then made another, crying out: "Drop that gun, Tracy!"

There were two flashes as a pair of shots slammed out with the officer and Tracy firing point-blank at each other. Breese dropped like an empty sack, while Fawley, who'd run across the road, gun at the ready, never had a chance to use it and fell mortally wounded.

With the hysterical screams of Mrs. Van Horn and Cudihee's bull-throated bellows ringing through the moonlit night, Tracy leaped into the brush along the road. The sheriff's bullets followed, but failed to find their mark, and Tracy was gone in the dark.

For nearly a week Tracy clung to the Seattle area, sleeping in the woods during the day only to emerge at first starlight and prowl about restlessly. Ranging first to the north and then, when his keenly-honed senses warned of nearby posses, he quietly drifted back southward. For six days he came and went silently as an Indian, appearing suddenly at some lonely farm or ranch to request a meal, then again vanishing.

During a three day period from July 4th to July 6th, Tracy had an unwilling companion, one Anderson, a hired man he'd taken along from a farmhouse near Puget Sound. Harry had informed the burly Swede he needed someone to carry his provision sack and whatever else he might commandeer. Actually, with the lonesome nights and empty days stretching on and on before him, Tracy felt the need for company. But Anderson's brogue was so thick Harry could barely understand him, yet he still felt the need for some sort of companionship. Even Dave had been there to talk to in the quiet hours of the night, and he came to miss Merrill more and more, despite his old-maidish complaints and carping.

Tracy also knew that with the gunfights at Bothell and the Van Horn farm, he'd aroused the countryside to a new fever pitch and he had a real bulldog on his heels in the person of Sheriff Cudihee.

While traveling in the daytime, Tracy appeared at the Gerrells' farm near Renton, Washington on July 6th. Here he put the women folk at ease, ate a meal, and attempted to send the Gerrells' son into town to purchase him a six-shooter. But having second thoughts of the stripling possibly informing on him, Tracy waited at the farmhouse most of the afternoon, then faded away into the timber before Sheriff Cudihee could arrive. Realizing he'd have to move faster and farther in the immediate future, he dispensed with the services of his stolid companion, tying Anderson like an unwanted pack horse, to a post in the Gerrells' barn.

Later Tracy would read in great detail of his conversation with Mrs. Gerrells and a pair of teen-age young ladies visiting at the farm, much of the newspaper talk manufactured as usual.

The following three days Tracy traveled through King County with the great, snow-capped pyramid of Mt. Rainer ever within sight, seventy miles to the southwest. Gazing at the blue and silver giant, he sometimes had the feeling it was watching him, waiting with inhuman patience to view his downfall. A hell of a big tombstone it seemed—but it could be a tombstone for tin stars like Cudihee and his medicine-show deputies if they blundered into his .30-30 sights again.

Tracy had read in one of the Tacoma papers, taken from the Gerrells, of his pleasure in the many violent confrontations with the lawmen, and even more so in the killings, murders, as the newspaper hack called them, but that was a lie. He was fighting for his very life, and it was either some counter-jumper's neck or his own. He'd convinced himself that such people were interested in just one thing—knocking him out of action for that blood money.

Chapter Nineteen

On Wednesday, July 9th, Tracy walked out of a wheat field at the E. M. Johnson farm near Kent, ten miles east of Tacoma. He was desperately hungry and determined to get additional weapons before heading on east toward Spokane and on into Idaho. He still relied on his Winchester, but sorely missed those six-shooters he'd left strapped to his bedroll near the Olympia docks.

"Good morning," Harry hailed the farmer who was just stepping from the back door of the plain little house. "You'd not be a bachelor?"

"No, I've a wife and two children," Johnson answered a bit stiffly, thinking this hard-faced stranger in dark slouch hat and ragged clothing might be one of the countless vagrants prowling the country in the wake of the latest recession. But when the farmer saw the .30-30 rifle dangling from the intruder's hand, he knew the man.

"Well, I'm Harry Tracy," said the visitor, "the fellow everyone seems trying to kill. And I've got to tell you that I'm plain beat out and hungry. So you march back and get me some grub."

Once inside the farm house, Tracy tossed his hat on the floor and seated himself near the kitchen stove. Noticing Mrs. Johnson standing nearby with two children, a boy of seven and a girl of six, Harry smiled in an effort to put the farm wife at ease, even remarking on the girl's doll and winking at the boy.

Once Mrs. Johnson had recovered from the initial shock of playing host to the man the newspapers were branding "The Lone Wolf", she turned her hand toward producing a hearty breakfast. When Tracy had downed a hot meal of fried eggs, oatmeal, batter cakes, and coffee, and assured Mrs. Johnson that it was the best he'd eaten in many a day, he turned abruptly to Johnson. "How much money do you have? You've got to get into the city and pick me up a pair of pistols right away."

Between the farmer and his wife nearly $30 was scraped up. And for the first time their uninvited guest showed obvious regret. "I don't want your hard-earned money, folks, but I've got to have two six-shooters, Forty-Five caliber. So hustle up, Johnson! Take your best horse, ride in to Auburn, and then catch the Tacoma train . . . and be back by six o'clock, or. . . ." Here he frowned at Mrs. Johnson, who hurriedly gathered the two children to her skirts like a mother hen throwing a wing over her chicks.

After seeing Johnson saddle his gray horse and start off at a gallop for town to catch the train, Tracy went back into the house with the farmer's wife and children. There he relaxed over another cup of coffee, again praising Mrs. Johnson for her cooking.

Throughout the remainder of a long day, Tracy drifted back and forth from the house to a grove of trees 300 yards from the farm buildings, explaining to Mrs. Johnson he felt locked up staying in the house too long. "That's what prison does to a person after a time."

While Mrs. Johnson contained her anxiety as best she could, the children played in and out of the grove, watched by Harry with a slight smile. Sometimes he seemed on the point of joining their games, but, with a sigh, he'd start up a one-sided conversation with the farm wife, who, although she'd lost some of her fear, answered only in monosyllables. This didn't bother Tracy, as he seemed eager enough to talk, even with an uncooperative listener.

It was then the woman heard something of his story, that he had no fear of posse men, but hated their dogs. He'd been forced to return the fire of more than one attacking force, he said, but took no pleasure in cutting down a fellow human, contrary to what the papers said.

As it grew on toward evening, Harry took the boy for a walk down the road and back, while the mother and girl remained at the house. Returning to the kitchen, Tracy drank more coffee and wondered out loud when Johnson might return. Near dark young Albert, watching for his father, hurried in to report Johnson was in sight.

Meeting the farmer at the door, Tracy took a single six-shooter, a .32-20 Colt, and a box of cartridges from the nearly exhausted Johnson, who explained he'd walked the length of the city of Tacoma, but had been unable to purchase more than one pistol.

Harry assured the worried Johnson that he'd done his best and he would get his money back in time. The weapon secured, Tracy left the farmhouse under cover of night, taking a flour sack of provisions prepared by Mrs. Johnson. He also rode off on the Johnsons' faithful gray horse, and that was the last they saw of Tracy, although the horse returned to the house within the hour. Harry had decided to cut the gray mare loose and continue his cross-country march until he reached more open range land, where a fast mount would be a vital necessity.

In the morning Johnson and a neighbor rode into the town of Auburn to inform the authorities, however, Tracy had vanished again.

But the dogged Sheriff Cudihee and a new, augmented posse came within rifle shot of Tracy the following afternoon, when Deputy Sheriff J. A. Bunce and his son noticed Tracy walking down the railroad tracks, between Auburn and Kent. For once the posse men shouted at the fugitive to halt before firing, but Tracy merely made for the safety of an adjoining woods. As their rifles and shotguns cracked out behind him, he felt the sudden sting of shotgun pellets in his right shoulder, but never broke step in his retreat. Running onward, Tracy saw another deputy, named Crowe, coming at him from up the tracks and whirled long enough to get off a snap shot. The .30-30 slug grazed the man's scalp doing little damage but stopped him in his tracks.

Cudihee again began to have visions of starring in the big city papers, for every indication pointed to the fact that he and his posse men were forcing Tracy toward a great, sprawling swamp to the east. Miles wide, with nearly unscalable cliffs on both sides, Black Diamond Swamp was so treacherous the sheriff was willing to bet his badge that his prey would never get out alive.

"This time, boys, we'll put the kibosh on that slippery devil," Cudihee expanded as he sat at a campfire on the swamp's edge and waited for the sound of gunshots, for he knew, while Tracy would put up a fight, they had him. Fresh footprints into the gloomy slough proved that. But Cudihee didn't know Tracy as well as he thought, for at that minute, as the moon began to loft up above the pines and cedars, Harry Tracy was already putting miles of swamp and forest between himself and Cudihee's riflemen, having cut back toward Seattle, slipping Indian-like through the posse's line at dark.

After backtracking from the swamp, Tracy spent a week in the neighborhood of Green River, getting by with the food taken from the Johnsons. As he'd dodged about the farmlands of King County and the country east of Tacoma, playing a deadly game of tag with the posses, he'd resisted leaving the vicinity of the Pacific Coast, for he still clung to the idea that, somehow, he'd return for Janet Warrington, when he actually knew that was almost impossible. But with the increasing pressure being exerted by the King County sheriff, he'd decided to head eastward toward Idaho and Wyoming. Now that he possessed a six-gun and ammunition, in addition to the Winchester, the next move was to find a decent horse with plenty of bottom to travel the grinding miles without faltering.

And while Tracy was about to leave Washington for good and the July days wore along, he might have been in Alaska or the South Seas as far as Sheriff Cudihee and the world in general knew, except for two reported appearances in the latter days of the month.

The first sighting came on Sunday afternoon, July 13th, when Tracy arrived at the house of Morris Garner, several miles from the village of Enumclaw, a good twenty miles from the sheriff's posse. As usual, he walked in, uninvited, and demanded a meal. After eating, he stayed long enough to insist on getting a shave from one of the Garners' three sons who'd been sprucing up for a dance at the time of Tracy's entrance.

Young Tom Garner protested: "I can't handle a straight razor that well. One of my brothers would do better."

Tracy then looked at another of the Garner boys, stating: "Oh, I'll settle for you. You look more like a barber. Come on and get at it. I've got to be traveling." Then Harry sat back with tilted head, so he could keep an eye on the room's other occupants.

Despite the long, incredibly arduous grind of the escape and pursuit and the possibility of the razor slipping in a wavering grasp, Tracy sat motionlessly, apparently at ease.

When the near incredible display of nerve was over, Harry ran a hand over his face, fingered his trimmed mustache, and told the boy he'd done well. After flipping him a coin, he walked out of the house with his Winchester, warning the motionless Garners against reporting his visit.

The sheer impact of Tracy's personality made such an impression on the Garner family they failed to inform the authorities for two whole days. By that time lawmen in that part of the state, including the dogged Cudihee, had only the vaguest idea of the elusive fugitive's progress.

From that Sunday until Wednesday, July 30th, while great interest continued in the newspapers concerning Tracy's whereabouts, he'd again, like some Apache, blended away into the rolling countryside of scattered farms, shaggy woods, and lonely ranches. But he was busy in that time breaking into a ranch barn, close to Lake Easton, in the middle of the night, making off with a superb riding horse, the pride of the foreman. Twenty miles east, the same evening, he roped a little brown mare out of a pasture near Blewett for a pack horse. The following night, he raided a crossroad store, southwest of Wenachee, and departed before dawn with a complete camping outfit of cooking utensils, another grain sack of supplies, a saddle, and a scabbard for his Winchester. And most welcome of all—another six-shooter and holster, with ample ammunition. Now packing a heavy .45, he put the .32-20 in a saddlebag.

Even though he was well outfitted to travel fast and hard, he still lingered in the wilds along the mighty Columbia, camping and hunting and soaking his shoulder in the river water to ease the sting of the birdshot the posse had fired at him. As he dug out most of the pellets with his jackknife, he found himself hoping Cudihee's posse or some other make-shift lawmen would appear. But the sheriff and two other posses were still wandering around back to the west, searching Snoqualimie Pass, and so Tracy was undisturbed for over two weeks.

At last the lonesome, lazy life he'd been leading palled on Tracy. Packing his camping gear and swinging aboard his black mount and leading the little pack mare, he rode out of the secluded valley and followed the bends in the great river toward the southeast.

The first inhabited place he came across was the orchard-rimmed farm of S. J. McEldowney, six miles below Wenatche on the Columbia. Arriving there at 10 o'clock, Wednesday morning, July 30th, he found McEldowney's father-in-law, W. A. Sanders, busy boxing fruit in the packing shed.

"Good morning, Mister . . . ?" Sanders greeted the solitary horseman who swung down from the saddle.

"Name's Tracy."

"Fine. Help yourself to some apples." The busy Sanders, catching something in the stranger's voice, glanced up to peer into the muzzle of a big bore revolver. He motioned for the man, who called himself Tracy, to have a seat on one of the crates, but continued to work.

Shoving the six-gun back in its holster, Tracy settled down to talk with the older man, eagerly chomping down several round, red apples.

At noon, McEldowney came to the shed, located about 100 yards from the house. Intent upon calling his father-in-law to dinner and seeing a stranger visiting with Sanders, he invited the man to come along and eat.

"Here's Mister Tracy," Sanders said.

McEldowney, failing to catch the name, merely nodded, but, when he saw the Winchester and pistols, he was instantly aware of his heavily armed visitor's identity.

Following the meal, the McEldowneys and Sanders were

escorted out onto the farmhouse's screened porch by Tracy, where they sat during the long afternoon, the tense monotony broken every so often into bits and pieces of conversation. For a while Harry entered into the talk but kept it away from himself and the intensive manhunt that appeared to have gone astray at last.

He did go as far as to tell husband, wife, and father-in-law that he was on his way back to Hole-in-the-Wall in Wyoming, then, noticing a recent *Daily Oregonian Statesman*, datelined the previous Saturday, picked it up, and began thumbing the pages. For a few minutes Harry read, with one eye on the paper and the other on the McEldowneys. Then he grew rigid and, gripping the paper, read again a brief news item on an inside page:

Salem, Oregon, Sat., July 26th—Miss Janet Warrington, said to be the paramour of the escaped bandit, Harry Tracy, passed away Friday, July 25th, in the charity ward of the county hospital. She had been suffering an advanced case of consumption and was taken to the hospital as a ward of the county, having lost her position with a local ladies' dress concern due to well founded rumors of duplicity in the notorious Tracy's desperate prison break. A Mr. Ogden Palmer of Chicago was said to be on his way to return the body to her widowed mother in that city.

Janet gone? It wasn't possible. It had to be some under-handed trick of the law to shove him into some wild move. Janet dead? And now that yellow pup, Ogden Palmer, would take her back to Chicago. But that would be damned small consolation for Palmer! Tracy knew, as sure as the sun rose and set, that Janet was his, had been his, and would have been his again. That was something to hold on to, that and the memory of the last time Janet had told him: *I'm as full of the Old Nick as ever . . . you'll find out.* He knew what she'd meant—that wonderfully crazy mixed-up night in Chicago and the incredible afternoon out at the fairgrounds when she'd been everything a girl could be to her man. No, he'd not forget Janet—now or ever.

Harry fell into a bitter mood. His somber expression and icy silence soon began to tell on his hosts. Mrs. McEldowney, in particular, began to feel that this smoldering-eyed stranger might be meditating them harm.

"Mister Tracy, it's getting on toward supper and I wonder if you'd stay for another meal?" She actually hoped he'd be riding on, and her plain, honest face betrayed her hospitable words.

Tracy looked up from the paper. "Why, yes, I'd be glad to put my feet under your table again." Then he cocked his head quizzically at her obviously disappointed expression. "Didn't think I was going to leave you-all so soon? I'll also have to ask you for some supplies . . . bacon, flour, and coffee for starters."

The McEldowneys and the father-in-law attempted to look well satisfied, but, Tracy could see, they just didn't have their heart in it. And he couldn't blame them. It was hard to put a good face on things when everything went wrong.

Janet! He still couldn't believe it. It had taken so long to find her, in fact she'd found him, and, when she did, he was already locked away from her. But when he'd broken out—he'd thought that, sometime, they'd be together again. And now? What in hell was he going to do without her? Even if he got to the Hole? He'd read somewhere how the light seemed to go out of the world when a particularly bitter thing happened—and, damn, if the late afternoon sun didn't seem dim to him, although it was still shining in a cloudless sky. Then he realized there were tears in his eyes—tears that hadn't been there since Mike Tracy had been killed by that falling timber. But he hadn't let anyone see those tears then, nor did he now.

"I'll need fresh horses." Harry stood up, shifted the Colt in its holster, and hefted the Winchester. "Let's go take a look at your stock."

McEldowney shrugged and preceded Tracy out to the barn lot, followed by old Sanders. There they picked out a fine, spirited black, similar to the one he'd been riding. As the pack horse still appeared fresh, Harry decided to keep her. "You'll have to only swap one cayuse at that." He grinned slightly. "But I think you'd better throw in a saddle. That one of mine is strictly mail-order catalog." He'd noticed an expensive, tooled, Mexican saddle hanging on a peg in the stock barn.

By the time they were through with the horses, supper was called, and, as soon as he'd finished and loaded the pack horse with supplies, Tracy prepared to leave.

"When I get to Wyoming, I'll drop a line with some money," Harry told McEldowney as he mounted and rode out of the farmyard. "I know this saddle's the apple of your eye, but right now I need a good one for a damned long jaunt."

Riding twelve miles south down the Columbia, Harry reached the Moses Coulée Ferry about 11:00 p.m., but didn't get across the river; the ferry attendant, an old Irishman with a wooden leg, explained that it was unsafe to cross at night for recent rains "had her a-booming." Eyeing the heavily armed posse man, the Irishman invited him to spend the night in his shanty, but Harry declined and camped on the bank.

In the morning he did take coffee with the old fellow and, after being ferried across the wide, brawling stream, rode off with the riverman's best wishes for running down Harry Tracy. "Ah, me bye, you'll need that pack horse loaded with luck to grab that divil. They say he's harder to catch than the Old Nick hisself!"

Tracy gave him a wave and put both horses to a gallop up the Coulée City Road, as if eager to come up with that slippery fugitive. He'd sold the old Mick pretty good at that. In fact, he'd lied so convincingly about his near misses with the foxy fugitive the old ferryman had refused payment for the crossing.

For the next two days he rode in a northeasterly direction across rugged, wide-open terrain. By-passing several small towns, he camped out, not encountering anyone as he traveled or coming across any habitation until he rode into a farm near Odessa in the afternoon. Again, as luck would have it, no one was home. Tracy thought about forcing his way into the shabby, unpainted, little house, but decided against it. With ample supplies, he merely watered his animals at the well, filled his canteen, and then, taking a piece of paper and a pencil from his saddlebag, he scribbled a note that he pinned to the well.

> To Whom It May Concern: Tell Mr. Cudihee to take a tumble and let me alone, or I'll fix him plenty. If your horses were any good, I'd have swapped with you. Thanks for the cold drink.
>
> Harry Tracy

Riding on, he wondered why he'd left an indication of his presence in the area. Word would get back to that damned fool sheriff, but too late—for he planned on being 100 miles away, perhaps into Idaho, by the time Cudihee could do a damned thing about it.

As he spurred up the black mare, he felt her stumble slightly but thought little of it until later in the day when he paused to rest the animals and discovered she'd pulled a tendon. Although the day was still warm, he felt an unexpected chill. Here he was out on a wide-open prairie with a lame horse, and that fool note was back at that farmhouse. He debated returning, then shrugged off the thought and rode slowly on, the pack horse gratefully adjusting itself to the easier gait.

That night he camped in a deep coulée ten miles north of Odessa, and remained there the following day, Saturday, August 2nd, reading a book he'd taken away from that crossroad store—*The Explorations of Henry M. Stanley.* Reclining upon a saddle blanket by a small fire and drinking coffee, Harry followed the adventures of the doughty newspaperman who fought wild natives, forded crocodile filled rivers, and eventually stumbled upon a man who didn't seem to know he was lost, a Dr. Livingston. Yet every so often his thoughts would wander back to Janet, a girl forever lost, then he'd push her out of his mind and grimly read on.

Late Sunday afternoon, Tracy, still favoring his mount, pulled up on a ridge where he could overlook the rolling countryside, and unsaddled. It wasn't a particularly good spot to camp but he meant to spare the black as much as possible. He built a small fire, was frying some bacon and had the coffee on, using the last of the water in his canteen, when he noticed a single horseman riding across the prairie. When the stranger, a young man in a summer-weight checked suit, bow tie, and patent leather shoes, came abreast of him, Harry invited him to dismount and have a bite.

"Thanks, mister, but I'm not hungry," the rider answered, giving Tracy a cursory glance as he passed by.

"Hold on!" Tracy got up with his Winchester. "Think you'd best come back and be more sociable."

Looking over his shoulder, the youthful horseman reined in, hesitated, raised his straw skimmer, and, wheeling his brown mare, rode back.

"I'm Harry Tracy. Take me to the nearest farm. I need supplies."

"That'd be the Eddy Ranch on Lake Creek."

"Fine." Tracy emptied the coffee on the fire, cooled off the frying pan, and packed. While he was saddling he glanced at the young man, sitting motionlessly on his horse.

"Any posses around here?"

"Nope. Guess they think you're still somewhere to the west."

"Good. Let's ride."

Chapter Twenty

The two riders pulled up on the brink of a grassy bluff over-looking a tidy farmstead with its barn, white house, and out-buildings. On his black horse, Tracy sat listening, but the lonely silence was unbroken save for the strident cry of a hawk, drifting through the hot evening sky where a copper-penny sun still burned in the west.

"That the place?"

The younger rider glanced over at the Winchester glinting on his captor's saddle bow and wiped a bead of sweat off his nose. "Yep, the Eddy farm."

They descended the slope amidst a little swirl of red-tinged dust, and clattered into the farmyard, scattering chickens and rousing an old redbone hound.

As they pulled up, the gawky young fashion plate with Tracy pointed out two chunky bachelor brothers. "That's Lou there on the settle . . . he's oldest . . . and Gene's comin' out the side door."

Lou Eddy, a neatly dressed man in shirt sleeves, removed a half-smoked cigar from his mouth. "Say there, George, ain't you sparkin' little Nelly Foster any more? Seems you're always makin' a beeline fer her place of a Sunday evenin'." He addressed the gangling young fellow but eyed the silent man on the black horse. There was something about the stranger's flat, watchful gaze that was bothersome, although he couldn't just say what—maybe it was the business-like looking Winchester now shoved into the saddle boot.

"Well," George hesitated, swallowing hard at his Adam's apple, "this here's. . . ."

"Tracy." The stranger briefly removed his old, dark crush hat, replaced it, and dismounted, pulling out that ominous saddle gun.

"Ah, Tracy." Both Eddys stood staring at their visitor. Suddenly Lou dropped his cheroot with a grunt, slapping the sparks from his trouser leg. "Drat!"

The Winchester in the stranger's hand swung back. "Sorry," he remarked dryly. "Sudden moves get me jumpy." He stood looking from the white-faced farmers to their neat homestead. "Many passers-by?"

"Not many." Gene Eddy kept his calloused hands carefully in sight. "Bein' off the main road to Creston keeps it sorta quiet, but we like it that way."

"So would I." Tracy smiled briefly. Turning to young George on the roan mare, he ordered him down. "Well, gents, this is how it is . . . I suppose you know from the papers, that I'm on the scout. Won't be here long . . . then it's off to the races again." He slapped George on the back.

Jolted, the young fellow spoke up. "Ah . . . Mister Tracy says if we act sorta agreeable, I can go along pretty soon."

"But your folks, George"—Lou, the talkative Eddy, spoke up—"won't they be a-lookin'?"

"Not likely. Pop and Mom's visiting an aunt over to Spokane, and won't be back afore Wednesday night. So there's just our hired man and hired girl back at the place . . . and if I'm gone it won't bother them none."

"Now that's settled, let's get these animals into the barn and give them a good feed and rubdown. Wouldn't have any mounts for swapping, would you?" Tracy's piercing blue eyes, never at rest, took in the barn lot and mounded hills beyond.

"Got one two-year-old, and a fourteen-year-old plow horse," Gene Eddy offered apologetically.

Tracy shook his head. "Guess not. We'll just rest my pair for a day or so. I always take proper care of mounts, then, when I need to hustle, they're ready." He waved the Winchester at his three captives and followed them into the barn where his black mare was unsaddled and stabled along with the brown pack mare and George's roan.

When they came out of the barn, followed by the old dog, Tracy bent and ruffled the redbone's velvety ears. "Seems good to run into a friendly hound for a change." He straightened slowly and adjusted the Colt six-shooter in its holster. "I'm a bit stove-in, and wouldn't mind a pick me up. Got anything?"

Lou Eddy, adapting to the rôle of unexpected host, poked a thumb at the house. "We got some right nice hard cider in the cellar, but she's kinda hefty. Of course, as Methodists, we don't hold much with John Barleycorn." His brother nodded silent agreement.

"Neither do I." Tracy gave his quiet laugh. "I've seen what it can do to a man, especially when he ought to have his wits about him. But you fellows needn't think I'm going to get myself tanglefooted so you can jump me."

Both Eddys politely shrugged as they led the way into the farmhouse, each thinking of their double-barrel Princeps Greener shotgun resting in the bedroom closet.

Tracy settled himself down into a kitchen chair by the south window where he could keep an eye on both the outside and his captives as well.

When Lou had fetched up the applejack the cool stone jug was passed around the kitchen table several times until young

George became melancholy over his absent Nelly. A few more nips and he gradually subsided, head resting upon the table.

While Tracy again reassured the apprehensive brothers he'd not be on their hands long, and that he'd soon let their young neighbor go free, he busied himself at cleaning up rifle and pistol. "Any arms around here?" Keen, cold eyes raked both men.

On being told there was a shotgun in the bedroom, Tracy followed the Eddys into the front of the tidy house. After glancing over the parlor with its antimacassar-covered sofa, the potted plants, gleaming morning-glory horn of the gramophone, and crayon portraits of vanished Eddys—all staring their disapproval at the intruder—he returned to the bedroom to pick up the shotgun.

Carrying the Eddys' weapon along with the rifle, he herded the farmers back out of the house to the barn lot, leaving young George dozing in the kitchen.

Tracy paused at the barn to heave the Greener up into the hayloft and then paced off sixty yards. Leveling his own weapon at a small shed near the barn, he casually squeezed off a shot. The brothers flinched at the flat *crack* of the rifle, glancing sideways at each other as threads of ice flickered down their respective backbones.

"Look that over gents," Tracy grunted. "That's just what's waiting for those bastards if they ever get near enough again." He jacked another shell into the Winchester's chamber as the three walked down to the shed and inspected the knothole that had been punched from a board.

"Mister Tracy, think you'll be staying long?"

Gene Eddy cringed at his brother's words. The damned fool would get them killed yet, sure as shooting.

Then Lou Eddy watched Tracy out of the corner of his eye

as they went back to the house and caught the outlaw smiling slightly. "You asked how long I'd stay?" He stood aside as the brothers preceded him into the shadowy kitchen. "I'll tell you. No longer than it's necessary, and damned sure before I wear out my welcome." Tracy resumed his seat in the kitchen's corner, letting the butt of his Winchester strike the wooden floor with a *klack*.

The noise roused George from his boozy slumber at the kitchen table. "What's . . . that?" The young fellow sat up, blinking, then grabbed at his towhead with both hands.

After supper and another cup of coffee, Tracy related his encounter with George when that young Lothario rode by his camp. George grinned feebly at the tentative laughter.

Harry, who'd moved away from the window, and now sat with his back to the inner wall, looked over his hostages. "Well, let's get the chores done and settle down for the night." He rose and beckoned to Gene.

"Want us to come?" Lou offered, bobbing his head while young George sat glooming at an untouched cup of black coffee.

"No, we'll take care of the animals while you and the kid do the dishes." Tracy followed the older Eddy to the barn, where they bedded down the horses and solitary cow. Once back in the kitchen, Tracy remarked that he'd be sleeping out at the barn with one of the three as a bunkmate.

Watching Lou Eddy at the table, apparently engrossed with the local paper, he helped himself to another belt of the applejack. Leaning over, he tapped Lou's paper with the barrel of his six-shooter. "Glad you keep up on affairs. Don't suppose there's anything new in your weekly bugle on the so-called manhunt?"

Eddy looked up hurriedly. "No . . . this doesn't say much. Just that. . . ."

"An early arrest is expected?" Tracy grunted and turned to Gene Eddy. "Well, guess we can split up then. I'll take your brother along for company. As he's up on all the latest, he can pass along the news while we bunk down." He poked the Colt at George, and slowly thumbed back the weapon's hammer. "Now, you. Behave yourself and keep Mister Eddy here company, and then maybe you can get home tomorrow."

Leaving Gene Eddy and George at the house, Harry and Lou made their way toward the barn through the warm, still evening, Tracy cradling the Winchester under his arm as Lou preceded him with a lantern and a pair of blankets.

Eastward a great orange-red globe was floating over the horizon's black curve. As the full moon drifted up into the hot sky, a coyote yapped its protest somewhere in the darkness, while a neighboring farm dog quavered despairingly. Tracy froze, motionless.

The startled Lou sensed his captor to be a wild creature, searching the night for unseen enemies, while the surrounding night was vibrant with unknown dangers.

A vagrant breeze, sweeping down from the bluffs to rustle the dry leaves in a nearby poplar grove, bent and tossed the parched grasses around their feet and keened around the farm buildings. Far toward the south, sheet lightning rippled its pallid waves, then the wind dropped.

The dark silhouette that was Tracy moved again. "Thought that'd be one of their damned hounds." He slapped Lou on the shoulder. "Come on, let's bunk over at your haystack. Too hot to stow away in any barn."

Once settled down, Tracy and his guest lay on the small stack south of the barn, watching the sheet lightning and idly speculating about the possibility of a storm. Lou attempted to draw his captor out by relating gossip from the nearby town

241

of Creston, but Harry would say little despite an earlier demand for news.

Tracy seemed so remote from the farmyard, the moonlit night, even the world itself that Lou, despite himself, drifted away into an uneasy slumber.

Tracy awoke at first light, momentarily confused as to his whereabouts. He stared around, saw the sleeping figure beside himself on the straw stack, and murmured: "Dave." But it wasn't Merrill. Then he realized just who this stocky stranger was, lying there, half covered with straw, snoring his head off.

"Roust out there, Eddy!" After digging an elbow into the amply padded ribs of Lou Eddy, Tracy yanked out his own bandanna and wiped away the heavy dew from his Winchester and Colt six-shooter.

By the time his captive host had gathered his wits, Tracy was standing erect upon the straw stack and looking over the Eddy farm. The early morning sun, flaming up in a welter of yellow fire, was transmuting the entire place into a wonderland of brilliant buildings.

But the magnificence of the dawning day was already threatened by a growing pall in the southwest, for the fragile pastel threads of the night's sheet lightning were being rewoven moment by moment into an ominous sort of storm fabric. One by one the Eddy farm's magically gilded buildings were fading back into a weather-beaten reality.

"Jump for it, Eddy!" Tracy poked the farmer with his Winchester, then followed him off the stack on the dead run for the house with the lightning's thunderous sword slashing the dulling daybreak.

Once inside, they stood drying their faces on the roller towel at the sink and listening to the rainfall's pattering counterpoint to the rumbling storm music. By the time Lou had the Arbuckle's boiling on the wood stove, his brother and young George were up.

They sat around the table in the lamplight, eating and making casual conversation between mouthfuls of hotcakes and ham. Tracy, who seemed more relaxed than on Sunday, found time to josh George. "Think your gal's got the county looking for you?" He winked at the brothers who were, apparently, determined to eat until the weather changed.

"Don't know." George was suffering from his bout with the applejack and barely touched his food. "You said I might leave today . . . didn't you?" His Adam's apple bobbed and his green eyes were opaque with a mingled anxiety and hangover.

"Too wet out." Tracy grinned, shifting the six-gun in his waistband, and forked himself more ham. "Young sprouts like you better stay inside on such a day. You could run head-on into a posse in this bad light and get some holes shot through your backside."

"Goldumned weather," Lou grumbled at the rear window. "This keeps up and we ain't gonna git our alfalfy out, and that's a fact."

"Might let up. Sounds like she's dwindlin' off northard," his brother reassured the partakers of the breakfast.

Within half an hour the rain had ceased, despite the intensity of the thunderstorm, now muttering and banging away to the north. It being too wet to get at the mowing, Gene Eddy suggested they might mend some harness in the tool shed that needed repairing before they could work the south field.

Harry, who'd been listening to the Eddys' Columbia Grand gramophone, which he'd fetched from the parlor and placed on the kitchen table, turned from the brassy tones of the morning-glory horn as it spun out Sousa's "Wizard of the

Nile" in a jaunty parade of notes that danced off the walls. "Give you a hand in a minute," he told Gene Eddy.

Grinning at George, he said: "Here's one for both of us, old sport." Rewinding the spring, he slipped on a cylinder and played "The Girl I Left Behind Me". When the pretty ballad was finished, he shut off the machine. "You take care of the dishes, then come down to the barn lot and join the fun."

Leaving the young man in the kitchen, Tracy, Winchester at his side, followed the Eddys to the barn where the horses were fed, the cow milked, and the pigs slopped. That done, he sat with the brothers on their collection of empty kegs in the tackle shed and worked with them throughout the morning, mending harness.

At dinner Lou pronounced the weather improved enough to allow work along the fence line west of the barn lot. "Dumned cow jest persists tryin' to squeeze through the breaks and git into the corn."

"Fences can be bothersome," Harry said as he finished off the meal with biscuit and honey. "Ran into trouble with a fence when I first came back West. Instead of fixing the thing, though, we took our wire cutters and coaxed out the stock to join our own drive."

The others waited to hear this tale of derring-do, but Tracy merely shrugged, and then winked at young George. "I just bet you'd be a curly wolf at Hole-in-the-Wall. Cassidy's gone, some say to South America. So there's room for a new bunch. Think you'd like to come out there?"

"Don't reckon his young lady friend would like him running off to jine such scallyhooters," Gene tentatively offered.

"Nor his ma or pa," Tracy grunted. "Are we going to do some work on that fence now?"

"Y'bet." Lou arose and motioned to his brother and George. "C'mon along, the tools are out in the shed."

"And you come too, Napoleon." Tracy reached down and rubbed the velvety ears of the redbone that had taken to following him wherever he went. "We could use ourselves a good watchdog."

On the way to the tool shed, Tracy and the others stopped at the barn to inspect the horses. "About another day and they'll be in good shape," he observed. "Because when I ride, I'll ride long and hard."

"And you said I might leave today, Mister Tracy." The coatless George rubbed his hands along the seams of his trousers. "Folks at the farm'll start gettin' curious and so will. . . ." His Adam's apple bobbed nervously.

"Ah, the girlfriend?" Tracy mused. "Oh, let her think you're off visiting some other sugar cookie . . . do her good to miss you." He tapped the Winchester. "Come along, old sport, you're sticking around for a while."

Picking up a roll of baling wire and the necessary tools, the party of four tramped through the damp grass to the west fence and was soon busily engaged at fence mending.

Finished near supper time, the brothers Eddy suggested repairing one of the barn doors. It was apparent to Harry they thought it would be safer if he were kept busy. *Devil's work for idle hands,* he thought. He didn't mind as he liked to be occupied. It kept away unwelcome thoughts.

That evening was calm after the morning storm. Supper over, the foursome gathered out in the front yard—where they sat on kitchen chairs as the sun became a red-streaked memory in the lonely sky. As the evening star began to burn its cool, bright candle in the apple-green west, a cricket tuned up, its shrill fiddle saluting the oncoming night.

Tracy, who'd remained silent during most of the afternoon, expanded to the extent of agreeing that George might leave in the morning. He knew if the fellow were held too long, there'd be some sort of a search for him.

"But if you trot around shooting off your mouth . . ."— Harry paused, puffing at one of Lou's Floradora cheroots— "why I guess I'd have to come looking for you."

George gulped down his glass of hard cider and he promised to head straight home. "Nothin' against you, Mister Tracy, and I sure wish you luck."

Tracy blew a long, wavering lariat of smoke at the young man, smiling slightly when the blue vapor curled around George's gangling neck. "I'm pretty sure you wouldn't cross me, because you must have read of my duel in the forest with that snitching bastard . . . Dave Merrill." He fingered the velvety ears of the old hound. "They say revenge is one of the strongest urges a body can have, and I think it must be so."

The Eddys, familiar with the yellow press' account of Tracy's duel with his partner, grunted mutual agreement and waited.

But once he'd mentioned that fight, now a month and a half past, another thought seemed to strike Harry, and he turned to Gene. "How long you fellows run this place?"

Eddy replied they'd tried to make a go of it for six years since coming out from Illinois the summer of 1896.

"And a pretty good go of it, at that." Lou snapped his own yellow galluses in modest pride.

"Well, you've come a long way with your layout." Tracy looked around at the tidy, prosperous farm, then fell silent, staring wordlessly at the thin bar of red that banded the slowly darkening horizon.

Young George, rendered garrulous at the thought of getting away from the Eddy place, began a rambling discourse on the prospects of the town's baseball nine. From there the talk veered this way and that, particularly with Lou's unbelief in such skyscrapers as the New York City Flat Iron Building. "Such things just ain't natural. They're bound to tip over sometime."

"Mebby so," his brother replied, "but that ain't as odd-like as these here dummed auto wagons. Think of it . . . no horses." Both Eddys glanced at Tracy, but he merely chewed his cigar and fiddled with the redbone's ears, clearly withdrawing into himself as the deepening darkness wrapped its quiet blanket over all.

"And them autos . . . that's what they're callin' the rig . . . folks say they're dozens of 'em out in the East and least nigh that many down around Frisco," Gene volunteered. "Yes, sir, the hull country's changin'. It's this here new centry, I guess."

"Buffalo Bill's keepin' up with the times," George interjected. "Uncle Walt saw his Wild West Show out to Nebrasky last fall, and old Bill's got red-coated Canuck Mounted Police on his program. That bunch always gets their man . . . er . . . so I hear." He glanced at Tracy in the deepening twilight. "Guess all's changin', I'd say."

"I'd say you're right," came the flat tones of the vague, shadowy shape that was Tracy, a shape marked as much by his commanding presence as by the bright orange button at the end of his phantom cigar. They looked upon an apparently disembodied face, briefly waxing and waning as Tracy drew down upon the stogie's stub. "Yes, those fellows seem to get their man." He gave his dry chuckle. "They could have used some down this way in the last few months, but I guess it's best they didn't for all concerned."

There was a brief silence, then the desultory conversation continued to drone on, while the crickets chirped lazily, and the silver face of the moon began to peer at them with quiet interest from the eastern horizon.

Within the hour, almost as with one accord, Tracy and the others returned to the kitchen, taking their chairs with them, all settling down for a last cup of coffee before turning in for the night.

Reaching into a pile of old newspapers that lay in the kitchen corner awaiting their appointment with the stove, Tracy pulled out several sections. He discarded the newsprint and took up the Hearst Sunday Section. For a spell he immersed himself in the garishly tinted doings of the "Yellow Kid" and "Cy and His Mule Maud".

"That's the way I get to feeling, sometimes." He indicated Cy soaring over a barn after having come into contact with the explosive hoofs of that demonic quadruped. "Just about when I think things are really the berries, I get the same sort of surprise." He downed the rest of the coffee and tossed the sheets to the floor. "But turnaround's fair play . . . as I guess I've already given those damned tin stars and bounty hunters a few surprises of my own."

Getting to his feet, he crooked a finger at Lou. "About time to hit the shucks." Picking up his Winchester and adjusting the six-shooter in his belt, he nodded to the remaining pair and accompanied Lou out to the haystack through the moonlight's white sheen.

Long after Tracy and Lou had bedded down in the soft hay, they lay unmoving, each enwrapped in his own thoughts. Once Eddy mentioned work needing to be done without getting any response. Thinking Tracy slept, Eddy kept still, not wanting to arouse his dangerous guest.

But Tracy was not asleep. He lay, hands behind head, staring up into the great, gleaming moon face above him—trying not to think of anything. At first he merely pictured figures drifting over the silvery moon surface, formed by the shadowy wisps of cloud floating through the nearly transparent night sky—first a sheep, then a ship, followed by a horse, a mule—like Cy's devilish Maud—and then he fancied he saw the Oriental-like grin of the Yellow Kid, and watched that barefoot urchin in the potato sack gown disport himself amongst the cloud shadows until the figure wavered and blended away into one of Buffalo Bill's Mounted Policemen. And at the very last before he slumbered—he saw the eyes of Janet Warrington, lost and gone forever, the girl he'd left behind.

Chapter Twenty-One

Harry roused up a good hour before the sun's red glow first tinged the eastern darkness. He couldn't tell what awakened him as the night had been peacefully quiet, and Lou, beside him in the stack, had barely snored. But he now recalled something like a voice whispering in his ear and he'd awakened from a dreamless sleep more rested than he'd been for many a night.

Rising on one elbow, hand on six-shooter, he peered through the misty star gleam until he made out the motionless form of his host, still out like a light. Tracy smiled, then settled down, Winchester and pistol at his side, hands behind his head. For a time he willed himself to sleep, but was unsuccessful, and so his thoughts began to ferret away at whatever had fetched him up out of the restful night. But whatever the voice's message had been, it was gone for good.

Once up and breakfasted with the Eddys, Harry sent young George upon his thankful way, the young fellow promising to keep his mouth shut. Coached to tell his folks he'd stayed over at the Eddys', it should work. In addition, the subtle threat that Harry would come looking for him, if he went back on his word, might carry additional weight. But only time would tell.

Throughout the rest of the morning Harry and the Eddys worked at repairing the last of the harness in the shed, then began to ready some planks for the new barn door. Dinner time came, and, as they went up to the house, Harry remarked to Lou about turning his horses out to pasture for the rest of the day. "They might as well enjoy themselves while they can," he said. "They'll have to work for their keep mighty soon."

"Thinkin' of leavin'?" the farmer asked as they entered the kitchen door. "Not," he cautiously added, "that it's any business of mine or Gene's."

"Well"—Tracy began washing up at the kitchen sink— "with young George loose since this morning, I don't think it's smart to stick around here long."

"Oh, he's a right good fellow," Gene said, bustling from the range to the kitchen table, cooking up fried ham and potatoes, while the blue enameled coffee pot chuckled and muttered to the fire. "A right good young 'un, and I surely don't think he'd go back on his promise to keep mum."

"Not saying otherwise. Guess he's too busy now getting reacquainted with his girlfriend to tell tales out of school." Tracy sat down, placing the Winchester beside his chair. "Think it's still about time to be on my way. Maybe tomorrow."

Both Eddys exchanged glances, then attempted to get the conversation moving, but Harry had fallen into another of his silent moods, staring almost unseeingly at them and his plate as he began to eat.

After dinner, Harry and Lou, followed by the hound, returned to repairing the barn door, while Gene hitched up the mowing machine and drove the rig into the north field to commence on the alfalfa, now sufficiently dry for reaping.

For an hour or so Tracy and Lou worked at the door, but ran into a problem when they found the screws were not long enough to hold the hinges in place. When Eddy went back to the tool shed to rummage about for replacements, Tracy took advantage of the break to visit his horses.

Although he hadn't let them out to pasture as yet, he took up a currycomb, and groomed his black mount, and then worked for a while on the little brown pack mare. Both looked in tip-top form, for the mare's tendon had mended nicely and the pack animal seemed to be getting fat from the good fare both animals had been receiving—grain, alfalfa, and bran mix.

They were certainly ready for the trail and so was he. Yet for the past day or so he'd a vague feeling that, despite those fumbling posses, things weren't working out just right and there might be more trouble before he saw Wyoming and the Hole. But he'd laid such thoughts to Janet—for how could things really work out when they'd never meet again. And it was the hope of seeing her sometime that had kept him going for those long months after Chicago.

Love was nothing but hell. He saw that now. A man could shrivel up and die if love or life went wrong. It didn't pay to grow attached to anyone—father, lover, or even partner—for life, fate, or whatever they called it, was just too damned quick to kick a fellow in the face—and when he least expected it.

Gene was still out in the alfalfa, cutting wide swathes, the *clicking* of his mowing machine reaching the barn lot in wavering waves as a wind had come up. The same wind had also pushed away the fleecy, white clouds that had been drifting overhead and now the fiery August sun was burning down with a renewed brilliance.

When they'd finished the door, Tracy wiped the sweat from his face and raised his head, for the rasping, chirping of the mower had stopped. "Guess your brother's had enough for the day."

"Probably so," Lou replied, ambling out into the barn lot to take a look, followed by Harry, who casually stooped to rub the hound's ears.

What they saw gave them both pause, for Gene was seated on the machine, hat pushed back, talking to a pair of strangers who stood by the road, holding their horses' reins.

As far as Tracy could see, neither man was armed, but it was too far to be completely sure. "Let's put the stuff away and then see what's what." He and the silent Lou took their tools into the shed, then emerged in time to find Gene driving back into the barn lot. The two riders had been joined by several other horsemen on a nearby hill.

When the mowing machine clattered up abreast of Tracy and Lou, both assisted in unhitching the horses.

"Don't know who they are," Gene answered Tracy's question, but he could see from the way Eddy's hands shook that he did.

"Seems our friend George didn't keep his bargain." Tracy laughed shortly, then turned into the barn, reëmerging almost at once with his Winchester. Yanking his hat firmly down over his eyes, he ran past the Eddys without a word, heading for the haystack. As he came into view, the four on the road opened fire with rifles, the bullets plowing into the ground around his boots.

Harry plunged on toward the stack, but, as he neared it, two more riders came up over a fold of ground with leveled pistols, calling at him to halt. Without slackening his pace, Tracy snapped off a brace of shots at these two, causing them to wheel their mounts back in haste. The stack was too close to the last pair and Harry continued to jog on across the open ground into the Eddys' wheat field, bullets whining past to ricochet off the rocks and stony ground.

Throwing himself behind a great upthrust chunk of

granite in the wheat, halfway up the hill, Harry settled down to return the fire. Squinting in the sun glare and picking his shots, he drove the horsemen off the road, then turned his attention to the pair in the field. Try as he might, when he sighted down on them, Tracy found himself firing into the sun, its glare blurring his sight and foiling his usually deadly marksmanship. Even worse, he was wasting ammunition, not hitting what he was aiming at—and that wouldn't do.

For several minutes, he crouched behind the rock, occasionally dodging the shards and gritty dust kicked up by ricocheting leaden slugs cracking against the granite surface. And that sun was still high! There'd be no darkness for some hours and it was impossible to stay where he was, for he could tell from the oncoming gunshots that some of the riflemen were working their way around to outflank him.

The moment the firing diminished, Tracy leaped up to rack off three shots at the group that had been shooting from below the lip of the nearby hill—then he whirled and sprinted toward another great boulder, fifty paces away. He ran with the rising wind at his back and the *chirp* of bullets about his head. One clipped the peak of his hat, and, as he grasped at the brim to keep it on his head, he stumbled and fell headlong. For an instant he thought he'd tripped over some rock—then he knew! He's been hit.

Down on his face in the wheat, he spat out a mouthful of dirt and grunted with the pain that swept upward from his right ankle to his hip. But he was only a few feet from the rock and there he wriggled on his belly like an Indian.

Once behind the momentary safety of the granite boulder, he attempted to make what repairs he could. Pulling off his belt, he buckled it tightly about his leg to stop the flow of blood. And as he did, he seemed to hear above the rustling whisper of the wind-tossed grain—*You forgot . . . you up and forgot!* Just those few words. But in his pain and momentary despair, he knew the voice, although he could see nothing save the great, golden eye in the blue sky and the countless amber tassels of the wheat, bending and bowing over his head in the sudden silence.

Those words had come, somehow, from Mike Tracy, his great friend of logging days, the man who'd warned him always to expect the unexpected. Lying there in the wheat and gritting his teeth at the sudden shafts of fire lancing through leg and side, Harry heard himself muttering: "You forgot yourself. You weren't ready yourself when it happened to you."

But the only response he heard was the exultant shouting of some member of the posse, baying hound-like in murderous exultation.

Then, for a spell, time seemed to lose any meaning, although the sun had slanted off toward the west a thumb's breadth, while he lay trying to think.

At last he had his thoughts somewhat straightened out and the voices were gone. He lay in the middle of the Eddys' wheat field, while faceless men were gathered close at hand, ready to reap him in along with the ripened grain. And there wasn't a solitary thing anyone could do about it—except himself. He'd always been a gambler, and now the stakes were the highest they'd ever been—his very life. He'd lost the first hand when they bluffed him out of the barn and then got him in the leg. But if he could work back through the grain to that barn, he'd get his horse and ride for it. He'd never been beaten by any posse before, and now, despite that lucky shot, he still could pull it off.

Grinning with pain, he lay listening to the excited babble of voices at the field's edge. Some Constable Straub's name was called along with Smith and Morrison, but Cudihee wasn't around, and that was good. Win, lose, or draw, he didn't want that bastard in this game at all.

Well—that was enough time wasted. Now the sun seemed to sink lower. Where was time going? Dragging himself slowly back toward the barn, Harry was careful not to make any more movement than possible in the grain. The gusty hot wind still tossed the wheat about, covering much of his progress. He had those hayseeds guessing for, from an occasional haphazard shot into the field, it was plain the posse didn't know his exact position.

Suddenly Tracy heard the baying of a dog. He froze on his face, waiting, then realized it must be old Napoleon, the Eddy hound. The shots and the clamor of the strangers seemed to have set the animal on edge and he was merely letting off steam.

Harry edged on toward the barn, gritting his teeth. But the oddest thing about it all was the remaining birdshot in his bruised shoulder that was kicking up more rumpus than his injured leg.

All at once, above the whispering swish of wind in the grain, came the sound of someone, or something, coming toward him. Rolling onto his side, he jacked a shell into the Winchester—and waited.

Then Napoleon was there beside him, wriggling with pleasure at the meeting. He attempted to shove the animal away, but the dog wasn't being put off so easily. Lifting its head, it gave a bay of delight—then a volley of rifle fire ripped through the field. With a yelp of canine despair, the dog, its tail between its legs, vanished, but the damage was done, for among the rifle slugs plowing the ground and clipping the grain from the stalks—one ball slammed into Tracy's other leg, right at the hip.

Numb with the shock of the impact, Harry rolled back

onto his face and crawled on. Overhead, the late afternoon sun had become a golden foundry furnace that would eventually mold this fiery day into some sort of peaceful eve, cool, quiet, and unending.

But Tracy was unaware of anything but the enormous distance to the barn, not on horseback, not on two good legs, but on hands and battered knees. Presently he gave it up and lay back, listening to sounds beyond his vision—the dull, muttering of faceless enemies, somewhere out there, the chittering rasp of grasshoppers balancing on wheat stalks before springing away into the declining afternoon. There also came the infinitesimal *chirp* of a distant cricket, and, listening, he hazily thought, that he might even hear the tramp and bustle of busy piss-ants near his head if he only tried. And somewhere, overhead, there came the rusty scream of a flock of gulls, drifting inland from the distant Pacific, on the look-out for pickings from barnyard and field. Staring upward, Harry thought they seemed familiar. Suddenly images flooded his mind like lantern slides of those lake gulls, sailing like paper-white angels above the heads of Janet and himself, when they'd lain in a world of their own on the green grass behind the Columbian Exposition building beside the glittering blue of Lake Michigan.

And with his mind oddly backtracking to that wonderful time, Harry knew that he would somehow see other segments of that vanished past . . . and they came, as transparent as colored glass, through the wavering wheat, untouched by buffeting winds or the murderous, raking fingers of the posse guns.

Thanks, Harry, for what you did came the vaguely recriminating voice of Dave Merrill, who stood in his rumpled clothing, arms folded and head cocked accusingly. *Y'didn't let them posses think they'd cut my string . . . but I'd been all right if I could have got me a doctor.* Harry's eyes blurred, and, when they cleared, Dave was gone and Flat Nose George Currie had drifted up, tugging at his mustache, to stand looking down at Harry. For a moment Currie was silent while the posse's guns cracked out again as they sensed somehow their prey was beginning to retreat from them.

You made one jim-dandy rider, Harry Bass. Currie smiled sadly—flat nose wrinkling slightly with the effort. *If I'd have had you with me at the Green River crossings, that tin star Tyler wouldn't have nailed me. But then it happens, sooner or later, to everyone, don't it?* Currie resignedly spread his hands and wavered away into the sunny air.

Where Currie had stood there was now another. And Harry would have rubbed at his eyes but for some unknown reason he didn't seem able to make the effort. *He was right.*

You was about the hull backbone of our bunch, drawled the voice of old Bill Madden. *And we'd 'a' been proud to have you with Tip Gault's gang, let me tell you.*

"But you . . . ," Harry husked, his voice now strangely distant to his own ears. "You aren't . . . ?"

Dead as a doornail, bucko! Dead as a rock. Madden's spikey mustache bristled with something like pride. *Passed on, if that's what the preachers call it, passed on last month right while you was fightin' half the state of Washington . . . and winnin' for a spell.*

"But what . . . ?"

Got tired of bein' penned up like some damned wolf in a zoo. Hull blamed world's a-changin', Harry. They went and killed off the buffalo, put the Injuns out to pasture, and then got to work on us longriders. Life inside or out just ain't worth the hangin' on. I guess you see that now, fer damned if you ain't up and cashin' in yourself.

Before Harry could answer, Madden hauled out a ghostly

Colt Dragoon and thumbed off phantom shots at the posse, grimacing toothlessly down at Harry as the big gun jumped silently in his withered fist. Then with the sixth shot, Madden was gone—pistol and all.

For a time Harry lay back easily, seemingly to almost float inches off the ground. It was as if he reclined upon the downiest of featherbeds. And like Dave had said when he had found the whiskey bottle at that farmhouse, he didn't care if school kept or not.

Thus he lay, mind seemingly as clear as a child's, not questioning the hallucinatory parade of wraiths that had come to him through the wheat field, nor did he question an oddly growing darkness, although the glowing circle of the golden sun was now nearly touching the gilded hills to the west.

So old Bill Madden thought Tracy was dying, did he? Well, the more he chewed over Bill's words, the more he came to think it might be true. But if he were dying, and he'd seen, or at least thought he'd heard or seen, some of the dead folks from his past life—Mike Tracy, George Currie, and poor old Dave, then where was the one person he longed for—longed to see above all others?

Where was Janet?

A rifle cracked out in the amber light, someone in the posse trying to get a rise out of him. Trying to seek out and cut his string.

Harry struggled onto one elbow and tried to lift up his faithful old Winchester, but it was asking the impossible. He couldn't even work the cocking lever, let alone fire back at those damnable tinhorns.

With a groan he sank back, all the way this time to the cold, hard ground, his head encountering a rock, but he was too lethargic, too weak, or too lazy he told himself, to move another foot.

Soon, maybe after dark, the darkness that now swirled about him, despite the gleaming sun, would blanket all and they'd come pussyfooting out into the field either to hog-tie or to shoot him. Either way, Harry wasn't having anything to do with such possibilities. He'd fought them for two months, and won every fight—and be damned if he wouldn't win this one the only way he could.

Painfully hauling out his six-shooter, Harry struggled to get it to his head, and, while he was able to cock the weapon, he was now too feeble to pull the trigger. For a long time he lay, tears of weakness welling into his eyes, then, gritting his teeth and staring up at the still blue sky, he steadied the Colt with one hand and pulled the trigger with his other thumb.

And in that fraction of an instant, Harry saw those white wings circling overhead were more than gulls. As the world he'd known transmuted into a macrocosmic, incandescence rippling forever onward toward the unseen stars, he saw the figure of Janet Warrington awaiting him in the midst of the all-enveloping light—holding out her arms. And Harry Tracy went toward her, as the millisecond closed.

Author's Note

Every novel, particularly if it be an historical, is a jerry-built affair cobbled together with fact, supposition, and out-and-out guesses. But it owes its existence to the person who went through those experiences and the imagination of the writer for gathering up those strands to form the end product. For myself I've found some reputable publications to use in tracking the elusive Harry Severns who became Harry Tracy through his admiration for an older friend. The most recent is the admirable *Manhunt: The Pursuit of Harry Tracy* by Bill Gulick, which contains many photos as well as valuable facsimiles of newspapers of that period. Other publications of passable interest include *The Outlaw Trail* by Charles Kelly, *The Gunfighters: The Authentic Wild West* by James D. Horan, and *Badmen of Frontier Days* by Carl W. Breihan. But as valuable as anything has been, were the many conversations with that stalwart biographer of the James and Younger gangs, Carl W. Breihan. His knowledge of Harry Tracy was the spark that ignited my book.

About the Author

W. R. Garwood was born in Mason City, Iowa, but spent his early childhood in New Mexico. After returning to the Midwest, poignant memories remained of the Sandia Mountains hovering on the horizon like lavender clouds while tumbleweeds cavorted past his little two-by-four home and shadowy coyotes ghosted through its yard at dusk. The West had stamped its presence upon his mind's eye. Always a scribbler, he went to Hearst's Detroit newspaper when out of school, gravitating from copy boy to cub reporter and eventually working on more than a dozen area papers during a fifteen-year period. From there he moved on to advertising agencies and was assigned to the arts and entertainment magazines they produced. It was a short stretch to using that talent in fiction by polishing up the personalities of whatever stars of stage, film, and niteries performing at Detroit's major entertainment venues. In the 1980s, Garwood began to draw on his early memories of the American Southwest, turning out five Westerns, including *Kill Him Again* (Bath Street Press, 1980) about Billy the Kid and *West Wandering River* (Doubleday, 1986) about Judge Roy Bean. Garwood lives in Central Pennsylvania. He is working on his next Five Star Western.